Jade

JONATHAN LOVEJOY

Armageddon Publishing
All rights reserved.

Cover: *Lemon*, 1899
William Adolphe Bouguereau (1825-1905)

ISBN-10: 0692508716
ISBN-13: 978-0692508718

For every Sarah

And the LORD sent an angel, which cut off all the mighty men of valour...

1 Chronicles 32: 21

The Jade Dragon

*J*ade Silk will past the test. The Jade Silk Warrior is ready. Known high and low, for the power I must command. For the power I wield in my sword. This Jade woman rises from the east, burning green and black fire. It is the song of vengeance heard round the world, when Jade East meets Amber West, and the blood must fly in the evening.

I am a woman of Asian descent. Still young at heart, though a generation has crossed my eye. I am Sarah Green. Once the mother of one daughter, but having left her when she was small. This girl grew up without her mother, who lives secretly in another town. It is a town occupied by buildings great and small, where I can hide at best.

No one from the life I knew can find me. And those I must find will have to pray. Because already, there is the blood of fifty seven women on my sword—each dedicated to the Lord. But Jade is the color of vengeance, as it is for Sarah Green, for she is not the lackey of some organization, nor the lapdog killer for a secret billionaire. I am the unwilling partner of Fate itself, which leaves me numb with want, then panting with desire, to roam the night like a shadow demon. To slice the head of who might be deserving, the head or the neck or the chest, gut or spine, but always a mortal wound upon my sword, which is light as a feather in my hand, forged in the fires of the rising sun.

I am alone in my apartment, oftentimes, the greatest serial killer of all time, not opposed to the sight and stain of blood. Fifty seven varieties, though not of culinary delight, but of human soul and scream. And now I wonder, I know, that I must reach the end of my tenure as a vigilante, but not until others have paid the price for their sin. Now, there are mothers *and* daughters who have inherited the call, I believe, and to the exclusion of all others. Mothers hiding in the suburbs, sluts and whores who masquerade as wives and mothers, brats and bitches who inhabit space as their female children. These are the strains of madness in my brain, when the killings move from righteous to unrighteous, and my sword must now drip with the blood of the innocent. It is time for me to get a home among them. To walk and work among the suburban moms and daughters, so that I can meet the ones who deserve a killing. It is the consequence of their lives, I believe. As well as the consequence for my own.

Tonight, I sleep with the curved metal on the wall. The Jade Dragon of my bloody dreams. As I remember the screams of Number Fifty Seven, of the last woman, the corporate shark who died, I remember the three angels who haunt me, who I must continue to run and hide from. The angel Sea Breeze, cut from cloth as blue as the ocean. Her angel partner Snow, weaved from cloth the color of winter white. And their angel lady Redwing, born of cloth as red as crimson fire.

n underground network of serial killing women, we are. But we do not use guns. We do not use poison. This, the firepower of cold steel, amidst the poison of dread and fear. Assassinations so mysterious, so secret as to have withstood the test of time, to have gone unreported through the generations to the modern day. When simple beheadings of corporate sharks and drug lords do not suffice, the horror of endtime truth so often reveals itself, upon the nude bodies of their dear wives and children. Women hung naked from chandeliers and second floor banisters, or nailed spread eagle to the walls and to the floor. Mothers and wives stripped of their dignity, their hands spiked to the walls of their wealthy suburban palace, with their feet spiked to the floor underneath, their bodies betraying a river of blood from the deep gash X'd into their skin. Two slices crisscrossed from under their breasts to their gut, even to the miraculous preservation of Olympian breast beauty, to preserve the power of their femininity in death. Healthy hipped, heavy breasted wives of the privileged, hung up and crisscrossed as a sign unto them, that there is no longer a place to run and hide, no detective work sufficient to decipher and track them down, as it would be paramount to trying to find the whereabouts of a shadow in the evening day.

These are the wives and children of evil men, I tell myself, at the massive suburban window, overlooking the lawn of beauty and privilege. Sarah Green, a.k.a. Jade Silk, whom some have branded "Lady Wolverine," because of the manner and appearance of my brutal trademark upon the women. An 'X' displayed upon their nakedness without pity or remorse, to satisfy a hatred built up from days of old, and a mother drowned in bitterness and hatred. I remember the feel and the smell of my mother's lipstick, the smooth flow of it across my naked body when I was 13, being made to stand naked in front of the bathroom mirror, as my mother's angry reflection stands topless in her jeans, Asian eyes burning green with fury as she takes the crimson fire lipstick, and paints it from her daughter's shoulders to the bottom of her flat abdomen one way, then crosses it diagonal in like manner from the other. The girl stays there, as a little girl reflection of the heavy breasted beauty who paints her in rage, seeing only her body fading away in the mirror, a light doused to insignificance by the burning red X that stands in front of it. And the red X is joined by a flash of pure white in her vision, as the mother slaps her with all her might. Then the girl stands there in false dignity, trying to evoke pity in the lack of expression, as the tears roll freely down her face in front of the topless woman.

"Put your hands behind your back," the woman says, but with such a controlled fury as to be more terrifying than a scream. Then the shapely hipped, heavy breasted woman walks out of the bathroom down the carpeted hall, leaving her daughter there to ponder the fullness of regret, and words spoken in youthful rage and stupidity born:

"Grandma says I don't have to obey your fat-breasted rules!" Having been built up by a fortress of lies, that offer no real protection when the storm of truth hits, having been made by her Asian grandmother to believe that she could share in the same power she has over her daughter, that grandmother and granddaughter could join hands in this new place, of maturity and independence over the young Asian widow, newly rich from her dead husband's will and testament.

Your mother's fat breasted rules make me laugh, the grandmother had said, voice rich in Jade accent from the East, giggling a quick and hearty laugh at her daughter's American ridiculousness, and her allegiance to the role of suburban widow queen. *Why you give Sarah so many chores like a maid,* she has heard her grandmother say. *How she do her homework after you work her like a horse?*

Sarah is my daughter Ma, and I'll do with her as I please.

So that how you talk to your mother now, she says. *Rich husband die and leave you all his money, so now you don't have to respect me? What happen to daughter who does not respect her mother?*

The question causes the pretty Asian woman to stare into space in frustration. Unable to speak.

Jade

As long as there is breath in your body, you will respect me. When I am in my grave, you will respect me.

I, Sarah Green, stand at the horizon of my future. Waiting for my beautiful mother to walk back into the space of my condemned life, as I gaze upon where the crimson X marks the place of grieving. Where X marks the spot of bereaving. The beautiful woman comes into the bathroom, still topless in like manner as before, in full condemnation of my audacity. Of my audacity to believe that I had joined with Grandmother in power. In power to subjugate her in her own kingdom. To join the grandmother at the center of tragedy, where the greatest insults lie in wait. To use the words *'fat breasted'* to her, as if I understood the rumbling beneath the mountain. As if I understood what will happen at Armageddon.

Mother places the *cane* at my body's undeveloped little attempt at a breast. In the whip lash of sound, I hear agony spoken to my breast, answered in the voice of a wasp sting that grows from my nipple into the rest of my body.

From the heart of memory. To my white finger at my palatial window. Watching it draw the invisible diagonal cross. The place where there is marked a spot of grieving. Of treachery, for the future of a woman I know.

And her daughter.

I am the Jade Assassin. In my sword is the sting of death. I lift the heads from all other assassins if I so choose. I shit upon their graves in the moonlight.

I am the bringer of sorrow in the last days. The bringer of Truth and Revelation. The rule of pain and suffering. My body is honed with fires of impossibility. My blade in the fires of magic. There is no skill, no training, no meditation above me in the night. There is no refuge from this killing in the shadows.

There is no battle here to be fought. No victory here to be won. No clumsy clattering of blade and steel. Only the wind of motion unseen. The letting of blood from the spirit of silk and green.

Jade

The nonsense of hand to fist is boredom to me. The kicking of feet is trite as children's play. I leap upon the winds of their hopelessness. I move in the speed of their thoughts and fear. I am the tragedy of their earthly prowess. I am the tears that mourn their lifeless clay. No human speed, no human strength, is anointed upon my lightest way. No human power withstands the hour of my darkest day.

Run from my shadow in the moonlight. Flee from the dark'ned fires of Jade.

Jonathan Lovejoy

The Pantheon

Amanda and Tiffany Bynum. The lady president and first daughter of this town. Filled with smiles and public good will. Mother and motheress extraordinaire. Though only an accursed few can see beyond this closeness. Through the voice of this public mother daughter friendship. To see what it is they have embraced beneath the walls of secret. An anal obsession in this wide hipped whore—nurtured by her daughter since the girl was nine. Back in the days when Mrs. Bynum was a housewife, to John Bynum's will and desire. An obsession she kept hidden from him, hidden away in the icy realm of rejection. The cold region of resistance.

A romantic liaison with her husband once in a blue moon, while she focused her attentions on her daughter. On her house. On her mother. On her sisters. On everything else in her universe except John Bynum. Mr. Yale Law School. In his magistrate's chair all day, dead from the waist down. Compassion seared with a hot iron. Charity frozen to oblivion. So unaware of what happens during third grade school vacations at home. While little Tiffany is at home with mother. Ignorant along with the rest of the world, as to what churns beneath cultured civility.

By the spirits who burden me with this calling. The vision of Amanda Bynum is clear. I see her at home when the girl Tiffany was but a child of nine. In the third grade, a little doe eyed, brown haired Rebecca. A nine year old doll in pink lips and pigtails. Laid out flat on the floor, surrounded by a rainbow of magic markers. Engrossed in her coloring books and Barbie Dolls nearby.

Amanda Bynum emerges from the kitchen. Faded jeans, tight navy t-shirt in place. Big, suburban hips on display.

"Come upstairs to Mommy's room," she says. Naïve, oblivious little Tiffany follows her pretty Mommy to the bedroom. Hearing her mother say, *"I want us to play a game that my mother taught me when I was little. It's got a funny name. It's called "Butt Bounce."*

I can see the little girl laughing at the comic audacity. Asking her mother what it is. Being ushered over to the bed. The mother climbs onto the king sized, comfort cushion mattress. All smiles and good natured fun. Facing toward the foot of the bed, lying on her stomach.

"This'll be fun," she tells her daughter. Coaxing her to climb onto the bed after her, and sit on her bottom. *"Climb up here and sit on Mommy's big butt,"* she says. Evoking more laughs and giggles unawares. More expressions of innocence untainted.

The girl climbs onto her mother with fun park enthusiasm. Straddling her mother's bottom without knowledge. Without reservation.

"Turn around," the mother says. *"Face the other way."*

This, she does. More delighted than confused. *"Now, bounce on Mommy's butt,"* she says. Fungalooga tone in place. Every pretense of innocent fun still in check.

The girl Tiffany begins to hop up and down on her mother's bottom, facing toward her feet.

The very first bounce rings a chime to her groin and the rest of her body. Sending a cold twinge up her back and downward to her bosom. A chord played in D major in her bra. Bound up and rounded under her navy shirt. A symphonic display of feeling she has missed for over ten years. Since before she was married. A private obsession, passed down the motherline through the generations. Having fallen from the top of the family tree to the bottom. From her daughter's bottom. To hers.

The nine year old girl goes at it with trampoline heat. Loving every spongy second of her mother's big, comfort cushioned hips underneath. Bouncing without knowledge. Without ceasing.

To her shock, her mother makes a loud, wailing cry. Pushing her bottom upward in her jeans. The daughter stops in confusion. Wondering if she hurt her mother. Feeling her entire body shake underneath her.

"Did I hurt you, Mom?"

But the mother cannot answer. Barely able to draw a steady breath. In grieving for the shaking to cease. Unable to speak to her daughter's confusion.

Jade

The daughter knows only to sit still. Feeling her mother's body tremble underneath her. Wondering why the back of her mother's jeans are now soaking wet.

Wondering.

$\mathscr{I}$ was an outcast from the 1st day I stepped off the schoolbus. Into that strange netherworld. That ghostly reality that they call public school. That silent hill. That place where Hell on Earth is a reality.

My first step off the bus was met by a girl spitting in my face, while her friend slapped me hard enough to ring my ears. When I showed up in class crying on my very first day, the teacher wiped my tears and asked me who did it, but I didn't know their names. What could I say of Patricia, a.k.a. Patty Price and her friend Rhonda, who never hardly spoke at me while Patty primped and pranced and stuck her tongue out with her hands on her hips all the time like it was her calling from God to do it. She even did it to the teacher who called me her little China Doll, even though I'm Japanese. The boys called me an ugly gook, and one of them looked at me up close and said *"girl you got some slant eyes."* And then he shook his head and walked away.

I am unfortunate enough at this moment, to be a prisoner of my six year old self from a generation ago, where I can see Patty Price talking to Rhonda and another girl at recess, where I am in the playground drinking the only carton of white milk the teacher ordered. Every day, the little red carton sits bright and conspicuous in the sea of brown ones, because I could not stomach chocolate milk. These four girls come up to me in such sweetness and friendliness, talking about my black hair, which one of them had already called 'greasy,' but suddenly now it was 'so shiny.'

"Let's take a walk," Patty says, and she puts her arm around me, and talks so lovingly, whispering in my ear about how I can come over to her house and watch movies on her mother's giant screen TV, and that *"we can go to Toy's R Us when you come over. And then we can go get milkshakes and French fries. You want to do that this weekend?"*

What am I supposed to say? What is a little girl dying of thirst supposed to say when offered something ice cold to drink? The lump appears in my throat, that warns of no speech, lest I succumb to tears of joy. I can remember being so blissfully carried away from the others, from the pathetic nothings, from the dull witted woman in charge of those accursed little demons. I have been chosen by the gods—I am whisked away to such a delightful journey on the breeze, carried aloft to a place above the others, where the elite are placed on the pantheon of worship, where they are looked up to as desirable, as the penultimate examples of how to look, how to speak, how to live.

Rounding the corner from the others, from the noise of their mediocrity. I feel so special when the three of them and myself stop just out of their sight, and she looks at me with kindness, and says, *"I have to tell you a secret,"* and she stands in front of me, as though about to whisper the meaning of life onto my lips.

Then suddenly, the world around me begins to move in such a way that I have not known, as a force from beyond where I can believe takes hold of my shoulders, and shoves me *hard* backwards, causing me to fall over one of the girls knelt down behind me. The world is lifted and turned topsy-turvy around me, and I perceive my body as falling from the sky above, where the ground awaits somewhere underneath me to cause pain and suffering. I hit the ground in a sickening thud, a flailing mess of Raggedy Ann arms and legs, losing my ability to breathe all at once, suddenly feeling my legs go immobile as one girl sits on them while another girl pulls my arms back, laying me out on the ground like a set of skins to be dried on the prairie in 1888.

And somewhere in this haze of breathless immobility, I see Patty Price in long, blonde pigtails, flying at me as if from on high, slamming herself into my stomach, to acquaint me with one of the types of fear. This, the fear of death. As the pain courses through my abdomen to the rest of my body, I am laid there un-moving, unable to turn myself over and breathe.

And Fate has mercy on me, causing her to shift her position, so that she can stare into my face, as God grants me a breath to breathe, to feel the cool, life giving air rush into my body just enough, to allow for the six year old wailing voice, and the pleading for them to have mercy. But this, they do not. Gathering themselves on top of me, so that I do not have enough breath to form words as I cry. Patty lays heavy on top of me, putting her hand over my nose and mouth, to acquaint me with the Fear of Death again.

"Is she crying yet? I don't see any tears. Pinch inside her thighs, Beth. I want to see her cry."

And suddenly, I feel the clamping agony in red inside my thighs. A biting pinch under my dress high up on my inner thigh, to add pain to this suffering, to make me think only of the compassionate young teacher, as I feel pain itself strike the fat of my inner thigh, which seems to give me greater breath to breathe, as she removes her hand from my mouth, so that they can listen to me scream. My feet are clamped, my hands are bound, and my breath is held in check as I squirm underneath them, feeling Patty's press, the pushing of her little groin against my leg while she is on top of me, to where I perceive the sharpness of her pubic bone, stabbing into me without mercy or fear.

The loudness, the force of my squealing unnerves her just a bit, and she puts her hand back over my mouth. Laying strong on top of me while the other two hold my arms and legs. Watching me.

Watching the tears fall.

Jonathan Lovejoy

The Jade Silk Warrior

he myth of the Chinese star is nothing of the kind. It is as real as the fingers that lift them through the air at lightning speed. We release them upon the current of still air we see, that guides it from our hands to the place in our victim's body. It is a talent for most who have thrown them. For a few, it is a gift. In the seven years I trained, I learned to pierce coins tossed in the air with them. Soft, gold coins, pierced by the silver stars I threw.

My Lady Master, my Mistress, told me of this only in passing. To amuse herself watching me fail. In twenty years of training, she said, she has never seen it done. Coins have been hit every so often, to be sure. But no star has ever pierced a coin. *Every one hundred years*, she said to me, *there is one warrior, who can pierce a gold coin at will. Every one hundred years, this is the Jade Silk Warrior.* This, she spoke to me in awe. In reverence for what it is she believes. That this warrior is sent by God as an avenging angel of death. As a sign of the end time. Legend speaks of seven such warriors. To signal the end of time. The end of mankind. The judgment of God over the wicked.

Legend says that there have been six. And there would be a seventh warrior born. Born in the age of knowledge and wickedness. When mankind is beyond redemption. A warrior passed from the body of Eve. *The greatest warrior in the history of the world,* she said. A sword that cannot be resisted. A shadow that cannot be fought. To see the eyes of the Jade Silk Warrior is to see the eyes of God.

This, when the walls of her training room were decorated by the gold coins. Pierced by the silver stars of Heaven.

I have no more to teach you, she says, the tears streaming down her beautiful face. Staring at me in quiet awe. Reverence hidden by a master's restraint. *There is no sword, no fighter on Earth,* she says, *that you cannot defeat. Your speed. Your strength. The grace in your movement. It is unlike anything I have ever seen. This cannot be taught. It cannot be learned. It is a gift from the Almighty. I have watched you defeat the best fighters in the world without effort. The walls are decorated with the truth. Out of respect for me, you put your sword at my neck on the side not for cutting. You, Satari Sakara—you are the greatest warrior of all time. You are the Jade Silk Warrior.*

And I watch her take up seven bright gold coins, tossing them all high into the air across the room, and I see seven lines of sight appear from my hands to these seven coins that fly. And I feel my arms move as though under their own command, as seven stars leave my left and right hand as they will, done upon a single motion from each arm, piercing each golden light from left to right in silver, to form a new message in the stars, told in the serpentine body of the Jade Dragon, whose tail is curved to strike as the scorpion's sting, behind the head that breathes green and black fire.

Upon the winds of this flame, I ride. In the heart of memory, I accept my first so-called commission. This, from a Japanese billionaire, looking to acquire a company to add to his ridiculous portfolio of conquests—a deal being held up by the strength of one stubborn executive, who will not vote in favor of this acquisition.

These assassins are trained to flourish in the shadows, he has heard, like those spoken of in legend and lore, but these in reality. In my reality, I appear at the house of this man at his door, in the armament of Jade, which is a silken dress of the finest emerald fabric, hugged to my body from my neck to my ankles, married to my long hair which is raven black, hung about my shoulders and down the length of my back.

This Japanese corporate king invites me into his beautiful home, unable to take his eyes from me in the awe of disbelief rather than reverence, a scent that flows from him like that of a wet dog. *Come to my office*, he says, shaking his head, unable to give me the courtesy of genuine respect. Through the grand livingroom we walk, past the great portrait of his lovely wife and beautiful daughter, both dressed in the beauty of ivory white.

They are very beautiful, I say. *Your wife and daughter?*

Yes, he says, without looking at me as the door slides open, stepping into his office. *Please, have a seat,* he says, moving to his leather desk chair upon a current of contempt, barely hidden behind a look of mistrust and bewilderment.

Jade

He tells me of the man I am supposed to kill. He speaks of his *"evil resistance,"* and how his company must be stopped from impeding the progress of the greater good. *If this man is gone, so too is his resistance, and then they will have to sell their company to me.*

But you are already so rich. Why do you need this company?

This will make me the richest Japanese businessman in the world. He stops speaking for a moment, to look me from my forehead down to the curve of my hips, then down to the black heels strapped to my feet, then back up to my shoulders, my large breasts, and eyes big enough to warrant them. *I ask for an assassin*, he says, *and they send me a whore.*

The types of fear are many, and uniquely distinguished. Among these is the Fear of Rage. The nagging terror that what has been said is going to trigger a chain reaction from the mind, to the soul, to the spirit, and to the body. I stand and look at him boldly, hardly able to hide my humiliation and inner fury. Turning to walk to the sliding doors, much to his satisfaction, I suppose. Believing that I am going to leave.

But I slide the doors closed. Feeling myself turned about slowly, as on a current of grieving. Strolling back to the peasant side of his superiority, on this side of the desk. Opening my jade silk purse. Removing my Jade silk kerchief.

Excuse me, I say in sweetness, in his native tongue. Tying the jade cloth around my eyes. Then reaching demurely back into my purse in the chair, for the requisite silver stars that wait. Taking them up smoothly, gliding back from the desk a single step, the cloth tied about my eyes. Then one step more, standing still as though in a stride frozen, my head lowered in what otherworldly concentration there may be.

Hi! Is the syllable that startles him like a firecracker from my mouth, as I drop forward to one knee in jade silk cloth, my arms spread out on both sides, unable to see in my blindfold the look on his face. I stand up smoothly again, in the full strength of my calling. Removing my blindfold. Strolling back to the desk, not bothering to look at what he cannot cease from gazing at, which is one silver star in the face of his wife on one wall, and one in the face of his daughter on the other. The glass in each picture is barely cracked, I suppose. Having not had the fractions of a millisecond to create them.

I do not kill fat, stupid men, I say. Placing my jade cloth back into its silken hiding place. Is the emerald shine of my fingernail paint to your liking, I want to ask him. *Is this man married,* I say. Not looking at him.

Yes. He has a son and a daughter.

This man's son will live, I say. *But his wife, and his daughter will die. And you will pay me three and a half million dollars today. And then three and a half million dollars when they are dead.*

That is ridiculous, he says. *The price was seven hundred thousand, and only after you do the job.*

I can only turn my head slowly. Ever so slowly, to look at the picture to the right of me.

Your wife is a precious jewel. A queen among women. I turn to look at the picture to the left of me, where the other silver star rests in the face of innocence. *Your daughter is the most beautiful flower in a forest of green leaves. A flower too beautiful to be seen. If you do not pay me in 24 hours from now, I will kill your wife and your daughter before your eyes. They will die in a way that is too terrible to speak of.*

The awe upon his face is now in the company of fear. In the company of sorrow.

And then I will cut out your eyes with my sword.

Jade

I turn my back to him. Walking slowly to the door. In grieving to sense the foolishness of a gun behind me. But there is none.

White Lotus Garden Cemetery. You will come alone with the money. If you are not alone, your wife and daughter will have to die. If you love them, you will not betray them with greed and stupidity.

I slide open the door. Breathing the fresh air of leather and wood lacquer, the smell of money flourished to infinity. Strolling out into the open space of this grand entrance room. Stopping to gaze once at the lofty painting of two ivory flowers in repose.

In the armament of jade, I stroll to the gate of the money prison. Opening, closing the elegant door behind me.

The door to freedom.

ade Silk will pass the test. The Jade Silk Warrior is ready.

My money will be wired to no bank. To no institution. No place. We will not meet in a crowded mall. A church. A courthouse. A school.

Like a shadow in 3D apace, the man walks from the dirt road where his car is parked. Whether or not he walks in fear, I do not know. Perhaps he has the heart of a warrior himself. A corporate king. A conqueror among men.

I cannot accuse him of cowardice. But this is bravery laced with treachery. Lust. Pride. Envy. Greed. No respect for human life. Caring more for money then morality.

The figure strolls in the starlight. In grieving for the light of the moon. Strolling unawares. Not knowing if he has seen his last sunset. If the sun will rise over his corpse tomorrow. Having placed his faith in the Almighty American Dollar. Putting on the whole armor of gold.

The corporate king moves to the middle of the stone sea. The nighttime wasteland of grave markers. Knowing that he had better not leave, until the leather briefcases are claimed. Until the dark comes to life and takes them away. Until the one he called a whore makes their presence known.

As he stands in the middle of the Dead Land, tiny shadows whisper at him in the starlight. Above him, the stars of the Milky Way Galaxy look down upon him in pity. In eternal knowledge. In grieving for his fate.

The man hears a tapping nearby. The tiny tapping of stone against stone. To alert him to the reality that even for a corporate king, the types of fear are many.

He remembers the motion of lightning. The whishing of silver stars in his office. The piercing of both pictures of his legacy. His life.

The man draws in the deepest breath of shock. Born from the glint of ice cold steel at his throat in the dark.

I have your money, he says. His voice trembling with truth. With revelation. *Every dollar is here. I swear it...*

Open it, the Jade Shadow speaks. *Do not turn around. On your knees. Open the briefcases.*

The dark figure kneels to the cold, grassy earth. Opening the root of evil to the night air. *It is all there*, he says. *See?*

Close them. Now, tell me... what part of your body does a whore want to cut off?

Please, he says, *I did not know who you were. Forgiveness. Mercy.*

Why do you deserve mercy? Do you want mercy for the family I must kill?

Please forgive me. Do the job, and I will pay you the rest of the money. I swear it.

Oh, but how much is a human life worth? How much is it worth, to have peace of mind? Stand up.

In the dark, the corporate king rises to his feet.

Fearfully.

Remove your coat. And I will ask you a question.

The man slides out of his fine, seven hundred dollar suit coat, of the finest soft and pewter gray sheen.

How much is your family's life worth?

The man breathes a trembling breath in the dark. The tip of the blade is cold at his cheek.

Ten million dollars, he says. *I'll pay you another six and a half million. You'll have ten million dollars.*

You will take these nickels and dimes with you when you leave. When I see you again, you will have all of my money in one lump sum. Take off your shirt. How much is your family's life worth?

He fumbles with whatever shade of gray masquerades in his silken tie fabric, removing the sky blue shirt in trembling style.

Twenty million dollars, he says.

Your t shirt. And your pants.

Thirty million...forty million...

He removes his t shirt and his pants in the dark. His pallid skin glows in the starlight.

Your shoes. Your socks.

Seventy million, he says. *His voice near weeping. I will pay you seventy million dollars.*

He hops clumsily from foot to foot. Dropping his shoes and black socks somewhere in the grass.

Your underwear.

Please tell me…please have mercy for me…

In the shadow of night, the corporate king stands stripped of his dignity among the graves. Understanding the nature of fear.

Please tell me…

His cold, fearful hypocrisy is cut off, by the feel of sharp, cold steel placed gently at his livelihood. At his place down below.

ONE HUNDRED MILLION! I WILL PAY YOU ONE HUNDRED MILLION AMERICAN DOLLARS!

Slowly. Completely. Death's cold touch lowers away from the front of him. From where it was secured at the bottom of the front of him. He feels the presence behind him move slowly away.

In the next instant, there is the sound of a quick whisk of the wind, and the sharpness of a pain he never thought possible, in double lash into his skin, making him fall forward naked to the ground in a burning emanating from his back.

Hush up, is the sound he hears spoken in feminine sharpness, in the heat of his native tongue. *On your feet. Take your whore's money. And your filthy clothes. Bring my money here tomorrow night. Alone.*

What about the job, he asks, unaware of the blood that drips from his naked back to the ground.

That is up to me now. Your only concern is your gift to me. The price you pay for your greed. For your stupidity. Tomorrow night. Here. Or the next time you see me, I will not be wearing a dress.

In the cool of the cemetery night, underneath the stars of Heaven. The man stumbles bare skinned through the dark, holding his clothes and leather cases, in grieving to see the cutting of his white skin to blood. The man runs breathlessly through the dark, cold and naked, thanking his God that such a vulgar price is fit to be paid, from just the outer edges of what fortune he hath acquired. It is the cost of a lizard's tail, to escape the jaws of a hungry enemy in the woods.

The man stumbles, in sight of the safety of black luxury, falling flat on his face. Struggling to get back up, leaving the paper set free from one case flown open, not knowing what sock or shoe has been lost, nor what destination these flimsy bits of paper hath chosen upon the night wind. The man opens the doors of black luxury, throwing the clothes and the two briefcases inside, one of them flown open and empty. The next moment screams in the flow of time, in the voice of a grave road being marked by spinning tires, and an engine revved up to a place of agony and warning.

In the cool of a cemetery night. A shadow stands alone underneath the stars. Watching the condemned soul in hopeless flight. Hoping to flee. Hoping to flee the wrath to come.

My body will tell me when she is going to die.

When I open my eyes, I can see the fat, stupid man bound with his stupid clothes on. On the floor nearby his eight year old son. Both of them tied with rope, their arms behind their back, mouth gagged so tightly with their mother's cloth. Navy cotton-polyester weave, cut from her dress. The pieces used to bind their mouths too tight for them to speak. Only the sound of speechless voices muffled were heard, as they watched Mother and Sisters be hung upside down by their feet from the upstairs railing.

When I open my eyes, I can see the pool of blood on the floor underneath her. Underneath the twelve year old girl who bled with hardly a squeal, her voice held in check by fear. Her innocent young mind spared the indignity of terror. Hung up, strung up in dim witted compliance. Hung slowly from the railing upside down. Naked. Naked while her father and brother watched it happen. When I open my eyes, I see the naked girl's arms and hair hung down as she hangs. Two separate drippings into the same puddle of blood. Drip, drip, dripping from her long hair. Dripping from the tip of her fingers frozen in death. Blood on the edge of its last dripping. Its last attempt to speak.

I can feel my body about to tell the secret. The secret of life and death. The meaning of it all. I feel my body begin to speak to me, as I hang with my legs and arms clamped around his naked wife. Feeling the last of her whimpering. Feeling the fat of her buttocks pressed to the front of me.

I hang on to her. Upside down behind her. Waiting for my body to reveal its message to me. To speak to me the third part of the truth. The sorrow. The pain. The fear she feels take over her again. The sobbing shakes her body violently into mine. The fat of her mother-hips quivers against my groin pressed to them. *Do not move*, a voice tells me. *Let your body become. Become one with her suffering. Learn the truth of her suffering.*

From the center of my soul, I feel a calling from divinity. As though from the mountains of where I have lived and died to the flesh. It is a burning of another color flame within. Not the rage of this flame. This, the fear of revelation. This, the sorrow of truth revealed. This, the third part of the truth. Burning blue and black fire. This, the third part of the truth. Which is cataclysm.

This fire grows from the center of me. From somewhere in the Great Beyond. To reveal to me that even I cannot hide from it. From the truth of this reality.

Mankind is evil.

These words grip every part of my flesh. Pulsating my breasts and my heart. My bowels and my womb. *Hold on to her*, is the voice that speaks again to me, as I hear the cry of the damned. The wailing of the forest banshee. The screaming of the Jade Siren. I hold on to this woman for dear life, as the spirits torture me into completion. Holding me in the fire. Listening to me scream.

I hold on to the suffering woman. A woman who knows nothing of pain. Nothing of pleasure. Of life.

Of death.

Jonathan Lovejoy

Mayor Bynum Burns an Endtime Flame

9

The Jade Dragon burns an emerald flame

A rage too unfathomable to name

To cook the flesh from the bones of men

In the judgment of God over wickedness and sin

Mayor Bynum burns an endtime flame. On the eve of eschatology.

My heart grieves for the young Tiffany, twelve years along the timeline. In the sixth grade, she is. Pretty little Tiffany Bynum. Three years forward from Butt Bouncing in her jeans. When she first felt her mother shake. When she first heard her mother scream. Twelve year old Tiffany's already a young warrior in training. A little motheress born and bred. Taught in the daytime and nighttime dark behind closed doors, to service her mother in every way. Having learned to crave the smell of her mother's cunt. The feel of her mother's hands at the back of her little head. Having accepted the indignity of her face buried in the smooth shaven place, the angry screams of her thirty six year old mother clawing at the back of her head, holding it violently between her legs as she twists about in rage, at last unleashing a warrior's cry.

Having sworn already to hardly ever allow her husband anywhere near her desire. To let him ride himself into a spinning frenzy no more than once every six weeks. To lie there on her back in The Whore's Standard. Legs flared open in requisite. Without commitment. Without passion. Leaving her bra on. That it may scratch his pathetic flesh in resistance as he rides. Hair and makeup in place. Genuine pearl necklace donned at his request. Pearl earrings to guard the necklace from harm. From the harm of understatement. From the loveliness of feminine isolation. Essential in their calling. To help him ride to his pathetic heart's desire. To aid his visual of feminine power. To effectively draw strength from him. Draw life from him. Once every six weeks, she will listen to his pathetic siren. His pleading to the gods for mercy. Her face grimaced in irritation. Her mouth twisted in contempt. Grunting in disgust. Sounds he mistakes as pent up passion. Revulsion he mistakes for eros and reverie.

Amanda Bynum burns an endtime flame. On the eve of eschatology. Having kept her true desire channeled and archived. Stored up and released upon her calling. At least once every two weeks for three years. With many stretches of daily shuddering. Training her daughter to appreciate her. To crave her. To give her absolution. An outlet for her pain. *Harder and faster, please,* she begs. On her back in her daughter's bedroom. Away from the prying eyes of another. Just beginning to explore her anal obsession. At the beginning of its early perfection. Having discovered a drug no prescription can fill. The drug that sends lightning to the body. That sends thunder to the soul. On her back, her legs open wide for her daughter. For her twelve year old daughter that wears about her hips that rod of correction. The staff of discipline hung in realistic form. Slamming herself hard and fast, in and out, deep inside her mother's rectum. Unprepared for what it is she is about to see. Of what it is she must see. *Fuck me like you're angry with Momma, please,* she says. Her buttocks propped up on a pillow this time. Laid on the corner of her daughter's bed. Her daughter in flat chested, young girl energy and power. Pushing harder and faster into her mother than ever before. Wearing a thicker, longer member strapped on. The memory of her mother's exhortation still ringing a chime in her ears; *I want you to slide your new girl cock deep in Momma's ass, and fuck Mommy like you mean it okay?* Desperate to obey. In grieving to please her mother. Driving herself beyond exhaustion. Having already had to stop once, to control the lightning that shook her own little hips. Lightning that came when the mother touched her nipple with her thumb. Resting a moment. Readjusting herself for the second part. The second three feet in this grave to dig. Angry young energy back to full fathom. Twelve year old fury and determination. Glad to hear her mother suddenly sound as though she is going to weep. As though she is suddenly afraid. And from the midst of the pounding fever, comes a stream of crystal water up to her stomach. Shot up in greater power than pissing. In white crystalline pain and pleasure too deep to know. This, as the mother screams bloody murder once, and then a second time, to correspond with two powerful crystal pissing streams up from the front of her. Wetting the girl and the pillows underneath. Washing away what is left of her dignity. What is left of her sanity. *Don't stop, please, don't stop,* she says. Realizing that for her daughter to stop now would mean agony. As to stop running from ground that crumbles from a cataclysmic earth trauma. *Please...harder and faster,* she says. And she calls the names of divinity, the names of God and Holy Jesus spoken in a feeble cry for mercy, as she erupts a second time, screaming no less violently, but a scream now laced with the soothing caress of ecstatic cooling for the flame. *Make Mommy cum again... please make Mommy cum again,* this butt woman, this anal lady speaks, feeling her daughter's training come to full flowering, slamming obediently into her rectum per this request, knowing not to stop until the journey is done. Pounding the member deep and hard into her, until she screams and erupts again, to raise her crystal fountain a third time, not able to see her body pump it into the air as she lies lost in madness, finally reaching for her young daughter to climb on top of her, to hold her mother down as she shakes from the trauma of this cataclysm. From the violence of new discovery. As what happens when a new geyser is born from deep within the earth, to devastate the raw ground that it seeks. The woman lies there. Holding her twelve year old daughter without shame. Without control. Her entire body shaking like the ground at the Second Coming.

Amanda Bynum burns an endtime flame. On the eve of eschatology.

Amazonia

Christ will forgive me for the lives I must take. Through him, I know I can avoid the Lake of Fire and Brimstone. Before God, what is the difference between Adolf Hitler, and a doll faced hit lady? What is the difference between myself, and a little white liar in my rich Virginia suburb? How can a serial killer and a breakfast cereal killing Mom stand equal before God on Judgment Day? They all deserve jail, they say. They all deserve Hell, they say. Break man's law, you deserve to be disemboweled. Break God's law, you deserve to be eaten by owls in the dark. No compassion from person to person. No understanding from one to the other. We are a product of the tragedy of human existence, which is Fate. We cannot get along because the curse of God will not allow us to get along. From Eden to the Great Flood. From the Great Flood to the Crucifixion. From the Crucifixion to the Second Coming. The fate of mankind is the expression of evil. And to receive the consequences of that evil. The endtime expression of God is the death of mercy. The endtime expression of God is Judgment.

The screaming chaos in this crowded mall punishes me for my audacity. The loud, noisy-pretty black girls shoving and cursing at each other like dogs nearly makes me sick to my stomach. I have no desire to see their anger grow into the rage of hair pulling and clawing at one another by instinct, with no knowledge of the power the human body is capable of. The writhing and clawing of yowling, toothless, clawless cats they are, the sight and sound of which rises me up to my feet, to walk calmly and frustratedly away toward the nearest exit, regretful that the summer clouds have gathered, to punish me again with a rising wind, and the first drops of a fervent rain. I feel no remorse nor pity, when I imagine the sexy mall momma naked at my mercy, screaming from the agony of a dislocated arm, as she learns the power of grappling combat and skill. Your lovely, yellow brown skin will not save you from the wrath to come, my Dear. With your white oppressors, you will burn.

The first drops of this endtime storm attack me the moment I open the glass door to the outside. I so seldom feel at home among the Virginia southerners anyway, knowing that they have had enough of my unfamiliar face. The rain beats me with every step I take toward my black Mercedes luxury, insistent to echo into my brain the feel of my mother's belt on my face, and the resounding prophecy, *"every step you take for the rest of your life is cursed."* I take the rest of these accursed steps through the cold, early drops of rain, finding my refuge as the world prepares for a storm of long and melancholy duration. The trees already bend and sway with warning, in grieving to give voice to the terror of what they know, of the coming fire rained from Heaven.

The last drop of rain hits me in the eye, on my way into my rolling refuge, to flash the strap of leather across my eye in the heart of memory, that sent me to school the next day with a swollen eye and a scar underneath it, and faint bruises at my neck where her belt was put around my throat as I was drug to the bottom of the stairs, escorted up the length of them in stumbling, then to her bedroom where I was stripped naked and whipped to bruises and blood.

And what is it that I had done? Merely a fifteen year old sigh at the refrigerator as I poured a glass of sweet red drink after school. When I close the big, silver refrigerator door, I am met with her beautiful, angry face in waiting on the other side. A determined, satisfied anger, where her weapon is wrought with skill, making the glass of red liquid hit the tile floor and shatter into a million bloody little pieces at my feet. What is a glass of sweet red drink to me, when I need that hand to protect my other eye from the pain she wields? And then, what breath it is I have is cut off by the black leather, that was pulled so quickly from her jeans and folded into action on my face and arms, and now around my shoulders as my white book bag too is somewhere amidst the shower of glass and blood.

The autumn of the white woods continues to fall throughout my teenage years, as the canopy of snow white leaves continue to be taken up in the winds of endtime wrath, and the coming storm of eschatology. She hits me because she must. Whether in rage or righteousness, whether in anger or absolution, she needs no excuse to bring the rod of correction down upon me. Of what correction this is, I do not know. Very likely, it is my punishment from her, for committing the sin of confidence, the sin of self worth, the transgression of hope for the future.

A fat...breasted...whore... are the words I hear in allegiance with the rain, and the sound of the belt across my breasts in my memory, as the world around me disappears in a shower of wrath and summer cold. *A fat...breasted...slut...* are the words that I hear, in allegiance with this cold, summer storm, and the sound of my mother's belt across my naked backside, with her own curves bound up so tight in her black bra and underwear, to mock me as the ultimate hypocrisy of delusion, of a woman so curvy having the gall to express contempt for those of another. But I stand in place humiliated, as it is my custom to do, trying so hard to transcend the pain, but being unable. The belt across the wobble of my tits is as fire, the lash of it across the wiggle of my ass is blood.

And so too, the skin of my back is not spared. From my shoulders down to the curve of my hips, and down to the bone of my ankles. Of what purpose does a disrespectful sigh mean in the grand scheme of these things done in secret? This has nothing to do with righteous punishment, but is merely the continuation of my training, of my preparation to live the rest of this life in abject hopelessness, and regret for the day I was born.

Why, Mother Dear, are you angry with me? Is it because I am a bastard child of rape, when you were encouraged to embrace your Asian heritage, and entertain the possibilities of marriage to your own kind? Do you hate me, Mother, because this young Asian man impregnated you, this Japanese martial artist, who held you down on a date, who placed it inside you and held it there to completion? Do you hate me, Mother, because your own mother despised you as a whore of all whores, even though you tried to tell her you were raped? Do you hate me, mother, because the half rich white man you married died when I was a little girl, and left you alone with mediocre money and a mewling munchkin with eyes even more Asian than your own? Eyes that you sometimes slapped when I was two, three, four, five, seven, nine, eleven, thirteen, fifteen— because they looked at you the wrong way? Do you hate me, Mother, because your own mother wrestled you into submission more times than you can recall? Do you hate me, Mother, because after you were Judoed by this woman, you were caned and whipped to bruises and blood? Are you angry Sumi Sakara? Are you angry, Sue Green? Are you angry with Little Satari, because she reminds you of what the Asian man did to you in secret? Because you buried your white American revenge (husband) in humiliation and despair? Because after he died, you had to return to the arms of Hitomi Sakara, from you dead white husband's loving arms, to return to your mother's unloving arms? Here, as a grown woman with a child, as a grown woman with ties in community, as a grown woman of means, you were beaten in private like a bald headed stepchild, like an unwanted child called "it," though you were a woman already in her 30's, with a child not yet older than five. Hitomi Sakara, the gigantomastic Asian witch, breasts hung too big and heavy to be imagined by most, hung in proportion to her lust, this Hitomi Sakara, barely able to draw her English from the waters of her native tongue, this woman at the shores of fifty years young, reintroduced your *'disobedient whore's ass'* to the cane, the paddle, the strap and the whip, until as a grown woman you were reacquainted with tears, and the fullest purpose for which you were born—to receive suffering, and to give it no less abundantly. To be made to nurse at the woman's Vesuvian breasts until her body told you it was satisfied—to be forced as a grown woman to watch your own youthful and sensual mother's body do the Armageddon quake, caused by her breasts' unnatural sensitivity, and supernatural erotic ability. Yes, Sumi Sakara, yes, Sue Green, your mother is the famed Breast Goddess of legend, who bears this erotic obsession in her bra, and bears it out on your caned breasts striped in blood.

In the cold, summer rainfall. In the revelation of things to come. I am privy to thee, Sue Green. Grown widow woman with her hands behind her back, with her little slant eyed daughter asleep in her mother's little southern house by the woods, bent over in your mother's bedroom away from prying eyes, as she takes her pound of flesh from your buttocks with her cane, from the front and the backs of your thighs and most painfully, from your long breasts hung down in swinging repose, striping them from the top to the bottom, until she hears your pain threshold crossed, and Sue Green is Sumi Sakara again, and little Sarah Green is Satari Sakara, who cannot hear her mother in her grandmother's bedroom sobbing in tears from the agony of the cane upon her breasts, burned upon her skin with blue and black fire.

12

Amazonia looms like a ghostly, rogue planet over mankind's next horizon, on our journey toward the end of the age. Increasingly, boys and men are becoming background and props on the stage of civilized life, where the lust *of*, and the lust *for* women is taking over from top to bottom. It is a natural progression, as our acceptance of it has taken seven thousand years to manifest, finally coming to fruition here at the twilight of humanity. The God of War is now the Goddess of War, as she wields her sword and bullet proof bracelets in the power of eschatology. The God of Thunder is now the Goddess of Thunder, as she calls forth the lightning from the heavens in Norse beauty and power, extolling her worthiness to wield the sacred hammer in endtime feminine beauty. The rise of womanhood is the death of motherhood. As women are content now to compete with their daughters in sexuality, becoming more sensual minded as they get older, carrying their youthful libidos from their young adulthood onward, being consumed by it until well past middle age, where the sin of gray hair is done away with in the salon cathedral, and the skill of makeup lays waste to the trauma of aging, until mothers look like older sisters, and grandmothers look like mothers instead. This is the generation of the sexualized mother figure, where teenagers rate each other's Mom on the MILF scale, as to how badly she is a Mother I'd Like to Fuck. Women twenty years older and twenty years sexier than their daughters, advertising nature's gifts of fuller hips, bigger breasts, and greater sculpted maturity about the face, until pictures of these women from twenty years before show a woman decidedly less attractive. It is an endtime phenomenon, where feminine sensuality blossoms with age, where the days of matronly, middle aged motherhood are gone forever.

These women are drifting in the lascivious mind. Boiling in lust, being consumed by a desire that cannot be satisfied, by a fire that cannot be quenched. It is the rise of infidelity and divorce, the decline of the nuclear family, where the husband and wife are no longer the foundation of stability. It is the age of boyfriends and second marriages, where the term *cougar* is no longer a curiosity, but a necessity in the English language, to describe these predatory animals of lust and sensual instinct and craving. And underneath the iceberg of public sensuality displayed, there is a mountain of unseen, unspeakable, unfathomable things that must occur, where the full truth of Amazonia is run underground, and suppressed from public consciousness; where an infinity of daughters know the touch of their mother's hand, and the feel of their mother's lips upon their skin. Sweating. Grunting. Cunting in private, until the prophecy is fulfilled, that even the women have abandoned the natural use of the man. Daughters pressed down, held underneath their mother's whim, underneath their mother's quim in the dark, in their prayer closets of depravity, where only the walls are aware of the depths of what apocalyptic secrets are nurtured and grown. How many others are there must I join with in spirit, as I remember the flow of my mother's milk in my mouth? Trained to enjoy the pleasure of breast sex, enhanced by the sensual flow of milk, where sometimes every stitch of clothing is left on, with only our breasts exposed, nursing each other to completion, until the feeling trembles us below the waist, expanding to the rest of our body.

Sumi Sakara, a.k.a. Sue Green. My mother's strongest explosions would happen when I nursed the milk from her breasts in full, oftentimes me being lucky enough to catch a good glimpse of her expression, to see it twisted in something like fear and awe, from the love of erotic energy she would feel coursing through her body. The nursing she forced and coaxed upon me was not merely a twisted love as much as it was just twisted *sex,* which is what it was to her throughout my teenage years until I abandoned her. The massaging of them underneath her clothes, then underneath her bra was the foreplay, and the removal of her bra and the naked squeezing of them was as the sin of intercourse, as she would often stand still as I stood behind her squeezing them, wobbling them, pulling them, shaking them, even clapping them together until she could take it no more, begging me to pull them into my mouth and *finish me,* she would say, and these times clamping my lips onto a single, dripping breast for one long, continuous nursing without stopping, listening to her stop breathing in pure shock as the nursing pulls energy up from her groin into her body. These would deliver to her a thundering orgasm, where I would feel her whole body shake like a jackhammer, though she might be fully clothed with the two of us standing up in the middle of the floor, with the sound of a soprano shriek leaping from her mouth at times. As early as the seventh grade, up until my junior year in high school, my last year in high school, I was a prisoner of her body's craving. A privileged witness to its magnificent sensitivity, a trait that can hardly be taught and learned at the level she displayed. A condition undoubtedly inherited from Hitomi, whose expressions of her psychology on my mother were almost exclusively breast centered.

In the heart of my soul's memory, somewhere along the timeline of grieving, I can see Sumi and her mother Hitomi, in their little isolated house nearby the Virginia wood. Hitomi's English is buried in Japanese tone when it is spoken, preferring to speak to her daughter and her sister Lin in her native tongue. I see Hitomi and her fifteen year old daughter Sumi, engaged in secret while Lin is away at one of her many jobs, able to keep their meager money flowing through her 80 hour work week, unafraid of a long day's labor at two supermarket bakeries, to care for her giant breasted sister and heavy breasted niece.

Lin, a.k.a. Linda Sakara is not spared the power of this perversion, loving nothing more than the opportunity to bury her face between Hitomi's J cupped mountains at every opportunity, or to nurse at them until her own mouth is sore from the sucking. Lin is away at her cupcake and cookie baking infinity, unaware of her sister and her fifteen year old niece (my mother) back at the house on Robin Hood Road. Lin cannot see her sister in her long, peasant skirt standing in the middle of the bedroom floor, topless, so that the two enormous jugs are exposed for her young daughter to play with.

Sumi stands obediently behind her mother, holding them up from underneath, slamming them together like two giant paddleballs, already understanding deeply from whenceforth her mother cometh, and to the divine pleasures of this breast obsession, which is so many could develop to a degree if they understood. But what is so rare and special as a breast goddess, superior to a breast queen, is that her erotic obsession is universal, and almost exclusively devoted to her breasts and those of another woman. For Hitomi, the other woman is her own daughter, a lust inherited from the old country, lost somewhere in the rolling green hills of the Japanese countryside.

Hitomi stands still, pressed back up against her strong young daughter, who attacks the two flesh pillows with skill and purpose, attacking them like she knows how, slamming them together in full clapping sound and without mercy, stopping every so often to give them a squeeze, the two of them so safe from eyes that pry, then returning to smacking them together again, knowing this time not to stop, until the stern, sober minded woman's body has ignited this flame. It is a condition that affects so few women in full measure, where the squeezing, massaging, sucking or shaking of their breasts sends signals straight to their groin, in a feeling so far beyond ordinary touching of the genitals, causing full arousal by breast stimulation alone. And this is not from any deep concentration in particular, but simply the prolonged manipulation, which eventually leaves the woman on the edge of devastation and ruin. And this is the precipice where Hitomi Sakara has been brought to again, by the capable hands of her fifteen year old daughter Sumi (my mother), who slows the rhythm down enough for the long haul, for the slapping together of her mother's J cups until the fires have been lit, and the chain reaction has been achieved.

And Hitomi feels the gradual, strong twinge of muscles down below, as the spirit within her begins the unmerciful caress and squeeze, enough to suddenly make her grab on to her daughter from behind her, and wonder if she has not made a tragic error in this decision. But in fear, her lovely features begin that familiar anguish, the wrinkling of the brow, the opening of the mouth, the loud and irregular breathing, the pitiful whimpering in want, as she is helpless to endure what the clapping together of her breasts has started in her body.

And suddenly, her hearing phases into a dull echo of itself, as she can no longer hold her eyes from rolling back, as her brain seizures a network of lightning to her breasts and her lower body, causing her to push back automatically against her daughter who holds her tight, as her body jerks many times in her daughter's arms, giving her just enough breath for one loud and pitiful shriek into the room around them.

Jonathan Lovejoy

The Stormkeeper

13

*I*n the aftermath of my soul's tragic recollection, the blue and black fire in my body is morphed to jade again, as I think about who it is that must soon die.

> *I have cried so many times*
> *But only for things that never were mine*
> *Heaven is sweet, love is unkind*
> *Thoughts are twisted inside your mind*
>
> *Culture Club*

Jade

I can barely see the houses in this pristine neighborhood. Cruising the fine, friendly streets in black Mercedes luxury, having more contempt than envy for their perfectly manicured hypocrisy, and exquisitely landscaped pretense in leaf blade and emerald green. These are the brick laid houses of lower million dollar privilege, where Fate has placed the mothers and the motheresses in comfort cushioned luxury, believing that they are beyond the judgment of the Almighty by status, and blameless in the court of Divinity. These are the souls of false charity on display, where trumpets of alms are blasted in the ears of God until he can endure no more, and his judgment is visited upon the palaces of the haughty and the well to do.

These are the homes where the evils within cannot be imagined. Where the chorus of voices are gathered in the endtime cry from the deep: *she puts the pillow over my head at night,* as the legion of teenage daughters call out to the Lord in their dreams, to send an angel of mercy to avenge them, to rescue them from the secret tragedy they must endure. Female doctors, lady lawyers and corporate executives, stars of the academic world and the local news world, married to husbands of means, daughters of fathers with old money—women who masquerade in the cause of female empowerment, who have relegated their daughters to a place of sorrow, to a lifetime of hopelessness, having touched them in places unspeakable, in ways unfathomable, done in the halls of privilege, behind the walls of secret.

And I have been cursed with the motheress eye, in that the spirits that govern my condemned life have spoken this gift unto me, that I know beyond the shadow of a doubt who has cursed themselves by entrance into this house, this accursed house of Mother Daughter Perversion, where innocence is plucked from the meadows of purity, and tossed into the fires of cerulean and pitch. These are the generations of mothers who fuck their daughters behind closed doors, who beat their daughters behind closed doors, who torture their daughters behind closed doors in the spirit of modern day witchcraft, of the kind sold out to the whims of Lucifer, who hath deceived the daughters of men, and have led them to the Forest of Depravity.

And these things are done in the name of Discipline, done in the name of correction, until these daughters drift through life in an emotional netherworld, in a kind of living death, a purgatory of spiritual confusion they may never awaken from. And this torment they feel pains them night and day, causing them to suffer without ceasing. Running from job to job, house to house, hopping from bed to bed, from medicine cabinet to liquor cabinet, looking for a way to throw the vengeful ghost that clings to them like a *ju-on* to their back; presiding over unjust court rulings, unjust gradings in their classrooms, unjust credit decisions in their banks and lending houses, unjust punishments in their jails and prisons; lives of fungalooga happiness washed over misery. Unhappiness meted out in constant bitterness toward the husband, resentful slavedriving of the children into a place beyond exhaustion, giving what love and affection there is left to the church, the community, the job, the secret lover—ever searching, never able to come to the knowledge of the truth. Enduring the weight of the white-skinned, black haired ghost that rides their back, until they are doomed to accept the truth.

And these are the ones who stand in their thirteen year old daughter's doorway at night. In the bedroom of their privileged home. Watching their daughter sleep. Confronting the pain that charges its way from their soul into their groin, into their breasts, into every limb and extremity—

pain born from the memories of over the knee hairbrush spankings, naked, upright paddlings with the wooden board, the switch or the cane across their naked breasts, the sound of their mother's hot, bellowing voice in their ears as she lays on top of them and swears to *God* that she will learn them to obey. Still in a simmering, seething rage of memory as adult women, their skin still itching in recollection, understanding at long last that there can be only one way for this pain to end, one solution to the problem of the curse clung heavy to their back. This ghost aches at their breasts and their groin, until there is but one solution that must be tried. One answer that must be given. And this is the Curse of the Motheress. The corruption that must be passed down to the next generation, as the threats and intimidation and manufactured discipline must finally have its harvest. And these are the mothers, in these privileged houses of wealth and means, these are the mothers who simply climb into the beds of their daughters at the next crossway opportunity, at their next convenience—either in their daughter's bed, or their bed, or a hotel bed, or a sleeping bag on a camping trip, or the bed at grandmother's house—to finally do what they have ached to do since the girl was nine, or eight, or seven, or six—having held it in for as long as they possibly could, until there are no more outlets through which this accursed ghost can be appeased. These are the mothers who whisper in their thirteen year old daughter's ear of The Mommy Game, of pleasures that must be wrought, of secret debts that must be paid. These are the mothers whose fingers tremble at the buttons of their daughter's pants, whose hands fumble at the fabric of their daughter's shirts raised, whose lips quiver at the touch of their daughter's lips, whose suckling tongue twitches at the feel of their young daughter's nipple—these are the mothers who can no longer bear the weight of the curse that haunts them night and day, until they must stand in the soapy shower with the girl, with their soapy finger pushed into the girl's bottom, or until they are on the toilet in the longest piss of their thirty three year old lives, with their thirteen year old daughters straddled across their pissing lap—or until they are on all fours over top of their daughter, who is on all fours underneath them on the bathroom floor. Or until their daughter lies underneath them on their backs, their young legs spread open, to receive the curse of their mother's life passed down.

As I roll slowly past this house of million dollar privilege, I am burdened by the sights, the sounds, the smells of Amanda Bynum's surrender, when her daughter bounced her blue jeaned bottom against her healthy bottom a generation ago. I am burdened by Amanda Bynum's surrender, as she snuck into her daughter's room the very next night, sneaking past the spirits in an empty house, as the reign of million dollar privilege had fully settled in, in the days when big money was young. In the shadows of this fresh new mansion home, Amanda sneaks back into the innocent presence of her young daughter, kissing her fully on the mouth as the girl lays on her back, sliding out of her long night shirt and underwear, in a feeling she has not had in a generation of years, placing the front of herself to the smooth front of her daughter. Holding herself up on her arms in full woman's strength above the girl, coaxing her to take a breast into her mouth, a feeling that twitches a lightning bolt to her heart and mind, telling her *you have to fuck her.*

I see Amanda Bynum lay down full and heavy on her nine year old daughter, her breasts in D Major mashed big and round against the girl's chest and shoulders, telling the girl Tiffany, *open your legs for Mommy.* This, she does. As the woman touches her big witch clit to the little girl's smooth self down below, shuddering in new revelation to the power of perversion, settling in for a rhythm that was passed down as privilege, a rhythm that her body has never known.

This wealthy young mother can waste no time on a slow grind, but must pound herself with slow, deliberate authority into her daughter, to establish this depraved dominance outright, hidden in the nighttime dark, believing she is covered from the prying eyes of every all knowing constellation in the heavens. But the message of her delusion is written in the stars, as they look upon the suffering of women and men, watching past the barriers of fiberglass shingles and wood, to see the whited skin of the naked woman, who pounds her hips up and down on top of the girl because she can't help it, because she must obey her body, and because she could not stop if she tried. The woman's body settles into a heavy, steady rhythm of its own accord, quickly gathering steam and momentum of feeling in her soul, which tells her not to alter her motion as she fucks her daughter—as you put your witch cock inside her pathetic innocence and kill it for all time.

Fuck her until I tell you to stop, is the warning whispered in her mind, causing her to shake her head in disbelief in the dark, that motion such as this can come to life and take over a person—mind, body and soul. In relaxed motion of purpose, she slams this endtime message home, that there is none good, that no, there is nowhere to hide from the coming judgment; that no, you will not be allowed the freedom to live without me, that yes, you are *Mommy's little bitch girl, Mommy's little bitch girl, Mommy's little bitch girl,* unable to keep the words from spilling out under their own power, followed by the sound of an animal that is a woman, a woman that is an animal—a grunting so deep, so gruff, of such protracted and melancholy endurance as to be terrifying, as the wave of energy passes slowly through every inch of her body.

I see Amanda Bynum. Laid upon her daughter in the million dollar dark. Her body shaking with sobs, her muscles twitched in the agony of weeping, the deepness of her voice now grunting with the sorrow of regret, as her soul absorbs the ingestion of this fruit as bitter wormwood, laid in grieving on top of her daughter in the dark. From the curse of what I see, I am lifted from the heart of the earth's tragic memory, carried back to the present day, in my death chariot on the streets of this town, down just a little ways from this gray brick house of privilege.

In keeping with the spirits of my calling, I see the silver SUV, shining its privileged lights in the lull in this twilight rain. When the SUV parks, I see a tall, lovely blonde with dead eyes and a pleasant, defeated expression get out of the passenger side, and walk around to the driver's side where the shorter, more beautiful, mature version of herself stands waiting, her expression colored by somber complacency, and epic confidence in her power over nature itself. As I watch the beautiful older woman take the pretty younger woman by the hand, the lull in the rainfall passes away in an instant, and I watch the two women fade to ambiguity as they enter the mansion, safe from the new round of driving rainfall that descends as a veil of mystery, hiding their life from the angry clouds above, and from the eyes that stare in the world down below.

hunder rolls over the death of cultured civility. To announce the arrival of the Jade Silk Warrior. And I know this journey hath been blessed by the Gods of who I am, as they have commanded every desperate drop of rain to cease, so that not a single drop of water has touched me on this night journey. The clouds flash and rumble with anger, the skies scream in rage at the inhabitants down below, in grieving to drown every soul in pent up fury. I stand tall and straight, having leapt from the roof to the railing of an upstairs balcony in the back of the house, knowing that my feet would not slip as I landed in kneeling position, guided by the spirits of what I must do.

Oh, how terrifying a sight it would be, to witness this leap of impossibility! What dark creature, what shadow monster must this be! I hop down to the lovely white painted door, hardly surprised that it is unlocked, as if presented as another sign to me, on my journey into this valley of death. I am standing in the nighttime dark of upper middle class cleanliness and luxury, oppressed by the smell of new carpet and money, fresh paint and perfume, with the hint of soaps and shampoos galore, and candies hidden in drawers scattered throughout. What human mercy, what compassion I am capable of is gone.

There are two high classed, high minded souls that must be separated from their bones tonight.

And I thank providence in my heart, that there are no other souls in this house for me to tie up and torture, no other souls to spoil the intimacy of what must be done. I am guided as on a current of knowing, my dagger strapped to my leg, my sword sheathed and ready at my back. The skin tight garment I wear is as black as pitch, in contrast to the white skin that shows on the side of each leg in unique design. My curved middle is exposed to my liking below my naval, underneath great bosoms bound tight in midnight fabric, to match the armbands on both forearms, one of which displays the elegance of a dragon silhouette of emerald green. Only my eyes are visible, above the silken black mask tied around my nose and mouth, to hide my expression from the women I must kill, and from these spirits that guide me to their doom.

On the current of bloodlust, I drift unbeknownst to them. Pulled along by instinct, moving from the small, isolated bedroom down the darkened upstairs hall, until I am able to see a gigantic television screen playing silently down below. On the sofa, engaged in a deep and passionate kiss,

I am witness to an endtime truth hidden in the shadows, as I see an older blonde woman of mature, sensual beauty in a pressing, aggressive press upon a younger woman's lips—a woman a generation younger than she, and many years less sensual and beautiful.

The two of them continue to kiss fully clothed, button down shirts and t shirts in place, kissing as if they can no longer perceive the world around them. As I walk (glide) slowly down the stairs, taking each step in abject silence, I begin to hear the strength of their breathing, as the older woman releases her kiss and turns her head, to receive the younger woman's kisses upon her neck. The woman devours her neck in vampiric lust, to where the sounds of a sucking kiss are present, causing the older woman to hold her head back and groan deeply.

And this I know is the most powerful sign unto me, that I am obeying what is written upon the celestial parchment, since east of Eden, at the beginning of time. As I step from the staircase around to the front of the sofa, my blood burns with the fires of my calling. Even I am amazed that though I stand between them and their giant TV, I am as of yet unseen. But suddenly, the older woman's eyes drift open just enough, and I am witness to the lightning caused by the spirit of fear, which makes her shriek a mezzo soprano syllable, answered by her daughter's high soprano in this duet of horror.

"Who *are* you?" Amanda says. "How did you get in my house?"

In apocalyptic shock, they are both witness to a nightmare phantom, transcended from their darkest dreams into reality. Standing in front of them is a long legged woman of nearly six feet, dressed in tight, night warrior's attire, staring at them with Asian eyes of fury.

"Tiffany, call the police."

The two of us, I and the daughter Tiffany are suddenly joined as one, as she leans over to the night stand for the little phone thing. Her motion seems to pull me along, unlatching, unsheathing my knife from my leg, lunging as if in a slow motion dream, watching, feeling the tip of the knife blade meet her hand over the oakwood endtable, slamming through it with all smoothness of purpose, attaching her to the wood through the back of her hand. The scream that pours forth from the motheress' mouth is touched by the spirit of death.

I stare at the gold handled dagger, in finely crafted emerald jewel design, watching the blood run, able to see the mother standing up slowly, with both her hands over her mouth. I reach back and remove my mask, tossing it away toward the silent TV playing, ignoring the image of blonde and brunette suburban violence ready to be born.

"Why are you doing this? You're beautiful. I don't understand."

"Take off your clothes."

"I can't. I can't..."

The sound of her ridiculous defiance moves my arm to action, sliding my sword out slowly. Touching it to her daughter's hand.

"Take off your clothes."

"I will! Okay, I will."

I return my sword to its place. Watching the middle aged beauty fumble with every button of her sky blue shirt. Sliding it off and away. Removing the like colored t shirt, her expression burdened by dejection. The big, white lace bra holds a symphony in F, of which I myself am familiar when I look in the mirror. She bends over, fit and voluptuous, sliding her jeans down, kicking hem to the side (where her low heeled black casuals had just gone to rest), standing back up in foolish pretend for just a moment, then reaching back and unlatching the big lace bra frac. The daughter strains her head back to look, her face red and wet with tears from the stress of her trauma. The woman bends over, sliding he underwear down from hips spread to infinity from the small waist, her breasts hung heavy and low in the F major key.

"Your big, long breasts are beautiful. When did you first put them in your daughter's mouth?"

"I…"

A quick motion to my sword handle in its sheath awakens her memory.

"I…I nursed her as a baby."

"After?"

"She…she was nine years old."

"Take off your daughter's clothes," I say. Lowering my head.

The woman walks nude over to her daughter, unable to gather control of how to proceed.

"What about the knife?"

"Take it out."

With both hands, the naked woman pulls the dagger from her daughter's hand, flinching when her daughter screams and double's over in agony.

"Bring it to me."

She obeys quickly, tensed up in modesty unclothed, then returning to her injured daughter. Slowly and deliberately, taking off every stitch of her daughter's clothing. The two of them stand still in front of the sofa, naked, trembling from fear and cold. Outside, the storm gives its rumbling account of the tragedy inside, unable to hold back any longer the deluge of pent up, drowning fury.

"Your daughter's hips are like yours. But she has no breasts. Very large black nipples. When did you first suck your daughter's nipples? When she was nine?"

The woman nods her head without a word, her lips tucked in, tears streaming down both sides of her face. Both mother and daughter stand nude, their hands clasped in front to hide their depravity. The daughter's hands and thighs are stained with blood.

"Stand behind your daughter. Hold onto her arms."

"No, please," she says, as I pull the sword free. "What can we do to change your mind?"

"It is as the wind and the sea. The tide, the sun, and the moon. This always has been…"

In a flash of motion barely seen, I slash the long blade diagonally from the bottom of her tiny breast to her lower abdomen, then diagonally from the other breast, to create the tell tale sign, the signature of who was here, and of what tragedy was meant to be. The young woman's body stiffens in shock, as she falls heavily toward the gray carpet, her mother still trying to hold her by her arms as she falls lifelessly to the floor.

The mother can only stand there. Not screaming. Hardly able to breathe. Watching the blood flow.

"Take me to your room."

Fully exposed, tense and cold in the storm, the mother turns to walk pitifully in front of me to the stairs, taking each step in greater false hope than the last, that somehow she will be allowed to live, and tell the world of what depravities there are in jade and blood.

In the upper room, I lay my dagger and my sword on the finely crafted, darkwood mirror dresser. Immediately removing my top fabric, to let the truth of who I am wobble free, in as magnificent a proportion as this woman, though firmer and rounder, with nipples poked further out even when unaroused, above a waist thin and deeply curved inward, the Nova Curve of legend. I bend over, the assassin stripped bare of her pretense, sliding out of my warrior's pants and boots, wearing only my jade dragon arm bands, and a head of long, silken black hair.

"Come here, Mother."

The woman walks cautiously over to me, in full naked repose, as the lightning flashes a violent, screaming message in the storm. In front of the mirror, I stand behind the busty, hippy woman. Watching her look at herself, to try and fathom the best laid plans, and how completely they do not come to fruition.

I take up the dagger. Running it gently across her nipple. Gently. Watching it grow erect from the cold.

"Close your eyes," I say. Taking her by the throat. "Receive your redemption, accursed woman. In *blood.*"

Upon this last word spoken, the last word she is destined to hear, I bury the dagger deep into her gullet, pulling it up in trademark diagonal form, then quickly crossing another long and deep cut across the first one. Gripping her tight as she stands stiff back against me, her eyes wide open, her body trembling from the strain, as she struggles to hold on to herself, to keep her soul from leaving her body.

I hold on to her. My arms wrapped tightly, her arms pinned to her sides as the blood flows free from her body opened up, her eyes at last slipping from clarity, her focus on a place beyond the walls of her suburban palace prison. I hold on. Feeling the life slip from this woman, unable to stop my body's acknowledgement of my calling, as every inch of my flesh begins to tremble and shake on its own, as I listen to the warrior's cry appear from deep within, answered by the flash and rumble of thunder and lightning from the storm.

The Nutcracker

" **℞**esidents *of Washington Township, Virginia are stunned today at the death of fifty four year old Mayor Amanda Bynum and her thirty two year old daughter Tiffany, a teacher at a prestigious local all girl private school. Both women were found murdered in their wealthy suburban home this morning. The bizarre, gangland style murders have police baffled as to who could have done these killings, as neither of the women is known to have any connections with the criminal underworld. The bodies of the mother and daughter were found nude in their Virginia mansion, in a standing position, with their hands nailed to the walls and their feet nailed to the floor. Both women had suffered a deep, X shaped cut in their abdomen, the apparent cause of both their deaths. I'm Cora Leeds, the Associated Press.*"

"You will obey me, or you will die."

I am seventeen, when the spirit came unto me. I am seventeen, when the spirit hath come.

In the Heart of Memory, I am in the studio of false hope. In a hall of mirrors, in my stretchy black cat suit. Alone, long after the ballet teacher and the other students have gone. I am free to do the things that have so little to do with arabesques and fouettés, or hopping up and down en pointe, or posing with my leg over the bar and my arm raised pointlessly in the air. *You leap like a gazelle,* the teacher often says to me, *won't you let me put you in touch with a real ballet teacher, honey? You've got too much potential to be hanging around here.*

But of what potential this is, I have no concern. For I have no aspirations of dancing the Nutcracker Suite at the Community Cultural Center or the Virginia Opera House, or anywhere near the grand world stage in the big cities here and abroad, one of maybe two yellow flowers in the majority field of white. The Busty Ballerina, too round chested to be taken seriously anyway, unwilling to let a doctor butcher my chest for thousands of dollars just to find that I am still never going to be a prima ballerina. I am content to dance in the shadows, to use these stretches and turns, these runs and leaps as an outlet for my pain—to sometimes wear my pink tutu in front of the mirror so that I can see myself act out the Chinese Dance with aplomb, knowing somehow that I would bless the Christmas stage with my presence, if it were meant to be, legs and torso being long enough to offset the top heaviness they would see, so that my tragic silhouette would be in perfect balance, hiding myself on stage in plain view, a flower plucked from the field of secrets, displayed for all the world to see. But I find myself more a student of Angela Mao and Michelle Yeoh in spirit, progressing myself from the mastery of advanced ballet to basic martial arts, needing to become well versed in the movement of the heavy *bo* staff in private, spinning it around with the speed of a majorette on the fourth of July.

I feel most at home with the heavy wooden staff, even filming myself to see how ridiculous I look, but being shocked at the apparent brilliance of what I see, as if I am looking at someone else, at someone who is ready to audition as a stunt double in a movie. This, I have shown to no one, making sure these studio doors are locked when I practice. I have turned and leaped about in a whirling of wood, knocking the heads off of ghosts and witches that appear before me like puffs of smoke, then vanish when I flash the staff through them in just the right way. I have a burning inside, a fire that has been growing since I was twelve, to give myself over to a teacher, Tae Kwon Do or Karate, maybe, though my heart tells me that I need to be baptized in the waters of Kung Fu. What nonsense is this, a suburban Japanese Virginia girl looking for a Chinese martial arts teacher! Where? But even my mother wrestles Judo for sport, using me as her practicing dummy every so often, enjoying the flop and wobble of my breasts as she flips me into submission.

There are times when I have wanted to hop up to her big head and wrap my legs around it, and flip her over onto her back with a neck so sore that she would think it was broken. Somewhere deep inside me, it is something that I know I am capable of. But I gladly put on my biker shorts and go topless with my giant breasted mistress, who flops around so unashamedly in those hanging G majors, breasts too big to be believed as she removes her bra that says 36 H on the band, but were smaller than the J cup mountains her own mother often smothered her with. I think that Mother enjoys to no end the topless combat, the intense wrestling of me into painful submission, teaching me all basic moves, which she allows me to practice on her until I get it right, then surprising me with some brilliant flip or spin to subjugate me again. Truthfully, her skill is apparent, though she never competed for an Olympic medal or a World Championship or any other such foolishness. But the speed and strength she displays on her sparring dummy, me, is enough to convince me that she knows what she is doing. She even encouraged me to take up Karate, though I wanted when I was younger to be a ballerina. She signed me up for classes when I was eleven years old, as every mother might vicariously do for her daughter. Especially when her own mother (Hitomi) told her when she tried ballet at sixteen, "*your tits too fat, look like pig,"* a comment which humiliated her so badly that she quit and took up Judo instead. Angrily wrestling Hitomi into agony as many times as she could, trying to dislocate her own mother's arm on one occasion even after her mother had given up.

"I am still your mother," Hitomi had said. *"You can break my arm into a thousand pieces, and I am still your mother."* Hitomi had grabbed my mother's big face and said, *"and you will obey me, or you will die. Do you understand?"* And my mother had lowered her eyes respectfully and nodded, saying *yes Mother* in her mother's native tongue. *"Next time I tell you let go, what you do?"*

"I let go."

"For what you did to my arm, I swear you will suffer."

"I'm sorry."

"You are not sorry," Hitomi had said. *"But you will be."*

That night, Hitomi boiled a big, metal serving spoon in a pot of water, and pressed it to the middle of Sumi's back. *"For your disrespect,"* she said. And when Mother wrestled the giant breasted Hitomi from that day forward, it was with reticence and hesitation. A natural barrier and inhibitor placed, so that Mother was never comfortable enough to advance, never comfortable enough to compete beyond her black belt.

What are the fires of motivation that burn? What are the barriers that rise and fall? That hinder us on our journey toward the horizon? What is this blue and black flame, that drives my mother to try and pull my arm out of the socket sometimes when she wrestles me? Why is it, that when the ballet teacher comes by the house and says, *Mrs. Green, I have a lot of pathetic, wannabe students come through my studio, and well, one of the reason we teach is because we never really made it ourselves, and so, we're always looking for that one student who can do that thing that we can't. And the truth is, Mrs. Greene, I don't know if I've seen a little ballerina that makes me think of The Nutcracker Suite every time she starts dancing. That is, until I saw little Sarah Green..."* What is it, oh dear Mother, that causes you to remove me from her class the very next day? Why, Mother, did you tie me up in the brown extension cords and throw me on the bed like a rolled up carpet, and beat me with a stick until my bones felt like they had been crushed to powder? Why, Mother, did you leave me alone in the room in the dark for three days, not coming into the room once, to see if I was still alive? Do you know the cause of such a mighty hunger and thirst, dear Mother, that courses through a daughter's veins when she is near death?

In the heart of memory, I am seventeen, when you decide that you have had enough of my insolence, my disobedience, my disrespect, when you go to the bookstore one afternoon to poke fun at your loser daughter, buying some book on flower arranging that you will never read, but the cover which is a coffee table wonder. The young, blonde chippie at the counter is too new and stupid, too young and dumb to know that the Asian girl is sworn to this deadly secret, when she says, "Sarah's still at ballet class, she won't be in until after seven o'clock."

The young, blonde chippie is too ignorant to know of doors open along the timeline, of portals activated by words and events, of Predestiny's awakening at such checkpoints along the way. She knows nothing of the look that settles over your lovely Asian face, Mother, as you suddenly seem to be looking through her to another place, another place along your journey. A place where East and West at last do meet, to provide a cataclysm of which they collide. She knows nothing of the look you bear, Mother. The enigmatic smile you give when she hands you your pretty flower book in the plastic bag.

Now go, Mother. Go to the only ballet studio in town. Whether or not I am there, is not important. You will drift through the next few days anyway, asking around, looking, until you find the ballet studio of my traiterism. The studio of my insurrection. The studio of my betrayal.

The beautiful Asian woman arrives at the ballet studio. The small little nothing of a created space. A monument to failed aspirations. A shrine to every broken dream. And in this little parking lot of this little so-called dance studio...is a car. A single, silver Sonata. A melody in stylish economy. Affordable mercy of design.

The beautiful Asian woman steps out of the car. Walking in the haze of disbelief. Opening the door into the tiny entrance hall, where the window provides a view. In time to hear Tchaikovsky carry her daughter's treason to heights of beauty. Watching the beautiful Asian girl in full regalia, hair pinned back, makeup in place, leotard as white as snow. Watching the final waltz of The Nutcracker lift her daughter up in leaps ad nauseam, around the length of the studio, ending with whirling perfection, as channeling the ghost of Margot Fontaine, then fading into an arabesque stance of the sugar plum fairy herself, where her body control is the stillness of a statue, whose beauty is as the stars of Heaven. Body bent, hands up, leg curved up in perfect position, as still as a marble statue at the top of a crystal fountain waterfall. It is the most beautiful thing she has ever seen, she is devastated to admit, as she turns away and goes to her silver SUV. Unable to quell the rising tide of emotion. Tears born from a perfect storm of feeling. Not the least of which is a rage unfathomable.

Sumi Sakara

Rides the Wind

$\mathcal{S}$umi Sakara rides the wind. On the eve of eschatology.

Arriving at her lovely suburban home. In the aftermath of trauma. Sniffing. Wiping the tears away. Walking those high heeled steps from the car into the endtime palace of perversion. The hall of hidden depravity.

Sumi goes up the stairs to prepare the chamber. The chamber of screams. She gathers the ropes. The whip. The curling iron.

Sumi Sakara rides the wind. Back down stairs to where the hours wait. Where the timeline must slow down to a crawl. Cooking. Eating. Drinking. Waiting. Waiting for the slant eyed bitch to come home. For the fat breasted whore to walk in.

Jade

Sumi Sakara rides the wind. Drifting the hours as though on a raft down a river. A river of endless searching. A hopeless sojourn for buried treasure. A wilderness of lost hope. A wasteland of empty promises unfulfilled.

The hours pass her daughter into being. This, upon the sound of her car's arrival. The Sonata's tragic, melancholy key.

In the dark of night, as a hidden shadow from beneath the stars, the daughter emerges. Drifting through the door in false humility. Gliding through lies across the floor. In the audacity of a fungalooga grin. In ignorance of what ails her. Of what tragedy must befall.

The mother steps forward to the daughter. Arm raised to gather truth. Flowing back toward the daughter in pendulum swing. Slamming the palm of her hand to the girl's lovely cheek. Knocking her off balance. Grabbing her hair with both hands. Dragging her kicking and screaming to the stairs. Dragging her, one stair at a time, to the top of their violent climb. To the invisible gate of the upstairs hall. Dragging her to the upper room.

In the bedroom, the beautiful Asian woman slaps the girl again. Then with the back of her hand. Knocking her half senseless to the bed. Stripping her clothes. Ripping her bra away. Binding her legs with rope. Pulling her arms tightly behind her back. Binding her wrists immobile.

I saw you, are the only words her body can utter. The only syllables she can grunt in loud whispering.

The mother gathers up the whip of legend. A small, black serpentine. She stripes her daughter's naked skin from her shoulders to her ankles. Cutting her daughter's white skin to blood.

The daughter jerks. She twists. She rolls and falls to the floor. This, in a flurry of wild lashes. Cutting her to blood on the bedroom floor.

The Asian woman drags her daughter in shrieks up by her hair. Like a tied up sack of laundry linen to the bed. Staining the white sheets with crimson. The mother breathes through exhaustion. Gathering the heated curling iron quickly from the nightstand. Not stopping her spit from falling from her mouth.

I saw you, she says. *You will obey me. Or you will die.*

The mother gathers the heated curling iron. The iron too hot to touch. Pressing it heavy onto the middle of her daughter's back. Burning the skin to black. Hearing her daughter's death scream.

She presses the curling iron a second time. To elicit a second death scream. Pressing it a third time. And then at last a fourth. Memorizing the fourth death scream. Feeding upon its disillusionment. The agony of its despair.

Sumi Sakara rides the wind. On the death of her daughter's sanity. The death of cultured civility.

Sumi Sakara rides the wind. On the eve of eschatology.

An American
Girl in Japan

A warrior's heart is forged in the fires of suffering.

These words haunt me as I disembark my heavenly ride. A million miles from where the heat of eschatology burned a dragon into my back. A fascinating raised scar it is, a mark of suffering branded by the Almighty himself, to mark me as a child of suffering. I endured the fall and spring of my eleventh grade year seemingly with a huge bandage on my back, until at last I was able to remove it forever. The shape of what I saw was in such elegant simplicity of purpose, in such glorious revelation to my spirit that I was overwhelmed with knowledge of the future, and what lay forward on my journey along the timeline.

I can barely see the stars through the glow of the ambient light over Tokyo, an American girl in Japan, though who would know it without me speaking? Hitomi and Sumi both made sure I was bilingual by the age of seven, but there is still the slightest hesitation of thought every so often, that marks me as a foreigner in disguise.

The truth is, I hardly know why I am here. The same way any lonely soul runs away from home to another part of the world, wondering where the hand of Fate will finally take hold. Wondering what lies around the next curve of the river traveled, what triumph or tragedies lie in store. Maybe, it is this dreadful uncertainty I feel that attracts the sympathetic traveler, a pretty woman much older than myself, who seems to know immediately that I am American.

Maybe, my looks have provided me some advantage here, I don't know. But the woman is deeply sympathetic to me—asking me do I have a job and a place to live, do I have any family here at all. And what am I supposed to say, my mother burned a dragon into my back and promised to kill me before I turn eighteen, so here I am? I make up some lie about being here for just a vacation, because my grandmother is from here and I've never been in Japan before. What will she think of me, if I tell her that I'm really here on the winds of a pipe dream, hoping to get to the nearest ballet studio and someday earn a living as a dancer?

Even as this kind woman takes me to her home in her car, the thought of my reason for coming here fills me with apprehension, like walking across a suspension bridge over a river gorge. "I'm a dancer," I hear myself say, causing her to smile and nod her head as if hearing confirmation, inspiring her to drop her guard even further.

"I knew you were a dancer the moment I saw you."

"You speak English?" My shock and relief are genuine.

"I love to speak it," she says, accent rich with her native tongue. "I hardly get a chance. But I speak it so badly I do not."

"No, you speak it great. Better than my grandmother, even."

"What part of Japan is she from?"

"She was raised on a small farm near Nagoya. Do you know anybody from there?"

"I was raised here in Tokyo. I just put my daughter on the plane for college in America. She's going to Harvard. I was on my way out of the airport when I saw you. The truth is, I stopped because you remind me so much of her, and you looked so lost it broke my heart. I want you to stay with me, my husband and my other daughter. Don't worry. My husband is policeman. We have weakness for hard luck case."

I try hard not to breathe this sigh of relief loud enough for her to hear. Feeling the release from the pressure of the city as we drive on, until at last we arrive at a modest, two story grey house as familiar as something out of a cluttered American suburb, with the glory of every landscaped bush and small flowering tree hidden in the dark. The spirit of working class comfort lulls me into security. Establishing me on the new road to my future.

We gather my rolling suitcase from the trunk of the silver BMW, walking down the concrete walkway toward the front door. In the dark, I cannot tell whether the roses I see are pink or yellow. The friendly, pretty woman unlocks and opens the door, yelling confidently in the purest Japanese imaginable, while I look around cozy, tastefully decorated working class home, wishing I could call my mother to have her wire them some money for my gratitude. But the thought of her suddenly fills me with a greater sense of flight, and the need to divorce myself from her, and try to cast her out from my memory.

I listen to her harp her husband's name over and over, suddenly as comfortable around me as if she had known me her entire life. Soon, the short, likeable workaholic she is married to lumbers down the stairs in his smiling, dim witted façade, drawn by his wife's word spoken as if I could not understand her *"come and look at this pretty American girl I found."* Police Chief Noriyuki Ogawa hurries over to me smiling, saying *"but you said she was American,"* shaking my hand, welcoming me hurriedly into their home.

At the top of the stairs appears another lovely women seeming about 30, of deep Asian features who does not smile, calling in Japanese to another woman who is younger and more sensual and beautiful than herself. The sensual young woman causes me to look to her for a refuge in this storm of strangeness, but having no mercy as she gazes at me, whispering something into the thirty year old's ear that makes her smile.

"This is my daughter May Li, and her friend Su Ling." Su Ling the elder manages a compassionate wave from the stairs, while May Li simply looks on at the Japanese American stranger down below.

"Did she try English on you," he says. I smile and nod my head. "And now you see how bad your English really is," he says, with her hitting him on the shoulder. "Your English like Kung Fu Theater," he says.

"It is *not*," she says confidently. "Do not listen to his foolishness," she says. "Big bad chief of police. Your English the worse in all of Japan. Where is the food. Did you eat?"

"We were waiting for you to come home and cook," he says. "Sarah, her food good. English, bad."

She lays into him with her native tongue, the two of them squabbling in Japanese from the living room to the kitchen. Leaving me alone in the middle of the livingroom. An unprotected target for two sets of eyes that stare.

*H*oney barbecued chicken is the cure for what ails me, as I remember the pleasant food and conversation at dinner. In their small guest room, I am held captive in a world of dreams, where dinner in a Japanese house in Japan dances around in my head in mocking, as if it did not really happen, and I will wake up and realize that I dreamt it all. And somewhere in the midst of a troubled sleep, I hear the strangest words and phrases spoken in Japanese, feeling a sudden agony in my arms and legs, but being unable to move a muscle. And as it is always true when one feels the presence of demons in their sleep, I struggle mightily to jerk myself awake, but am unable, somehow knowing that panic is not an option, as I am unable to move or scream.

And suddenly, I feel myself being slapped in the dark, and a voice I find vaguely familiar says over and over in Japanese *"Wake up...wake up,"* until I am finally able to pull myself back from the dead. The first thing I see in the brightly lit room is the woman from the airport standing over me, leaning over the bed with no clothes on, her B cups bulging at me in mocking, above a waist carved in middle aged thickness, down to hips wider than I had imagined before. *The middle aged woman is beautiful unclothed* are the words that mock me, as I notice her naked husband on the side of the bed with a camera set up on a tripod, fiddling around with the thing in final preparation.

"Is she awake," he says. "Strap on your dick, Momma. She's awake."

From somewhere in the midst of my confusion, I am touched with just enough clarity of thought. Enough to know that the third part of the truth is about to descend. This truth is cataclysm to my soul, that yes, I am lying bound on my back, with my legs both folded and tied tight individually, so that they will stay back and spread open, with my naked middle blared wide open for them to see. I try to speak, but my words are cut off by the tight cloth tied tight around my mouth, gagging my tongue back so that only a pathetic moan is possible. I watch this voluptuous hipped woman pull up around herself a strap on member, in the shape of that which pertaineth to a man, hung down long and realistic in form.

What tears and pleading there are stored inside me have begun, as I shake my head and try to say the word *please* from behind the cloth pulled tightly across my mouth.

"Lick her first," her husband says. Staring into the camera. "Then fuck her."

Jade

This voluptuous hipped woman whom I trusted, this middle aged mother-looking Asian woman climbs onto the bed, as if obeying an inner voice, an instinct that cannot be contained. And I close my eyes to what I see, feeling her take my breast into her mouth and suck it as if there were milk to be had. She does this for several minutes, then releasing the nipple on one last high, sucking pull, saying in her native tongue *she has beautiful breasts*, moving back toward the foot of the bed, where my legs are rope bound wide open. The ropes that bind my arms behind my back are so tight I can hardly feel anything, except a growing, nagging pain in my shoulder. The ropes are crisscrossed over the front of my body, framing both my big, wobbly tits for their perverted pleasure.

Who are these people and why are they doing this, are the words in my brain, along with *do they really have a daughter going to Harvard,* or was she just lying to a confused, lonely young girl she found ripe for the picking? What perverted scheme is this, how many girls have they filmed over the years. The bright lighting pointed at us lets me know that they are probably *not* beginners, and I suddenly feel as though I have been abducted by aliens.

This lovely, sensual minded alien crawls to the center of my chastity, lowering her head down to my proper place, pulling the skin of it into her mouth, flicking and licking it strongly with her tongue. The feeling is such in my body that cannot be denied, and the loud, long groans I give are not from pleasure, but from the anger of violation, the rage of resistance that comes from it. The pleasure I feel moves through my entire body in waves from where she licks and sucks, as I lay bound tightly, each of my legs roped in bent position, so that it would be impossible to stretch them out straight. Her weight on them keeps them easily spread open, as she takes her part of this wine of perversion, and this end of the world depravity laid out as a gift at her feet.

She slurps and licks as if she were hungry and it were food for her nourishment, giving no compromise to the act, doing it with fever and purpose, until she sees my leg muscles tense up on their own, and hears my voice exclaim my terror in a higher pitch. In her native tongue, I hear her say *"I made her cum in my face,"* as she climbs on top of me with a look of total satisfaction on her face, sliding the member inside me to the noise of a loud, long animal growling from me, as if the more noise I make, the more power I have to stop her—but this noise only serves to feed the monster she is, and she begins to hump herself into me with greater speed, until I see the anguish on her lovely face move over into pain, and she begins to cry out pitifully as if in need of help, louder and louder until she expresses one long, forceful yell, ending with the word *"fuck"* spoken in her native tongue, as if it was nearly too intense for her to endure. The woman lays heavy down on top of me, breathing loudly in my ear, ignoring the tears streaming down my face, and the sobbing she hears muffled beneath the cloth in my mouth.

"A worthless dog," are the words I hear spoken from the woman's mouth, from somewhere in the dark. I am lucid enough to tell that I am still in the closet where they locked me last night, after I was raped by the woman a second time, and then by her husband. After he raped me, she

put her hands over my nose and mouth until I passed out, waking up a few minutes later in the closet, my leg ropes undone, so that I am able to sit up nude in the dark, with my hands still bound behind my back.

"She's a worthless, dumb American Jap. Her breasts are too big and fat," she says in her native voice, just outside the closet door. She opens the closet fast and with purpose, gazing angrily inside as if I could possibly *not* be there and make her furious.

"Oh, you are right," the other woman says. A less beautiful, less friendly middle aged Japanese woman. "You are right, her breasts are *so* big. You did not tell me she was beautiful. I run a farm, not a whorehouse."

"Who says she is beautiful? She's a Jap American dog. Look at that muscle tone. She can work like a mule."

"I don't know, I don't know."

"She is nothing. She has nobody. No one in the world cares that she is alive. We are done with this slut and we never want to see her again. You take her or she just might end up in a whorehouse."

The heavier, meaner woman kneels down to look at me. "Hey," she says, holding my chin. "Jap American Barbie. Look at me! You too stupid to stay in your own American house, huh? Then you too stupid for anything but farm work. Stand her up Li Su. Let me look at her."

My hostess Li Su Ogawa grabs me by the neck and the hair. Barking at me to stand up straight and to open my eyes. The front of my thighs are stained with blood.

"Ohhh," the other woman says, grabbing my face. "Tall and pretty, like prima ballerina." Both women laugh a cruel, genuine laugh, followed by a slap hard enough to flash lightning in my vision. When I can see again, I watch her sniff at me with a wrinkled nose and mouth, telling me I stink like a horse.

"I will be glad to see this Barbie Doll work, until her fat tits dry up."

In the next instant, I feel a twist at my nipple that arcs a shot of pain to my voice, causing a shriek that I clearly did not mean. Li Su Ogawa puts her hand hard over my mouth while holding the back of my head, muffling the second shriek while the farmer's wife (her guest) twists my nipple without mercy.

"I give you... a *good* price for her," she says. Rubbing her thumb across my nipple.

Gently.

In the Land of the Rising Sun

$\mathscr{S}$omewhere in the heart of the East. In the land of the rising sun. I rest uneasy, in the world after the sun has gone below the horizon, at the door of the evening day. As to where it is in the world I am, I do not know, considering that I was in the trunk of the old Accord for a least two hours (I suppose it could have been three) before she stopped. Then, at least another hour before stopping again. Opening the trunk into a world beyond the corruption of the cityscape, beyond the ugly concrete and steel madness of endtime desperation. I was met first by the gazing of blue eyes, round W.A.S.P. eyes from a land I once knew. The older woman and the eighteen year old blonde beauty pull me up from my repose with the care of pulling a rolled up rug, bumping and scratching my naked skin on my way out of the trunk. The girl walks me compassionately across a grassy lawn toward a small, wooden shack, where there are five other girls inside, none of them a day older than me. I notice that two of them are clearly American.

"Don't just sit there," my blonde angel says. "Somebody get her something to put on. Get me something to cut these ropes."

One of the Asian girls hurries over with a knife, finally releasing my arms and wrists into a new agony. The pain of fresh blood flow, and the reawakening of bones and muscles that were in the sleep of death. I am finally able to cross my arms, painfully in front of my breasts, while a girl whose hair is red as fire brings me a t shirt of the deepest forest green.

They help me slide the t shirt over my tragic condition, escorting me to what looks like an unoccupied bed. One of eight small beds in the room, with four on either side.

"What is this place? What are we doing here?"

"Its just a farm," the blonde says. "But we can't leave."

"Why not?"

"Because they'll kill us," the red head girl says. The fire in her eyes is tinted the color of jade.

"Kill us? Why?"

"We're slaves," she says. "They make us work for free."

"Are we like... *sex* slaves?"

The girls all look at each other without saying a word.

"Not really," the blonde says. "We don't have to go outside the family."

"You mean, we'll have to do things with the family?"

Just the father and the mother. But he hardly ever bothers us. Truth is, I think he's fucking his daughter."

"God, is everybody in Japan crazy? Are they all perverts? How did you all get here?"

"We were all separated from our families. This nice Japanese Lady took us into her home, and… well, you know the rest. Her husband is a policeman."

"I know."

I look around at the six girls, all standing and sitting close by. All of them beautiful.

"What's to stop us from just leaving tonight? To keep going until we find a road or something? You girls speak Japanese don't you?"

"We don't know where in Japan we are. If we try to get to the road they'll find us. And there's nothing around here but grass and trees. Past the crop fields there's nothing but a forest, hills and mountains. There's nowhere for us to go."

"But there has to be something we can do. Not all the police are bad, are they? If we can sneak to a phone we can call for help."

One of the Asian girls shakes her head at another, and the two of them walk away, as if it is part of a song they have heard sung too many times before.

"There are six of us. There used to be seven."

"What happened to her?"

A pause…

"They made Mary Ann and me dig her grave."

The types of fear are many. And uniquely distinguished.

"That's Mary Ann." She points at a lovely brunette American girl, with a kindness about the eyes, and a depth of sweetness in her melancholy expression. "I'm Annabelle, by the way," my blonde angel says. "Annabelle Blue."

21

Annabelle Blue come blow your horn

The sheep's in the meadow, the cow's in the corn

Where is the little girl who's watching the sheep

She's under the haystack fast asleep

22

The League of Shadow Assassins is the key. The reality from which myth and legend are born. A league of female shadow warriors, looming over the dark heart of mankind. The blood of their swords is rich with depravity. Blades dripping with every comeuppance overdue. Known far and wide by the wealthy elite. Who hire them in the shadows of revenge. In the dark promise of killing.

The League of Sister Shadows is the key. Deadly enemies to cultured civility. Riding the corporate elevators in the night. Drifting like a whisper in the suburban grass and woods. Finding their way into the heart of safety. Severing the heads of them who are guilty. Guilty by association. Guilty by predestiny.

The female shadow warriors hold the key. To unlock the door of fear and tragedy. Trained to ignore every cry for mercy. To drown sentiment in a puddle of blood. To understand that there are none who are righteous, no, not one. And that all have sinned. And come short of the glory of God.

These are the shadows of vengeance. The sword of Death and Hell in the latter day. Waiting to hear the call. Sang to them over the forest and fields of longing. Over the mountain landscape of fear.

Annabelle Blue

Rides the Wind

23

nnabelle Blue rides the wind. On the eve of eschatology. In shock and disbelief from what she sees on the TV screen. Of what she hears on the morning news. The assassination of the Virginia mayor and her daughter. Of the X carved in their naked bodies in blood.

Annabelle has a flash of revelation. Remembering that Lady X marks the spot. Remembering the way Satari Sakara had leapt and flown above the rest of them. The way she had flipped so high above her during swordplay that she lost her bearing looking for her. The way that the next moment of her life was filled with agony. Pain, when the Sakara Sword had come down twice instantly upon her back. Making her stumble forward in surrender. Not yet ready to die. Knowing that Sarah Green has a growing reputation among them. Unafraid to maim. A destroyer of those brought in to fight them in training. The so-called masters of swordplay. Speaking no disrespect of them with her lips. Speaking no respect of them with her sword.

Annabelle Blue rides the wind. On the wings of fear and despair. Having to climb the stairs of her lovely suburban home in Virginia. The wife of a surgeon. Mother of two daughters.

Annabelle goes into the private bathroom. The one adjacent to her bedroom. Removing her navy button down shirt. Removing the navy colored bra she loves. Admiring the high, rounded form of her breasts. A key played in C major. Loving the beauty of the pink areola. The nipples in perpetual raised slope and form.

Annabelle turns her back to the mirror. Picking up the hand mirror, so she can see. Looking into it, to see the full reflection of her back in the big mirror. To see the faint remnants of a scar. A scar crisscrossed in X. A scar born 20 years ago.

Annabelle Blue rides the wind. On the eve of eschatology.

Futanari Queen

"*Stroke Momma's cock,*" the farmer's wife says. "*Stroke Momma's cock so I can cum on your tits…*"

This, I do. Stroking the fake member she wears, lying on her back. Lying across her legs naked, my breasts swollen from the seed I did not know was planted inside me. In her mind, she is a futanari queen, about to release herself all over my breasts, being among the many women who suffer genuine penis envy in the bedroom. These women strap on the phallus without reservation, to express the fullness of their endtime lust—some pegging their husbands or their sons anally, but so many more of them giving themselves over to Testros, and the desire to listen to their daughters scream.

So many of these older women have been fortunate enough, lucky enough, to find a secret younger bedroom slave, some weak minded little sex kitten who worships the lovely ground they walk on, who worships their money or their position in the community. But for this farmer's wife, her only position here is on her middle aged back, watching me pull on her penis with the developed skill of a trained whore, having already known this same depravity I left behind. It is the promise of an orgasm unparalleled, which is half brought on by the imagination, that the cock they wield is an outgrowth from their own bodies, until they are unable to separate it as such, and this imagination is suddenly their reality.

The feeling of the leather harness, or the rubber dong against their witch clit is suddenly expanded, until the member seems to carry nerve sensations of its own, and their witch clit becomes a witch cock, ready to transport their body to oblivion. I watch the farmer's wife, observing the control I have over her at this moment, inspired to speak the words, "*I am a disobedient whore. I deserved to be punished...*"

And I see the fearful anguish in her face break, transforming into the arrival of agony, as her eyes roll back, and she throws her head back against the bed in suffering. But I know to continue this stroking, until her breath returns to her body, and she must let out a single, ghastly shriek into the bedroom, then beginning to grunt and shake, until I begin to cease the stroking of her Witch Cock, while she holds on to one of my milky white, milk endowed, milk fed breasts at the nipple, trembling from the aftermath of the sickness coursing through her body.

It is a lesser evil than being beaten or starved. Or set to work long hours in the fields, until our backs and hands ache so badly that they feel like they may break down, and cease to be of use from here to the grave.

"Come," she says, in breathless native speak, coaxing me to crawl my round bellied, balloon breasted body up to where she can use me for the rest of her maximum comfort.

The farmer's wife takes one of my breasts into her mouth, and I feel the expression of the milk begin to flow into her, sucking me deeply, holding onto my other breast for comfort, moaning, signing deeply as she sucks the milk without ceasing. In pity, I slide my hand down from her B cupped tragedies, down to her waist, then mercifully under the phallus still strapped to her. Under the leather, I feel the swollen, wet warmth she is, touching her at the center of herself, causing her whole body to twitch, in recognition of its painful post traumatic arousal. In understanding for her hopeless condition, I feel the knob of her girl cock still at attention, stroking it slowly, firmly while she holds the breast in her mouth, breathing already giving the signs of what is to come. I know what to do in this survival mode, what to do to ensure that maybe, I will not be bashed over the head in my sleep, and buried deep in the woods of farming country.

With this naiveté in mind, I feel the new growth of her down below, so firm, yet so slippery in my hand, as she begins to writhe in controlled frustration, until I stop moving and say "be still, Momma." This, she does. Still unable to release the breast from her mouth, moaning pitifully now, as if in grieving to be able to start wiggling pointlessly all over the bed. "Lie still," I say, feeling a rush of new, wetter arousal from her down below, along with the tell tale sign from her breathing again, coming hard and fast through her nose, as she begins to moan louder in muffled warning. I can hear the sound of desperation, the echo of fear in her pitiful voice, as every hidden muscle in her body begins to tense up again, along with the muffled whimpering, until at last, with my breast still in her mouth, the tension in her body breaks again, causing her to bellow deeply, which I hear coming out through her nose, and from somewhere deep inside the recesses of her immortal soul.

nnabelle and me are two of the greatest tragedies of human existence, which is Fate. By no fault of our own, the two of us are among those cursed with a dark destiny. Chosen by Fate herself to experience the pain of an altered timeline—to be denied the cushioned safety of home and family, to be thrown into the valley of thorns and thistles, where every step, every turn is but a grim reminder that to be born is to be cursed, and to live is to suffer.

We are not together in school, somewhere back in the states. Walking the halls as Diana and Aphrodite, two teenage goddesses for the teachers and students to worship. No. We are just two *"dumb bitches,"* they call us. The blonde girl whore and the Jap American slut, the farmer's wife calls us, not afraid to bring the cane down on either of our backs for no particular reason. The fact that I am fat with child is hardly a deterrent, as my arms, neck and back bear the unhealed scars of my predicament. *"The child is not yours,"* she has told me already. *"Sluts cannot be mothers."* I often pray that I don't really know what that means. Maybe, I am missing something in the cultural translation when she says the child is not mine. I have been haunted by this day and night as I cook and clean, watching her, her husband and two daughters eat my American food without taking a breath to tell me how much they hate it. They always ask me to cook that "crusted chicken" they call it, and the "cheese and noodles," which is just southern fried chicken and macaroni and cheese, which thankfully I learned how to cook myself from my great Auntie Lin. Who dreamed of opening her own Chinese restaurant back when my mother was a little girl. *"A Jap cooking chink food,"* my grandmother used to say, always laughing her skinny bodied, giant breasted laugh at Auntie Lin.

Who knows why Auntie Lin was content to work 40 years in supermarket delis, becoming an expert at cooking basic American food. Who knows why she never was able to take the step forward, to open *Jade East,* to delight the Virginia natives with her take of General Tso and lo mein. What spirit entered grandmother Hitomi, to be so cruel and unsupportive to great Auntie Lin, to make her certain that she could never run a business in a foreign land. To make her give her cooking talents to the basic American repertoire, until she learned to chef with the best of them. What spirit hath entered my mother, to make her burn the dragon into my back, to cause me to flee to the far east in fear? What spirit hath entered the policeman's wife, to cause her to deceive me at the airport, a deception which hath taught me the depths of what churns beneath cultured civility?

I am heavy with growth of that lesson inside my body, sweeping and mopping the floors as if it actually makes any difference, cooking and doing the dishes what seems eight hours a day at least, sometimes with her twenty eight year old daughter who still lives at home, a corporate queen who loves to play dress up and escape the farm ten hours a day— enduring her contemptuous, needlessly jealous looks, and deeply vulgar things whispered in my ear when no one is around. Though this woman shows no predilection against men, she never misses an opportunity to push up against me when I am at the sink, rubbing my backside and my rounded waist as if I am a horse in a stall, saying something far east of pure English like *"How you feel—you feel good?"* Then repeating it in her native tongue *"How are you feeling? Are you feeling good?"* To which I know to reply with great appreciation, *"Yes, thank you very much."* Then she will whisper in my ear, *"After you have your baby, can I taste your milk?"* And I will be forced to look at her with genuine shock, unable to turn her a pure answer, as she laughs at me and taps me on the bottom over my old country dress, going to her room to her TV and computer all night. I am not allowed to have a television or a computer or a phone, being told that if I am ever caught on either one that I will be *"whipped until the blood runs"* from my skin. This is something I know she is desperate to see happen, not shy to be her mother's enforcer, bringing the thin switch cane across the back of my dress many times already just to watch me react. For some reason, I cannot get used to the pain, though I have been acquainted with it all my life, still being unable to endure the numerous belt whippings and switches across my hips and the backs of my legs, done simply because I am *"a stupid slave girl"* and nothing more.

Jade

Tonight, Mika (the twenty eight year old daughter) seems so much friendlier than usual, making me believe that maybe, in some unknown future, there is a prayer answered that all is well.

"You can watch TV with me in my room." Of this, I am so deeply delighted, needing so much the emotional rest and refuge from being lonely. We both know that Ni Li Yung (the farmer's wife) does not want me anywhere near a television. But I would seriously *kill* for a two hour break from this reality, even if it is only to watch *Sorority Death House.*

In her room, I feel the ebb and flow of spirits I have not felt in the seven months since I have been here. These are spirits of independence and hope, echoes of complacency and confidence, and good feelings about the future on this side of eternity. She sits me on the edge of her bed, on this little corner of paradise, in the shadow of her room's homage to American horror classics, a poster of *Alien* not being the least among them. It feels more like an office than a bedroom, with many shelves filled with books and DVD's, horror posters and plants, a computer desk in the corner, and a 55 inch monster of a television across the room.

Apparently, when she is not using her legs and skirt to climb the corporate ladder, she is watching horror movies and helping her mother discipline us into submission. Why Mika is not married and sheltered in a suburb far away from here is no mystery to me. It is the call of the blood that runs through her veins. The call of the sadist. Which drives a soul to look for victims wherever they are lucky enough to find them. On her mother's farm, there are seven wayward girls trapped here with no where else to go, all who were lured and channeled through feminine lust and perversion, a need by these women to kidnap young girls and enslave them to work, and sometimes torture them in the name of discipline, all the while maintaining the façade of a normal life, and the pretense of people who would never be involved with such a thing.

The beautiful Japanese newswoman captures my attention on the big TV screen, while the news headlines scroll across the bottom of the screen in Japanese, reminding me that I am displaced, as foreign as a meteorite rock that fell from the sky. Suddenly, I hear the sound of two barking voices from down below, seeming to get closer to the stairs, then louder as they move up the stairs toward the upper room. Amidst the sound of these arguing Japanese voices is the sound of heavy, determined footsteps, clumping angrily toward the open door. In the next instant, Li Ni (pronounced Lee Nī), the farmer's wife, comes barreling around the corner in full race walk, startling me like a bolt of lightning, strapping me across the top of my head with her leather belt, making me cower all the way to the floor, as she wails into me like the professional abuser she is, lashing into my back like a nun on a monthly rampage, whirling her lashes down onto me in forward motion, reversing her arm with a backward lash, then bringing another series of forward blows down onto my back hard enough to make me feel as though I might need to cough between sobs. All I can see is the dark brown wooden floor beneath me through the flashes of light, unaware of whether or not the oldest daughter is standing at the open doorway, with both hands over her mouth in sheer delight.

On my hands and knees, I sob and whimper uncontrollably, until she says, *"Shut up!"* In the aftermath of this trauma, I hear only her breathing, colored by the soft tinkling of the belt buckle nearby. The voice of the newswoman hangs over our scene, like a ghostly echo from another reality.

"If I catch you in here again," she says breathlessly, *"I'll beat you the same every day for a week. Now crawl out of here."*

I turn on all fours, crawling obediently, flinching from the force of her kicking me in the backside. The lashes across my back hurry me along, bringing forth a new wave of sobs and whimpering, as I crawl down the upstairs hall to the small, bare room with only a bed and a small book shelf. In the room, I endure three more lashes on my back and a verbal warning, that next time I am going to be stripped naked and strung up whether my "bastard baby" dies or not.

In genuine rage come and gone, the farmer's wife walks away, uttering something in Japanese, too angry to see the look of contented mischief, the mischievous content on her daughter's pretty face. A minute later, I hear a knock at the door. As it is written, there is always so much to fear, from a fateful knocking at the door. The door opens, and in walks the corporate cutie, trying so hard to hide her desire to emit something close to laughter.

Yes. I can see her...

Trying not to laugh.

"I'm sorry," she says, sitting down on the bed beside me. Putting her arm around me, leaning my head against her shoulder. Kissing me gently on the forehead. Of what kind of compassion this is, I do not know. I only know it causes me to break down again. Sobbing with a hope as false as Mary of Nazareth, before the crowd began to chant the name Barabbas, over the name which is above every other name.

Jonathan Lovejoy

Tears and Blood

he child in my womb is a girl. I know this from the trip to the clinic, which was done after hours, long after the stars had come out at night. The woman doctor was compassionate enough, I suppose, though not to the point of seeing to the strangeness of all this, and whether or not I was with this woman of my own free will. *She's a pregnant runaway,* the doctor was told, which is truly not that far from my reality. As soon as they found out I was carrying a girl, they suddenly began treating me with slightly less bitterness than before, though I am not exactly sure why. I do know that boys are more highly prized in this part of the world, and it is no secret that a bucket of cold "baby water" has met with more than a few female babies born. This is the mercy of an icy death for them, one that catches them off guard, before they understand that they are alive, and that the few breaths they have taken are something they should be fighting for.

Its been two months since I have felt the hot lash across my skin. It almost seems that the child in my womb is opening a doorway of possibility, a new hope, that gives me a reason to want to live, to not take the knife and open my throat and my wrists late one night when they are all sleeping. So many times, I have tried to have the courage to drink rat poison, to crush sleeping pills in a glass of the horrid orange drink they buy, or to just run away from here and take my chances, hoping that I would be found and killed, and buried deep in the forest wood. But Fate has decided to keep me alive to suffer. Though I go to bed every night in some degree of tears or another, I know that I am going to wake up again the next morning, get up from the confines of a troubled sleep, and be forced to cook breakfast for them.

I had not seen grits or bacon when I first started cooking for them in my sixth month, and I took a shot in the dark to see if I could get something else for breakfast besides rice and bananas. Now, Oscar Mayer Bacon, scrambled eggs and grits are something they have even eaten for supper on occasion. They even eat eggs and grits with fried chicken wings, though I can't quite see the appeal for that one. Grits in the morning, grits in the afternoon, grits in the evening. *"Grits, grits, grits,"* they like to say, mumbling in Japanese all around that English word at the dinner table. My Auntie Lin taught me how to cook them so that they are not grainy or watery, with just the right amount of butter and salt. Even Annabelle and Emma noticed that as soon as I was taken into the house, the food they were given was vastly improved. *"Better than the half raw vegetables and rice we used to get all the time,"* Annabelle said. *"Is that your food?"* I seem to be hungry all the time now, though they will not allow me to eat enough to get as plump as I might normally be.

Of what weight I have gained seems to have settled in my belly, bottom and bosoms that have grown too big to imagine.

Sometimes, I think that when my baby is born, they are going to have mercy on me. They are not going to make me go back into the cabbage fields all day, or put the cane across my back because they caught me standing up straight for too long. When we harvest the crops for them, with seven girls doing the work of 10 paid laborers, oh how their money rolls in. It would be like a company with seven employees paying them absolutely nothing for working twelve hours a day. Oh, how many enterprising minds around the world would do this, if they knew they could get away with it! But what demon beyond the dollar drives these people to kidnap runaway girls, and keep them suppressed and subjugated from the world? Inevitably, we just run away again, so why do they go through the trouble? So many farms are glorified brothels, where the girls are known to be genuine farm girls by day. It is only a matter of time, I suppose, before they recruit enough girls to begin this, though I don't think they are in any hurry to do so. They seem to be pure farmers, with only the money from the farm being their concern, along with the pleasures of their farm hands exclusively for the wife, the husband, and just recently, the oldest daughter, who is the most violently insatiable among them. I know that her session with me is coming, something that she has held in these many months, waiting, I think, until after my baby is born, and she can nurse at my breasts with greater enthusiasm than the baby will. I know, I feel, that there is a deep and tragic soul to her sickness, one that she shares with her mother, but is more apt to display it in violence as foreplay, even to the completion of the act itself. Why else would she trick me into watching television with her, knowing how her mother would react? What did it do to Mika's mind and body, to watch me be beaten by her mother? Mika, what does it do to you, my dear woman, to kiss me on the lips when I cry?

The morning after this trauma brings with it another revelation, another part of this Hellish truth that I'm in. I notice at breakfast, Mika is dressed in leisure attire, in tight, faded jeans and a white T shirt with a Pepsi logo on the front, in keeping with the soft drink she loves. There is always a blue Pepsi can somewhere nearby her, which is how she prevents her big bottom from getting any smaller, I suppose, giving her an extraordinary figure. Truly, the hips don't lie, even on some Asian women, I see, letting me know that the incredible bubble and spread of her backside in her business skirts and country dresses was no illusion. Her loose fitting khaki pants and knee length shorts are suddenly and boldly gone, to reveal that what lies beneath is the strength of feminine beauty and power.

"Mika wear her big butt pants today," her mother says, which tells me now how its possible that in seven months of being here I have never seen them. I notice that her mother's comment embarrasses her genuinely, causing her face to turn rosy pink underneath the smooth, fair complexion, as she reaches for a slice of bacon to decorate her plate.

"Your butt fat like Kim Kardashian," her mother says. "Eat banana instead." And I am amazed that Mika cannot see the humor, and cannot look anyone in the eye for at least a half minute, as if she has been humiliated almost beyond a place of recovery. I continue to look at her, waiting to make eye contact with me so I can smile away the pain for her. But all I see on her face as her embarrassment fades is a growing contempt at her mother's comment, and a fierce determination to regain her power among us.

"Mika, why you stay at home today?"

"I gave them my month's notice already, remember? We talked about it."

"Yesterday was your last day?"

Mika does not answer, as she fills her plate with grits and scrambled eggs, from the serving plates just put on the table.

"Number one daughter," her mother says in half sarcasm, smiling as she fills her own plate. "Give up big city office job. Stay home to help her poor mother run farm." The look passed between them is of such profound understanding as to be terrifying to behold.

"Dad says you're a spoiled lazy pig," the sixteen year old says, only a year younger than myself. The next second of her life involves the agony of her ear being twisted by her big sister. The sister's scrunched face and exaggerated wailing in her native dialect is more hilarious than heavy. The mother snaps Mika's name twice, making her reluctantly let her sister's ear go in a pinching, twisting pull. "Next time I'll get a pair of pliers you little b—

"Mika! I said stop! You're old enough to be Suka's mother. Instead you act like a little noisy baby like them."

"I'm not old enough to be her mother."

"You twenty eight years old. You old enough."

Mika can hardly return to her meal at the table, staring at her sixteen year old sister with daggers.

"Suka, learn to keep your big mouth shut like Mai Li and you won't get beat up so much by your sister."

"She better not touch me again."

Suka's voice is low. Almost whispery.

"What was that?" Mika asks calmly. Falsely. "What was that you said?"

A pause. Ripe with tension.

"I said you're a fat, lazy pig!"

The tension in the room is suddenly broken by Mika's hand around her sister's throat and her other hand in her hair. The table clangs and scrubs over the floor from the violent motion of the two fully grown sisters, as Mika pulls her wildly swinging and kicking sister to the floor. The room is a theater of chaos, with the mother screaming her older daughter's name, which sounds like *"Bika-ta!"* screamed over and over, while she tries desperately to pull them apart, but being unable, before her oldest daughter fills the room with the sounds of her fist and her younger sister's face in a bloody tragedy.

Her stronger, heavier mother gets a good hold of her punching arm, at last being able to pull Mika off Suka just enough to gain control. The mother slams her oldest daughter up against the refrigerator nearby, screaming at her to *"Stop it! Stop hating your sister! Stop killing your sister!"* This, in the noise of the sixteen year old's coughing, and repeating that she can't breathe and she can't see. I go around the other side of the table, away from the two white tigers in heat, past the sweet, quiet Mai Li (who looks like she has seen a ghost), helping Suka up to her feet, noticing that she has blood all over the bottom of her face.

I take the crying young girl through the tiny livingroom and up the cramped staircase, to the privacy of the little space upstairs, to the privacy of the little space upstairs that passes for a bathroom. I wet a warm, white cloth, contemplating the nature of violence and provocation, as I try to find the original color of her skin underneath the steady flow of tears and blood.

Jonathan Lovejoy

Mika Yung Rides the Wind

28

Mika Yung rides the wind. On the Eve of eschatology. Standing naked in front of her bedroom mirror. Apocalyptic lust strapped in harness about her hips. Gazing at the realistic member hanging down, in awe of what it means. In grieving to feel the fullness of its calling. Pulling upon her firm, rounded breasts. Thanking providence that they are heavy enough. Long enough for her to raise to her lips to drink.

Mika puts one of her breasts to her lips. Pulling the nipple deep into her mouth. Wrinkling her brow, at what monumental feeling she hath born into her body. Nearly giving in to the epic ability passed down. To give rise to deadly energies in her body with minimal effort. Able to shudder her body through deep concentration alone.

Mika Yung rides the wind. The wind of a lust too big to endure. A desire too devastating to ignore. Tucking her member, her weapon into her underpants. Staring at her comfortable, cozy country dress. Thinking of one.

Mika goes outside into the quiet, country night. Looking once up at the stars that stare. Resisting their warning for her to flee. To flee the wrath to come. Walking slowly through the warm, rural night to the work house. To where six girls sleep without hope. Where they rest without comfort.

Mika goes inside the sparsely decorated room. Where eight beds languish in the dark. Walking boldly as the six girls lie sleeping. Turning her gaze over to Mary Ann White. Toward the sweetness. The brunette loveliness. The softest, most voluptuous curves among them. One of the American treasures found and taken. The most trusting, pathetic, and naïve among them.

Mika goes over to her bed in the dark. Aching in her groin. Having to swallow mouth watered desire. Mika sits on the edge of the bed. Slipping the covers off the sleeping girl. Running her hands up the girl's creamy white skin. Feeling her smooth thighs, from her knees to the high curve of her hips. Sliding her hands underneath her white nightshirt. Rubbing her tiny waist, sliding her hand up to the girl's firm, heavy bosom. Breasts high and rounded. Both firm and squishy to the touch. Feeling her own breasts react to the merest touch of the girl's nipple. Holding it hard and fast, the whole front of the girl's breast squeezed in the palm of her hand. Content to massage and squeeze the big, soft flesh. Squeezing them to satisfy herself. Squeezing until desire peaks in her body.

In the dark, Mika's body is struck by lightning. Causing her to twitch a premature shudder. Making her have to roll the sleeping beauty on her back. Waking her up. Holding her face close to the brunette's soft, pink lips. *"I'm going to put my nipple in your mouth,"* she says. Undoing the top of her dress. Sliding a breast free in the dark. Placing the nipple into the grieving girl's mouth. Nearly twitching again from this contact. Feeling every awkward suck pull energy up from her groin. Expanding beyond herself, into the member she wears strapped on.

Mika Yung rides the wind. On the wings of a gift passed down. Moving slowly, steadily as if possessed. Climbing on top of the girl in the dark. Comforting her whimpers in the dark. Raising the girl's night shirt all the way up, exposing her breasts in the dark. Drawing energy from the girl's whimpering, from her pleas in the dark. Whispering *"I have to do it,"* in her ear. Mashing their breasts together. Whispering loudly to God in her native tongue. Sliding her hand down the front of the girl's underwear. Causing another whisper to the God of Heaven and Earth. Allowing the girl's whimpering to grow. Until her voice rises from whimpering to pleading.

Mika Yung places her hand to her member down below. Her hand trembling as she pulls it from her underwear. Touching the tip of it to the girl's proper place. To her improper place. Listening to the girl's pleading become loud and desperate in the dark. Placing her hand over the girl's mouth at the moment of truth. The moment when truth takes hold.

Mika finds the place of what must be. Feeling the panic in the girl's body. Hearing it in her muffled voice. Sliding herself all the way into the girl. Feeling the girl's muffled screaming vibrate her body. Chanting to herself in her native tongue *"I'm going to have to cum."* Over and over she whispers this to herself. Barely moving at all, letting the girl's suffering draw her body's energy. Letting the girl's fear blaze this blue and black flame.

Mika Yung rides the wind. Breezes drifted from generations long gone. Passed down the timeline, across the forests and fields of Japan. Settling into her body. Into her bowels and her groin.

The feeling strikes both her breasts at once. To release her whispering chant into a wailing one. Yelling the words louder and louder in the dark. As if to call for mercy where none can be given. To give cushion to the blow in her body.

Spirits grip her hips, her breasts, and her groin. Tormenting her to tears without compassion. Shaking every inch of her body without pity in the dark.

Mika Yung rides the wind. The aftermath of her body's trembling. In the wake of her soul's pain and suffering.

Mika Su Yung rides the wind. On the eve of eschatology.

Jonathan Lovejoy

Earrings and Necklaces

29

Mika burns the pain in the lesbian dark
In the power of her easy command
As she causes the girls underneath her to suffer
Like lesbian putty in the palm of her hand

Closeted so deep, she erupts like a volcano. In pain. In rage…
In fear.

30

$\mathscr{I}$wake up in the middle of the night, thinking that maybe I heard a scream. This, on the heels of a fearful premonition that startled me awake, where I could feel the presence of Mika Yung standing over me, looking down on me in the dark. Somehow, I know that I am witnessing the birth of a new star with her, the trauma of ignition, when the energy that has threatened for her entire life has at last been given permission to go critical, to begin a process of self sustaining life. It is the acceptance of who she is underneath the public façade, who she has always been underneath the pretense. Moving so fast in the opposite direction, deeply committed to makeup and hair, to earrings and necklaces; to tight, pretty skirts and dresses, but all the while, refusing to commit to the trappings of boy-girl nonsense, largely refusing the infinity of advances, though showing no signs of being completely opposed to them. Running as fast as she can in lipstick and lavender pearl, high heels and *haute couture*, trying to get away from the roots of who she is, but still being unable to cut the motherline string, and move away from her mother's farm to the city. Seeing other women in the corporate offices where she hides in desperation from the truth that stalks her. Having to catch herself many times when she is lost in the daydreams of Eve, imagining slipping the shoes off a lady coworker, sliding her hands up the woman's skirt to her thigh high stocking. Pulling the stockings down and away from the woman's feet, and then putting the woman's toes hungrily in her mouth. Licking the fresh, clean soles of the woman's bare feet, sucking the woman's toes with violent enthusiasm.

Mika so often has awakened herself from one of these office fantasies, not knowing the source of them, nor being able to resist the rise and fall of their force and power. Giving in to the spirit at long last that has tormented her since she was a little girl is in school, when she would imagine that she was sitting in the pretty lady teacher's lap, kissing her firm on the mouth. When she would imagine that the teacher was taking of her clothes (Mika's clothes), and kissing her little thirteen year old bottom. She has at last given herself to the spirit of who she is, the spirit that has hit her when she would be in the elevator, and an attractive young woman would get in with her alone. Braving the involuntary vision of herself stripping the girl's jacket from her. Then tearing at the buttons of her blouse, ripping it open, then pulling the woman's bra down just enough to get to the nipple she hides from the world in false modesty, then breast raping her with her lips and tongue. Mika's attempt to fly from here, to run the course of the so-called normal and well-adjusted—her attempt has had the success of a kite, that celebrates its prowess and freedom in flight, but is nothing more than a glorified captive of whoever it is that holds the bottom of the string.

Over the years, there has been a gradual winding down, a gradual pulling in, with her mother's perversion waiting like the center of gravity so near and far away, until she finally realized that there is no more wind left strong enough to keep her aloft; there is no more fire left to try and rocket burn herself away. Over the years, the kite string has been getting shorter, until at last she finds herself again in the hands of her mistress, as much a prisoner of her mother's perversion as the unfortunate slave girls too stupid and afraid to run. We were all outcasts anyway, with nowhere to live, nothing to eat, no loving home to return to. The seven of us were ripe for the picking, for the lady cougar prowling the streets, looking for someone whom she may devour.

If we were to run away, where would we go? We are all underaged, like ripe fruit in the midst of greedy fat faces, all looking to take a bite from us, to nourish the heart of what lust torments their body and soul. We are all on the edge of whoredom, I think. On the edge of being sold into sex slavery, as it seems to me that it is what we are being gathered and nurtured for. Were it not for the strong, obvious legitimacy of this working farm, the growth and export of everything from radishes to watermelons, I would be one hundred percent sold on the idea of our whoredom. But it is a real vegetable farm, and we are real, unpaid workers here with nowhere else to go in life, with no one else in the world who cares whether or not we live or die.

The full flowering of this has gathered her attention like a butterfly to a red tulip. Something that her mother started only a few years ago, when the first Asian runaway was brought here by the police chief's wife.

"Take her to a whorehouse," Ni Yung had said, to where the police chief's wife had answered *"a whorehouse won't pay. But you will. It will be one less worker you'll have to pay. And besides that, you can keep her all to yourself at night. Look at her."* Ni Yung had been unable to resist the prospect, the perverted possibility, and had agreed to pay for the sixteen year old girl, hold her captive and force her to work under threat of brutal punishment. Not more than a few weeks had passed before Ni was in the young girl's room in the workhouse, sitting on her bed at night, whispering to her in her ear about how beautiful she was, with her hand on the girl's leg halfway up her thigh. Confident enough in her own middle aged heat, that she was not matronly enough to be repulsive, and just pretty and shapely enough to cause perverted desire.

It is the thing that saved her two youngest daughters from losing their virginity to their own mother, the way that Mika had lost hers on her sixteenth birthday, when the mother had laid on her and pushed the silver vibrator all the way up into her daughter, then laid on top of the girl until the vibration sent her body into spasms. From this, Ni Yung had never recovered from. Setting herself up as a victim of this perverted possibility. When the police chief's wife had chosen her as a possible candidate for this depravity, Ni Yung and the policeman's wife had enjoyed a divine spark, and instantaneous connection, as two extremely attractive and sensual middle aged women, who had abandoned the natural use of the man in their hearts, and who had given themselves over to this end of the world depravity.

Even the two of these women, the city wife and the country wife, have not resisted their call to one another, where they have shared every so often their unique place in the sun, in the shade of depravity's light, in the shadow of perversion's heat, when the city woman stood in the country bedroom behind a locked door, fully clothed in her casual midnight cloth, with both her breasts exposed, feeling the country woman holding one hand between her legs over her underwear, while she licked one nipple without mercy, Ni Yung shaking her head back and forth in rapid motion with her eyes closed and her tongue out, rubbing her tongue across the nipple without ceasing, while pressing her hand up the city woman's dress. Ni Yung had kept this up for several minutes, until the city woman had to grip the sink to keep from losing her balance and stumbling backward from the violent shaking that started in her body. From this Armageddon Orgasm, the two women had developed a permanent bond, exchanging these pleasantries among themselves every now and then, while the chief's wife continues her abductions from places in the city, bringing girls to Ni Yung's farm to sell for a high price to pay. Talking heavily, deeply among themselves so far beyond the feeble economics of this slim trade, the both of them being private consumers in this latter day intrigue, in the expression of end of the world lust to bear.

A universe away from the only place I ever knew and called my home, I lay in the bed in the dark, in the farm house of Ni Li Yung, listening to the front door open and close under the stars that stare. The shuffling downstairs moves to the narrow staircase and climbs the stairs in earthly nighttime loneliness, moving slowly down the hall, stopping at the door of Mika's bedroom. Then I hear the late night noise move delicately, deliberately, to my door. Opening it without pretense or reservation. In the eternal darkness, in the wee hours of the night I lay still. Suddenly unable to breathe, as the unseen shape steps into the room quietly, moving in authority over to my bed. Something tells me to take a breath, then take another, to breathe long, loud breaths of camouflage, to convince the demon that I am under the protection of sleep, in sacred ground that cannot be disturbed.

Then suddenly, I feel the air move at my face, at the temple, brushing my skin, then back through my hair. Something tells me, *breathe deeply, pretend you are going to wake up.* This, I do, playing it for all its worth, even moaning slightly, then moving my hand under the shirt across my body for effect.

Let the mother have her sleep whispers in protection, to the spirit that hath come for me, causing it to turn in the dark and walk reluctantly away. The door to my room closes again, allowing my heart to resume a normal rhythm, as I hear the nighttime noise move down the hall toward Mika's bedroom. Closing her bedroom door, in the quiet of nightfall and despair.

Farm Girl

Princess

31

The weeks pass into oblivion. Until I am at one with the sufferings of Eve. In the small, dreary space of my upper room, I am the origin of the death screams heard throughout the entire house, sprawled naked onto my bed, bloated and bellowing on my back, while Mika stands unmercifully over me, watching me with eyes of curious disdain, while her mother is at my feet, telling me to "push" in my native tongue, something I want to do and not want to do at the same time. If I don't push, this think will stay inside me, feeding on me from the inside, sapping my strength, tormenting me with sorrow and pain. But if I push, I know that it will claw its way out of my womb like a creature desperate to be free, splitting me open in agony passed down from East of Eden. *You're being picked on by God*, a mocking voice says to me from deep within. *Grim. Tragic,* it says, to only add to this end of the world suffering I feel. But another voice comes to me in mercy, and tells me *push with a warrior's heart.* Allowing me to find my sanity, taking a deep breath, so that I may scream this last death shriek in rage rather than regret. And this, I do. Angrily telling the woman above me to take my hand, grabbing it with the intent of trying to crush her bitchy fingers.

I take this last deep breath in determination, and I grit my teeth in preparation, holding my head back in apocalyptic concentration, letting this end of the world scream come out of my mouth in desperation. I feel the thing pass through the front of me like a damned watermelon, until I briefly understand that death is better. And then I feel myself emerge from the flames of Hell, the other side of which is paradise. And more suddenly than what can be imagined, the spirit of death departs, and the Armageddon agony drifts away like a fog in a summer morning breeze.

The baby-screams of little Hitori Lin Sakara pull at every cell in my body, while the farmer's wife takes hold of it in a plush, white towel quickly stained the color of a crimson flood. A lesser, ridiculously benign pressure appears again, as an accursed clump of God knows what is pulled out of me onto the soaked bed. I release the hand of the farmer's daughter, watching her take up the shears in obedience to her mother, and cut the gray, wiggly thing that once sustained its accursed little life. In the spirit of reluctant compassion, they place the howling, trembling thing into a soft, cushiony blanket, handing it to me without a word.

Somewhere in this space, I am vaguely aware of two women milling around, gathering the remains of this tragedy up and away. As I stare at the writhing, desperate victim of the very breaths of life she breathes, I am even less aware of the two women in the room, and whether they leave in admiration or pity, for the girl with dragon tattooed in fire on her back, and the helpless, condemned little soul she holds in her arms. I stare into the tiny Asian eyes of this little beauty. In grieving to hide her from the third part of the truth. That to be born is to be cursed.

And to live is to suffer.

32

My child's suckling lips are a pleasure beyond comprehension, so much that I am glad to be alone when it happens. The method of this madness never ceases to amaze me, while I stare down at this tiny precious at my swollen breast, feeling my body react on its own regardless of where my mind is, until I just have to close my eyes and give in, often imagining myself alone on a dance stage in total isolation, where Tchaikovsky's divine melodies bathe me again with Christmas light. And once, as my body was close to the mighty twitching I could not prevent, I was revisited by something I have seen, something I have felt before, as I saw the glowing green eyes of a dragon the color of jade, burning the world in green and black fire. At the moment this dragon appeared to my sleepy brain, my baby's suckling energy expanding throughout my body until I shook like a little girl on a snowy day. The feeling was so epic in my spirit, in my tragic soul, that I had to life my other breast to my own mouth, to ground the lightning energy coursing through. I lowered my breast in trembling sighs that I held in check the best I could, opening my eyes to look down at her, noticing that her eyes were wide open. Staring at me with otherworldly awareness, as if to judge me for my body's depraved calling, whether it be natural or no. I close my eyes again, to try and let the rest of this powerful and secret thing run its course, opening my eyes again, noticing that the otherworldly stare I saw had come and gone.

Every single time I nurse her, my body is burdened by an arousal that I cannot shake, though not always to the jade dragon fire. Sometimes, when she is done, I will try to get her to take it back into her mouth, even pushing a drop or two out onto her lips, just to see it run in a hopeless little stream away from her little tongue down her cheek and away. She will not nurse when she is full, much to my dirty little dismay, oftentimes, leaving both breasts exposed anyway, watching her struggle sometimes to be free of it shoved in her face.

If I am alone holding her, I will lay her on the bed on her back, watching her kick and squirm in epic satisfaction, while I reluctantly cover myself in my silken robe the color of black and emerald green, given to me in a flash of pure kindness by Ni Yung, the farmer's wife. *"Farm Girl Princess,"* she had said without smiling. *"Princess Sakara,"* she said, wrapping the beautiful robe around me while the child lay on the bed." *Nurse your baby in Jade Silk. Now baby get nice and fat."*

I stand at the daytime window of my little upper room. My jade silk robe hangs up on a hook nearby, with the only other dress they gave me besides the country flower one I have on. It is an old, faded piece of dark blue cloth with pale flowers that do not aspire toward the color white. As my little month old reason for living sleeps soundly on the bed, I look out over the cool, springtime planting fields, watching the six other girls hoe and weed themselves into another sore back, thankful that Fate has divined me a new path, another way to spend my days and nights, away from the backbreaking days in the cold sunlight, both sweating and freezing in the cold, late spring air.

Already, the world is poised on the edge of another summer, having lifted and carried me to another world. I still dream my unlucky dream of finding a dance studio that will have mercy on the dumb American Jap girl with a baby, and take her in on the ribbon of false hope, and patronize her pathetic longing for a time. But for now, maybe I have found something that might resemble what I need most in the strange, oddest of places in the world. Maybe, as I gaze almost lovingly at the silken green cloth in black dragon pattern that rests on the hook, I am suddenly touched by a brief security, a sense that somewhere in their hearts, Ni Yung and her family have grown to love me, and will adopt me in spirit as one of their own.

Little Hitori is bounced so happily from room to room, even causing the two youngest daughters to come inside at least once every day, to pick her up and talk to her in the most delightful baby talk in their native speech, so filled with long, drawn out syllables of hilarious mystery to their little adopted niece. The baby laughs as if she can understand them, so tickled by just the sound of their voices, always being happy to be held and carried away by either one of them. They love to babysit, to watch her while I continue my household cleaning and cooking chores when they are home from school. They are the closest thing to sisters I have ever had, and even Mika Su has allowed herself a less bitter and strict tone with me. Perhaps I am another daughter for Ni Yung and her husband—the slant eyed American girl in Japan, who has brought with her a special blessing upon their farmhouse.

The door to my room flies open rather suddenly, where it seems that Ni Yung flies in on a current of bitter urgency. She lifts my baby from her resting place quickly into her arms, and hurries out of the room. I turn from the window to follow her, running smack into Mika who blocks my path.

"Where is she going?"

"That is not your concern," she says, her scornful compassion from the last month fading into pure scorn.

"But…where is she going with Hitori?

I begin to call out my baby's name desperately, sounding like *"Hito-san! Hito-san!"* Rushing violently past my captor, who was clearly unprepared for such a show of natural strength, as I burst past her like my old high school girlfriends on a sales run at JC Penney, hurrying down the upstairs hall in something like a full run, just in time to see Ni Yung hand the baby to a very beautiful woman of obvious wealth and means, escorted by her husband hurriedly out the front door.

I fly down the stairs as fast as I can without falling, nearly leaping toward the front door in the midst of a scream of my baby's name— slamming hard into the strong farm woman, nearly overtaking her until she is joined by her oldest daughter. The two women do not speak, but seem to enjoy the violent struggle to hold me, sandwiching me tightly between the two of them, holding me as I exhaust every remaining strand of energy I have left, holding me tight for several long seconds, until they have me penned immobile on my feet, still begging whatever God that is listening to please have mercy on my immortal soul, and rescue me from the blue and black flames of this fiery Hell on Earth.

33

*I*n the aftermath of trauma. In the wake of grieving undenied. I stand still between the two women. Hugged and supported by the both of them. Unable to cease my whining, my repeating of the name 'Hito...Hito...Hito....'" After long last, Ni Li tells Mika to take me upstairs. Back to the place where life has mocked me these long months. Has lied to me with infinite aplomb. Making me believe that there was hope. That there was a future.

Mika takes hold of what is left of me. Escorting me up the stairs, down the hall, and into the tiny space of a back bedroom. Closing the door. Sliding the small bolt lock into place. Walking me over to the bed. Sitting down beside me.

"Your baby is safe," she says. "Look at me."

I struggle to hold my head up. Making a profound effort to focus her face through the tears and sorrow.

"What kind of life could you give little Hito San. If you love her, than you will understand that this is best for her. Do you believe your daughter is safe?"

The question only causes me to lower my head again, and endure another wave of pain and sorrow. Mika slides closer to me. Pressing her lips to my forehead.

"Satari," she whispers. Touching my chin. Raising my face up to hers. "Sata San," she whispers. Moving her face closer to mine. Closer, until her lips cross the barrier into truth. Touching her lips to mine. Touching with the merest, the faintest breath of what must be.

She places her lips upon my top lip. Placing the kiss so lightly upon it. Moving her comfort to my bottom lip. Pulling back slowly to look at me.

Without unlocking her gaze from mine, she moves her hand to the buttons of my dress. Taking each one in slow deliberation. Refusing to unlock her gaze. Sliding her hand inside my dress. Placing it firmly at my bosom. Firmly at one of my breasts. Showing me the growing anguish in her expression. The growing rage of instinct in her body.

She slides my dress down from my shoulders. Past my breasts to my waist. Exposing me topless. Keeping my eyes locked to hers in grief and fear. She turns her gaze slowly to her hand at my nipple. Pinching it slowly. Completely. Slowly. Completely. Slowly. Completely. Until she sees the white of life. The sweet elixir. The desperation of her heart.

Squeezing slowly. Completely again. Feeling the white liquid run from my breast down her fingers. Watching it in the pain of awe.

Mika lowers her head to my bosom. Licking the milk with her tongue. Causing me to twitch in the midst of sorrow. My twitch raises her head back up to me. Locking my gaze again. Pushing her lips to mine in a full, heavy kiss of agony. Pushing her tongue deep into my mouth.

"Did you taste it," she says. "Did you taste your milk on my tongue?"

I can only nod in surrender. In grieving. Watching the stress in her eyes grow. The pressure on her features raise. Until she must lower her head again. She pulls my nipple deep into her mouth. Sucking a long, powerful stream. I hear the faint gulp. The loud swallow of the milk at the back of her throat. Forcing her to drink. To nurse. Breathing in a deep breath through her nose. Exhaling a whimper.

I watch the pretty woman take her part of this nourishment. This feeding to her soul and spirit. Unable to hold the grunting in. The roughness of her voice in truth telling. While her cheeks are dimpled in sucking form.

Mika stands me up from the bed. Taking both my dress and hers off. Slipping every stitch of underwear to the floor. She lies on the bed on her back. Coaxing me on top of her. Placing me up to straddle. Taking both my breasts in her hands. Expressing the milk in two slow, steady streams. Feeling the white shower wet her face. Closing her eyes in suffering. In the pain of desire too deep to know.

Mika pulls one of my breasts down into her mouth. Releasing the nipple in kissing pull. Switching. Sucking the other deeply. Back and forth. Breast to breast. Milk stream to milk stream. Feeling my groin tighten against her on its own. Feeding on my suffering. She presses forward this motion. Seeing what deadly consequences may arise. Perceiving my body's impending doom.

In the aftermath of trauma. In the wake of grieving undenied. She feels my legs tense up against her body. Watching my face contort with pain. With the agony of truth. Hearing my voice wail my sorrow to the heavens. A voice of depravity discovered. A voice of weeping.

In the aftermath of trauma. In the wake of grieving undenied. I feel her body begin to tremble. A continuous wave of spasms. Hearing her voice moan at length. A voice trembled in quivering.

I feel the sucking end of its own volition. Watching her draw a breath in preparation.

Watching her scream.

34

I belong to Mika Su Yung.

I am hers to do with as she pleases. Taking advantage of my grief, visiting me in private at least once every day by necessity. In my little room. The bathroom. Even sneaking me into her room late at night when her mother is asleep, to keep the leather belt off my back, or the wooden spoon from the top of my head. My new body is the fulfillment of a lifelong dream of hers, I think, having such huge breasts bloated with milk, and such fleshy hips for her to spank and grab. It is a powerful dominance she needs to express, though not to impress her mother, but to satisfy what monumental urges have built up inside her over the years. Using me as an outlet for every imaginable depravity, biting and choking not being the least among them. I thought I once knew the depth of feminine lust, when my mother would have to sometimes visit me in the night. But when Mika wakes me up in the middle of the night and takes me to her bedroom, I am in touch with even another level of Amazonian desire, so apparent when she runs her hands trembling up and down my body as if in the early stages of withdrawal, barely able to control herself when receiving her drug again. Her kisses are filled with otherworldly desire, seeming to drink in my very essence when she lies on top—laying heavy on me, pinning my arms tightly to my sides. It is her favorite way to gather her body's energy to completion, pressing her lips hard to mine, then slamming and sliding herself against me hard enough to shake the bed, leaving her kiss locked to my lips while she bellows like an animal in heat; her deep, rough screams pouring muffled into my mouth, while he earthquake energy passes through her body.

Being used as a sex doll by a beautiful woman might be the less of evils for me, I suppose. At least it keeps me out of the fields, and off the streets of the city, where I surely would have become a whore in a whorehouse by now. There is something about me that makes other people want to hurt me. And they do it through the cane or the lash, through a sharp look or a sharp word, or through dominations best left unspoken of to others, done to me since I was just a little girl. Mika thinks nothing of mashing me naked up against the window in my room in broad daylight, risking me being seen with my fat breasts pushed against the glass, while she slams her naked body against me from behind, ramming her hips into me as if she would die if she stopped. She has this motherline ability passed down, but perhaps unique to her, I think, that she only need to set herself into a steady rhythm, and she will shoot off like a rocket into outer space, as strongly as if she were being licked to death at the center of her flesh and bones. It is a remarkable thing to bear witness to, especially for me, a motheress by trade, a motherloving slut by definition. If they didn't see it on me, if they could not smell it on me, would they be so drawn to me in perverted lust?

What have I done, to cause my life to turn out this way? Sometimes in the night, after grief has caressed me to sleep again, I'll wake up howling pitifully in the dark, hardly able to catch my breath, feeling as through something or someone were laid heavily on top of me, trying to smother the life out of me. I try not to accept the truth when it happens, that I always seem to think it is my captor, releasing the fullness of herself onto me in the dark. Here, in the family kitchen, as I prepare my American style food they have come to love (cheeseburgers and French fries), I watch the 28 year old daughter, remembering the violent depth of her need to satisfy herself on me in the night. Every so often, she will cut a sneaky glance toward her mother that unnerves me—knowing in my heart that something is amiss.

Maybe I'm just worried, because one of the Asian girls has suddenly turned up missing, though I cannot imagine why, as I remember that none of the three Asian girls would be inclined to try and escape. And sometimes, I can remember the time I was awakened by a scream, finding out later that Mika had raped Mary Ann White in the workhouse, which every other girl heard while it was happening. Thoughts of where this other Asian girl might be often haunt my own thoughts, as I always shrug it off as just post traumatic stress; nerves because of what I endured when little Hitori was taken. But as I put the serving plates in the middle of the table, the smiling, knowing glance I give Mika is laced with worry, because I know that down to the core of her being, Mika Su Yung is a sexual sadist, and I can't help but wonder, as she devours her thick, juicy hamburger like a greedy carnivore—I can't help but wonder how long it will be before the truth of who she is begins to blossom, and the tree of her life begins to bear the first fruits of its calling.

35

*T*he milk of kindness has gone from her private sessions with me, which are now textured by a growing bitterness, colored by a rising intolerance for my pathetic condition. Her pulling at my breasts now is not laced in loving kindness and compassion, but a determined shortness of temper, where she will stop drinking and snap at me, *"I told you to concentrate!"* Slapping me in the eye twice and calling me a slut, which is what I am, then returning to my breasts as if they were milk bottles hanging from a mannequin doll. Her comfort in this no longer encompasses mine—I find that she is more content to suck on them too hard, until have to squirm and whine from the sharp pain it causes. And I notice that she does not stop, becoming more enthusiastic in hurting them, sometimes holding me down on my back, sucking on them very long and very hard, most content when she knows it is causing me pain.

When she lays on top of me doing this, her leg straddled over one of mine, I will feel the strong, involuntary squeeze of her groin against my leg, which she actually tries to pretend does not happen, looking up at me to see if I am in any way judging her or mocking her for her body's sickness. I always pretend I did not notice, even when I feel the new wet on my leg after, her body's own betrayal of just how strong this phantom climax really was. Her soft, loving charge of me was merely her soul's new awakening, to set her on a new path, that will soon have me in the grips of behind closed doors reality, and the burning of blue and black fire.

What pleasure she ever intended for my breasts is turned to pain. Any reluctant compassion for my failed motherhood she may have had has twisted and contorted itself into contempt. "You cry too much," she says. Standing pressed firm against me, our naked breasts pushed tightly together. "Your tears make me sick." And I suddenly feel the flash of light in my brain, from the heat slapped across my face. And though I try as hard as I can to prevent it, refusing to blink away the itching in my eyes, the welled up tears roll anyway, as I stand here as dumb as a dead tree stump, not knowing of the possibilities of a life away from the gray world, and the dreariness of death and despair.

"See?" she says. "Cry baby." And with that, she takes hold of my hand, and lady licks my face from my cheeks up to my eyes, swallowing the salty taste with hunger and desire. "Your pain," she says, "is everything to me. Your happiness...is nothing."

The wave of sorrow pushes through me without mercy, pricking my heart, causing me to lower my head in defeat. But she grabs my hair. Pulling my head back up. Looking me in the eyes.

She steps back from me just enough, taking hold of my nipples without softness or care. And I suddenly feel the sting of angry wasps at the front of both of them, causing me to send a deep, woman's scream, short and quick, out into the walls of this house. By now, every soul here and about is somehow aware that the maid is sometimes in Mika's bedroom after dark. Being made to suffer.

"Save it," she says. Twisting them once again. "Save it for when you *really* need it. Now, grab your nipples," she says sharply. "Pull them. Pull them hard."

I pull them hard out in front of me, seeming to pull my breasts out to infinity from my body.

"Hold your tits tight," she says. "Pull them out as far as they can go."

She smacks my feeble hands away, grabbing them, pulling them farther out than even I had done. Holding them pulled, stretched straight out by the nipple. "Like this," she says, yanking them once, then letting them flop back into place. This time, I obey. Pulling on them for all its worth, which is my safety from her wrath. Holding the big things out far and long from my body.

She steps beside me, and in the periphery, I see her draw her hand back on the pendulum swing, flowing down and around, whacking full into the fat of my bottom. Wiggling it for her profound pleasure.

"Soft fat butt girl with big tits," she says. "Stupid, Jap-American Barbie Doll."

She whacks my bottom again in the same place, warning me to "hold my tits out," which I do. She whacks me, repeatedly, burning the same spot with fire, until I have to wonder how many more spanks can I take, until I have to cry out from pain again. But the hardest hit on them is the last, lurching me forward. She stands close behind me, hugging me around the waist tight. Breathing heavy in my air.

"I'm going to hurt your tits," she says. "So I can hear your scream."

She picks up the ropes gathered, binding my arms up tightly behind my back, so that my hips are completely exposed underneath them. She takes the cane from her bed, holding her hand over my mouth, and proceeds to stripe the skin on my backside with bloody welts, feeling my buried scream vibrate her hand pressed tightly over my mouth.

"You scream when I say scream," she says. Keeping her hand locked over my mouth. Returning to a quick, welting rhythm on both sides of my buttocks, until I can no longer hold still, infuriating her, causing her to hurt me harder and with less rhythm and precision, all over my thighs and legs, telling me "shut up and stand still! Or I'll take you outside and tie you to a tree and let the bats eat you alive!"

I do what I can to obey. Quivering in place and screaming into her hand while she hits me. Burning the red lines into my buttocks from top to bottom.

She walks around the front of me. Looking me up and down, her face calm and steady with delight, and a hidden smile of sinister satisfaction. She touches the cane across my breasts. Gently.

"If you scream, I will take you outside. Tie you to a tree. And beat you with a stick like a dog. Do you want that?"

"No," I say. So pitifully in her native tongue. Shaking my head.

She stripes the cane hard across my breast at the nipple. Causing me to scream with my mouth locked completely closed. I can only shake my head in disbelief that such agony is possible. As if I have been lapped by a string of pure fire.

She does this again quickly. Watching me scream again with my mouth closed, hopping up and down enough to shake both my breasts, enough to flop them hard up and down against my body. From the haze of tears, I see her lay the cane down gently on the bed, staring at me with her mouth hung open in lustful shock. Never taking her eyes from my body. Burning the image of my suffering in her mind forever.

With my hands still bound behind my back, she steps behind me, escorting me to her bedroom mirror. I can feel her nipples pressed against my back, with her groin pressed hard to my sore bottom.

In the mirror, I see the tragedy of human existence. Displayed in red, wet eyes and ponytail braided hair. Standing with her fat breasts hanging bloated and heavy from her naked body. Her expression burdened by the pain of loss, and the grip of hopelessness born and bred. I see the other woman's pretty hands reach around me from behind, barely touching the front of them, but still causing my whole body to flinch in fear.

"Now," she says. "You may scream."

This, I do. Remembering vaguely the sight of this tragedy in the mirror, which is a pair of pretty hands at both my nipples. Twisting them without remorse. Without pity. Very quickly, the twisting turns to a full, hard squeezing, with her holding on to me tightly. Steadying herself. And then remarkably, in otherworldly cause and effect, I feel the energy vibrating her body from head to toe. Feeling the quivering moan at my ear, while I open my eyes to the scene in the mirror, watching her beautiful face bear the agony of truth, as it moves like electricity through every trembling inch of her body.

Jonathan Lovejoy

Jade

The Workhouse

The morning drifts in on a current of grieving, echoed by the lonely cooing of the mourning dove. In my old, country flower dress, I sit on the edge of my bed, gazing out the window across the open field, listening for the voice of hope in the song of the dove. But all I hear is the voice of hopelessness, colored by the tones of despair. I know that there is nothing left for me to do but go downstairs to the kitchen, and try and focus on the one pleasure it seems that I have left.

With my hair still in its long, ponytail braid. I head toward the top of the stairs, passing Mika's room with trepidation, my skin still on phantom fire from last night's burning. With shame, I walk past the girls' room, past Suka and Mai Li's door, imagining what in the world they can possibly think of me now.

I glide slowly, in soreness through the morning daytime dark, anxious to begin burying my sorrows in the preparation of another meal. Through the kitchen window, I can see the barn close by, and the work house far off in the distance, where the other girls sleep under nighttime lock and key. The door is dead bolted, and pad locked from the outside, so that thoughts of escape for them are impossible, as each new day fades into night.

"We're always so hungry," Anna told me the last time we talked, which was more than two weeks ago. They are only allowed a banana, plain cornflakes and milk in the morning, and they have to work all day in the fields until after sunset. Then they have to go back into their quarters, the workhouse, I call it, three pretty Asian girls and the three lost Americans. All six of the girls are runaways from dreadfully abusive homes, fathers and mothers who beat and raped them constantly, two of the three Asians unlucky enough to have been put in contact with the wrong police chief, who introduced them willingly to his perverted wife. All of us were brought here by the same woman, all of us having endured the indignity of a session with her in private while her husband filmed her tragic needs being met. One of the Asian girls endured a double penetration rape, but not from the police chief; instead from his wife and a female friend of hers from the same neighborhood. This Asian girl, named Tiyoki—she said that it felt like her *"guts were tore open"* inside, and she said she felt sharp pains in her stomach that took forever to go away.

And tragically enough, all three American girls had well to do, workaholic mothers and fathers ambitious enough to have corporate jobs in Japan, who now languish in a Hell of regretful worry, not knowing whether their pretty little punching bag is dead or alive , or where it is in the world she could have gone. Emma tells me that she was the classic red headed stepchild, whose stepmother kept the father antagonized against her all the time, with constant, naked belt whippings from her father that her stepmother supervised every time, until Emma knew that when she saw the spots of blood on her white nightshirt, she would have to run, and try to get back to America anyway she could.

The police chief's wife had seen her crying at the Tokyo airport late one night, after having slept there for two nights already, pretending that she had just as much a right to be at the Tokyo airport as everybody else. The police chief's wife had been able to get her trust immediately, having lured the fiery red head girl away from her Hell of loneliness and fear, into the Lake of fiery pain and suffering. All of the abuse she thought she had received from her father and stepmother was suddenly enhance by ten, as she endured a whipping across her breasts that left them cut and bleeding. Emma said that she almost felt relieved when they brought her here, because for the first time in many years, she did not have to worry about being scolded or belt whipped almost every day.

And the lovely, sensual Jacqueline Smith-faced Mary Ann has something with me in common, that there is something about us that made our mother's have to do it—she was literally "fucked" by her mother almost every night since she was fourteen—nightly grindings that graduated to full blown strap on intercourse by the time she was sixteen. Mary Ann said that her mother rode her like a cow town whore, whatever that means, driving herself strapped on until she had to bellow for God's mercy in her daughter's ear. Mary Ann said that she hated it, and it made her wish she was dead every time. She knew that her mother was more than glad to come to Japan with her father, so that she could pull Mary Ann closer to her, to press her down further, easier said and done because of the cultural isolation, and the now completely sexless marriage to her father. Mary Ann says that she knows it broke her mother's heart when she left, but she also knows that she couldn't have endured another riding from her mother. *Leave or die*, were the words that had filled her spirit before she left, knowing that suicide was going to be her only option. Mary Ann said that her beautiful, but socially isolated, stay at home mother seemed to do this out of pure craving, but as if it were a natural one, always shocked at the moment of every orgasm, which always devastated her forty year old body to ruin. *Why do we have to do it*, Mary Ann would say. *Because my momma did it to me*, Mrs. White had said. Mary Ann had cried, telling her mother that she wanted to stop. Her mother had looked her deeply in the eyes, telling her simply, *we can't*. She had hugged her daughter in something like defeat and regret after, telling her how much she loved her "little girl."

Did the blood from Paula White's wrists decorate the tiles of their Tokyo bathroom floor? This, I cannot tell. Of what spirit was it that guided Mika Yung to her bed late that night in the workhouse? Of this, I cannot tell.

And the blue eyed angel. Annabelle Blue was the victim of a mother who was drowned in envy, that her younger daughter had taken on a look by nature equally as blonde and beautiful as her own. Spitting venom at her like a cobra every day, not afraid to bend her arm behind her back during the heat of any argument, beating her open handed across her back, long blonde hair and hoop earrings firmly in place, while the father was otherwise occupied in his Japanese corporate nonsense, trying not to notice the explosive energy created between his wife and his daughter, and the fear and pain it was causing his son and his other daughter. Annabelle's father, corporate champion Michael Blue, had broken up so many physical fights between his wife and his daughter that he got used to it, until one day she convinced him to hold her still while the mother administered a severe, underwear paddling that left her buttocks cut and bleeding.

The promise of these had been too much for Annabelle to deal with, and she left her family more in a spirit of rage and independence than fear. The kind, sensual, English speaking lady at the airport had been an oasis in her storm of angry confusion, promising her that she would pay for her ticket and give her money to help her when she got back to America, if she would just let her take her home and give her food and rest for the night. *"My daughter used to dye her hair like yours,"* she said, *"until she finally stopped pretending she was a pretty blonde American girl. I just put my daughter on the plane to Harvard in your country...come, come, I take you home to see my other daughters for the night. I buy you plane ticket tomorrow, tomorrow night you go to America."* At the police chief's home, Annabelle said she was *"forced to choke on the woman's cock"* until she couldn't breathe, while her husband was in her face with that *"stupid camera."* Between the four of us, Mary Ann, remarkably, was neither bound nor beaten, but was simply made love to by the chief's wife, who had laid her on her back and nursed her breasts, she said, *"until they were sore."*

In the wake of this tragic daydream, drifts two upon a current of laughter, drawn downstairs by the smell of bacon, and the promise of scrambled eggs cooked to perfection. "Ohhh," the mother says. "Let me

look at her. You have fun last night. Sound like you have good time."
She pats me gently on my bottom through my dress. "Bring Tropicana to
table," she says, joining her former corporate queen of a daughter, who
now boldly walks about the house in her "fat butt" jeans like there's no
tomorrow. After I bring the orange juice, the two of them get as quiet as
whispering customers in a restaurant in front of a nosy waitress. I feel on
conspicuous display as I pour the juice for them, wondering why it is
taking so long for it to pour, so I can hurry up and get away before it
happens.

But to my horror, Mika can hold it back no longer, and the snicker
that scrapes at me through her nose is a model of classic cruelty. "Hop,
hop, hop," she says when my back is turned, which makes her mother let
out a loud, deliberate laugh, one so determined to *not* care if it is genuine,
it manages to be hilarious in the effort, causing both women to suddenly
explode with laughter so loud and so genuine that it touches my soul with
fear, and chills me down to the marrow of my bones.

37

The strange, sudden disappearance of Tiyoki Nataka haunts me to no end this morning, until I have to risk going outside, walking to the part of the field where the beautiful blonde girl stands with a garden hoe, chopping the weeds from around the growing heads of cabbage. Their work is inspected closely by the farmer and his wife every day, and if they are not satisfied, the girls are sent to bed without any supper. I approach this beautiful American doll, in her old Japanese flower dress, feeling the strain of her backbreaking work in my own body.

"What are you doing out here? Did they say you could come?"

"They won't notice."

"Oh yeah? Since when?"

"I just have to ask you a question. What did Tiyoki say right before she vanished?"

"Like what?"

"I mean, did she say she was going to run away?"

"Her and Yu m i were the only ones who said they never *would* run away."

"What about Tina?"

A glance past me, over my shoulder, causes me to turn and look myself.

Worriedly.

"Tina's with us."

"What do you mean, *with us*?"

"You of all people should know what I mean," she says. "After what Mika's been doing to you? Look at your arm."

I cover the red scar on my arm, lowering my eyes, trying not to look as hurt and ashamed as I really am.

"I'm sorry," she says. "I'm sorry." She takes hold of my arm, sliding my hand away from the angry, red line scar on my forearm. Rubbing it gently. "How did it happen?"

I can only lower my eyes again, tucking my lips and shaking my head. She reaches over and hugs me around the neck. Whispering in my ear.

"We're getting out," she says. Looking at me, to see if my eyes judge her as insane.

They do.

"Emma and me can't take it anymore. Mary Ann and Tina say their going with us."

"But you don't know where we are. You don't know how many miles thick those woods are. There's not even a road to follow out of here. There's nowhere to go."

"We don't care. You know things have been getting worse since Mika left her job. She comes out here and hits us sometimes. Did you know that? And they've been giving us less food. And they lock the door right at sunset. They didn't do that before. We've all got bad feelings about things, Sarah. I feel like if we don't get out of here, we're going to die."

"But they need us to work. Why would they—"

"Satari!!"

The sound of my Japanese name harps at me from a distance, to remind me that the types of fear are many, and uniquely distinguished. I turn fearfully toward the house, as Mika rushes toward me in her white T shirt and faded jeans, carrying a long, thin stick the likes of an old broom handle. Annabelle, Emma, Mary Ann and the others are witness to a beautiful, shapely Asian woman bringing this stick down hard over my back, hitting my arms and sides without mercy as I try to run away, losing my balance and failing clumsily in the field, while she hits me several times hard over my dress, hitting me on the thigh, then kicking me hard in the backside as I get up, stumbling again toward the house, barely able to draw a breath through the shock, though my mouth is hung wide open, in the burden of the heavy weight of tears that threaten to flow.

38

$\mathcal{I}$n the kitchen, Mika screams at me in her native tongue, calling me a bitch, slut, whore and a stupid dog without batting an eye.

"What is all this?" her mother says, aroused from her room by the noise and commotion. "What did she do?"

"I caught this stinking whore in the field talking to that yellow-haired bitch."

The mother looks at me and shakes her head, making that judgmental clicking sound with her tongue, as if she truly feels sorry for me.

"Even after we open up our home to you. Treat you special. Let you work in the house like number four daughter. You still disobey."

She steps closer to me. Pinning me up against the counter.

"She is yours," she says. "Teach her to obey."

She clicks her tongue again, shaking her head, turning slowly to walk back into her room. The space she voided is immediately filled by her daughter.

"Walk," she says. With no tolerance for pretence. I know to move with purpose into the living room and up the stairs, with her following closely behind me. Still carrying her punishment stick.

Up the stairs, I walk nervously down the hall, bewildered when she goes into her room, wondering if I should follow her, but being afraid to. I take the safe route to my room, closing the door and bolting it, in false hope that if she hears the bolt click she might go about her own business. But down inside, I know that I *am* her business, confirmed by the sound of her footsteps moving down the hall and stopping outside my door.

There is a pause to eternity. To give me time to consider my own audacity, for believing that I could lock out this beating.

"Open this door!" she screams, slamming on it at the same time, making me jump out of my skin, reluctantly unlocking the door, but being far too afraid to open it. No matter. The next instant flows on her satisfaction, as she turns the knob slowly, and walks into the room. Closing the door behind her. Locking it again.

In bitter nonchalance, she kneels down at my feet, removing my shoes. Reaching up my dress, pulling hard at my underwear until they are down and away. When she stands up, I am doubled over in agony unfamiliar, feeling her hand up underneath my dress, clamping the flesh of my front as hard as she can, causing me to half to yelp, holding onto her as one would cling to a rope over the side of a clip.

"Pissy little *cunt*," she says. Hissing the words at me. Squeezing it hard again, hard enough to hear it in my voice.

"I won't go outside again!" I say, twice to her in her native tongue. Without a word, she slaps me very hard two times, then rips my dress off over my head, pulling at my bra as if she has the strength to rip it, giving in to the clamps in the back, eventually undoing them, then pulling the bra violently away from my body. The sharp pain I feel next flashes from my nipple to the rest of my body, while she pulls the back of my hair. I can only shake my head and cry out *"no!"* over and over, as she askes me the questions *"do you want to disrespect me? Do you want to disobey?"*

The sight of me shaking my head in such desperation delights her to no end, and she twists the nipple and grips my hair again, watching me stand fully erect and helpless in her power.

"Put your hands behind your back. *Put your hands behind your back!"*

This, I do. Feeling her grip go from the top to the bottom once more. Fully erect and trembling in the scream. In a brief reprieve, in the lull of silence from my shrieking, she kneels at my feet, wrapping the ropes tightly above my ankles, then just above my knees. She shoves me roughly to the bed, binding my wrists tight enough to make my hands numb.

And then, as if revisiting me from somewhere in the timeline, I feel the requisite gag go over my mouth. Cutting hard into my jaw muscles, making them sore enough to feel as if they could never be right again. By now, her expression is phased from delight to darkness, being burdened by a somber frown, seeming possessed by instinct, a need that she can no longer suppress, a desire that cannot be contained.

She stands up with the punishment stick, whacking it hard across my legs at the bottom, holding the sick with both hands, whamming it again at my legs, repeatedly at the side of my knee, then up my thighs, saying "*stupid... American...dog,*" and "*dis...obedient...slut,*" hitting me as if she is trying to break the stick, seeming angrier with each passing blow. The pause she takes is as much for a deep breath, as to find another place on my body she has not bruised. Soon, my arms feel the wrath of Mika's stick, eliciting a new wave of gruff, muffled screams from underneath the cloth. Then she shocks me with a sudden whacking again on my legs. Making me think I heard my bones crack, feeling like they have surely been broken.

From the throes of a brief rest, she emerges, bringing another series of blows hard over my thighs and the sides of my buttocks, bringing the scream again back to the surface, where it struggles to life in one last hoarse, haunting cry of the damned. From this burning, I perceive her exhaustion, having gone well past forty blows, standing with the stick sill in both hands, holding it still across the side of my buttocks while I lay still, sobbing in shock and disbelief at the depth of pain and suffering, my voice still deeply muffled in the cloth pulled tight around my mouth.

She takes a deep breath. Raising up in defeat, spitting on me, enough that I feel the wet of it on my shoulder and my breast. She is arrested by the sight of my breasts for a moment, laid flat and heavy on the bed while I am on my side. She waits patiently, until the last of my sobs drift into a muffled whimper underneath the cloth. Turning at last on a current of bitterness unrestrained. Walking defeatedly out of the room. Wondering, as I, who on God's earth could care whether I live.

Or die.

The Asian

Corporate Queen

Rides the Wind

39

*T*his Asian corporate queen rides the wind. On the eve of eschatology.

Feeling the burden of corporate pressures. Pressures to conform to office politics. To look and dress in lipstick hypocrisy. Watching all her office coworkers mill around in hopelessness. All crushed by the lust for capital. The craving for security. Desperation for a normal life. She watches them. Sickened by the weak, pathetic men. Disgusted by the macho strength of the others.

She watches the women. Enamored by the curve of every waist. The width and roundness of the hips. Gray and navy skirts pulled tightly across them. Legs exposed in high heels down below. Breasts pitched in every key great and small. Poking at her in mocking through the white blouses. She watches the cute smiles. The pretty smiles. The beautiful smiles painted in lipstick. The silken black hair long. In braids. In loose ponytails.

The Asian corporate queen rides the wind. In pressures from a calling. Lifting up from farming country, to touch her in her office space. *Bika-ta,* the voice says to her. Capturing her soul in a whisper. Caressing her spirit in a sigh.

The new girl in the office is a breast queen. Plain faced and sweet. Breasts pulled up big and heavy in her bra. Stretching the limits of her wifey blouse. Hips spread the width of her gray skirt. Legs thick and shapely down below.

The farmer's daughter watches this woman. Enjoying the changes in the color of her blouses. Relishing which new cloth will hold the promise from day to day. Which color cloth will tickle her desire.

The farmer's daughter can endure it no longer. Resisting the pull. The calling of her instinct. The cry of the banshee. She drifts to the station of the busty new girl. Finding out her name. Asking her out to a formal dinner. The first refusal. Staring confidently at her bosom.

Days later, she feels the whispers flow around her. Feeling the laughter prick her skin. Being told in fleeting compassion by one of them, that she was heard *"hitting on the big breasted girl."* The big breasted girl who is married. Someone has been saying *"you're a dyke,"* they tell her. *"Because you asked the busty girl to dinner,"* they say.

The farmer's daughter learns the source of the rumor. Confronting her in the break room. Humiliated by her bold refusal to deny. Walking out in rage pressed down. Enduring the wave of cruel cackled laughter in her native sound.

The Asian corporate queen rides the wind. From a lunch hour come and gone. Alone in the elevator. So rarely and so conspicuously alone. The door opens on the very next floor. The predestined source of this calumny. Of this clamour.

The Asian corporate queen knows the cry of Fate. The call of Destiny. Grabbing the other Asian girl by the hair. An Asian girl who calls herself Angelica. Smacking her across the face while pulling her hair. Braving her own hair pulled. Her own blouse ripped and torn.

They fall to the elevator floor. One girl in rage on top. A cruel, rumor queen in confusion on the bottom. The girl on top repositions herself. Biting down hard through the blouse at Angelica's breast. Holding the girl underneath her. Listening to her scream.

The elevator door opens again quickly. Two other hopeless, helpless corporate queens pry the women apart. Holding one back in quiet rage. The other in weeping despair.

The farmer's daughter returns to her office space. Simmering in rage. Drowning in apprehension. Waiting for the fall. The fall of the corporate axe that never comes. In the wake of a rumor lived and died. Touched in her soul by the whispers of a calling. From the forests and fields of farming country.

The Asian corporate queen rides the wind. On the eve of eschatology.

Resurrection Rain

The suns and moons over this tragedy do rise and fall, to oversee the passing of the days into night. It has been two weeks since I felt the punishment stick on my back, since I was laid three days in the tomb. This, the mausoleum which is the upstairs hall, and the chamber room where my coffin bed lay. I was left tied up on the bed when the beating was done, left naked and tied up in the dark for three days, where an old horse blanket was tacked to the window, keeping me in the dark. I felt as though I had been buried alive, in the agony of deep hunger and thirst, feeling as though my hands and feet were petrified, and hopelessly lost to gangrene and amputation. I laid there in something beyond despair, believing in the cause of suffering, and that for some, there is no joy that can be had in this life, and that they were merely born and bred to suffer.

At the end of the third day in Hell, as I drifted off to sleep, believing that it was to be my last night of life, the door had opened, being unlocked from the outside, then somehow in an unseen shuffling of motion, the dark blanket was taken down from the window, to bathe me in the merciful light of the Moon. I then vaguely felt a fumbling at both my dead hands and feet, until it seemed as though maybe my arms and legs still worked, and that my hands and feet were still attached to them. I lay free from rope bondage, blessed by God to see the Moon at the end of my third night in the belly of the whale, sometime before the crowing break of dawn.

In the heart of this memory two weeks ago, I lay there on the bed, trembling from the phantom cold, naked, too afraid to move, terrified that if she were to hear me, than I will be beaten again. I lay there for the rest of the night, watching the night sky fade to the morning day, the deep morning twilight, nearby the break of dawn. At daybreak, she comes into the room in the guise of reluctant compassion again, just enough to see me to the edge of the bed where she sits beside me, looking me uncompromisingly in the eye, asking me do I know why I had to be beaten. I only have the strength to nod my head slowly, seemingly with no more tears left to cry, though I have to lower my head anyway and sob just once, holding the rest back so as not to anger her again.

"The next time you disobey me," she says, "what do you think will happen to you?"

"I'll be punished," I say, my voice barely able to sustain itself above a whisper.

"No, no," she says, smiling with false pity and deceit. "Next time...will be the beginning of the end. Have you seen what a sledge hammer can do to a piece of wood board?"

My body finds a reservoir of brief tears somewhere, squeezing them out as I shake my head 'no.' The sobs have been trying to hide my voice quietly, twitching my whole body.

"Awww, shhhh," she says. Touching her lips to my ear. "All you have to do is what I tell you. And you'll never have to worry about the sledge hammer."

She slides her hand down past my knee to my shin. Patting it with the palm of her hand. Tapping it with her fist. Gently.

"You thirsty?"

I nod my head, in the wake of another squeak and sob.

"You want Tropicana? I'll go get you a big glass of Tropicana," she says, caressing my thigh as she stands up, walking out of the room, not locking the door this time. Before long, she returns with a tall crystal, glass of sweet orange elixir. I take the glass from her with all my strength, so as not to drop this gift more precious than gold, noticing that my hand trembles slightly. An invisible hand steadies my glass, guiding it to my mouth, while I close my eyes to better hear, to better *feel* the gulps of this orange life go quickly down my throat.

"No no no no no," she says sweetly, stopping the drink at the glass half empty. "Not too fast. Drink slowly."

I obey the best I can. Taking another huge gulp, but taking the glass quickly away. Obediently. The last swallow is more precious than the first.

"When I get back, we'll go take a shower. Okay?"

She raises my head up, watching me nod obediently. Endeavoring a smile at me.

She takes the beautiful Jade robe from its place of honor, draping it around my shoulder.

"Obedient girl," she says. "Farm princess."

On the current of satisfaction, she turns with the empty glass, taking it down stairs. Somewhere far away. When she returns, she escorts me from my tomb to the resurrection rain, to the bedroom shower down the hall. She removes my silken jade robe, and the plush white one she is suddenly in, getting inside the cramped little shower with me. Washing my hair gently, lathering the soap at my breasts, caressing every bruise and scar on my body from head to toe.

Gently.

Two weeks away from my orange juice elixir, from my resurrection under the nighttime Summer Moon. I pour what skills I have into a Mexican feast, cooked by an American girl in a Japanese kitchen. A meal they have never tasted before, that I know can cleanse any cultural palate, and place the heart and soul in post culinary tranquility. The buzz around the kitchen is considerable tonight, as the house girl is back from the grave, healthy enough to work and cook, preparing a meal by special request that gets their attention, as the unfamiliar spices waft temptuously though the house, lifting the family to giddy promises of culinary delight. Do they eat crispy and soft tacos with cheese in the far east. They do tonight. Courtesy of the American girl in Japan.

Even I have to admit, my appetite has returned, at least for tonight, and I intend to pack it in with the rest of them. A quick taste of the seasoned ground beef tells me that yes, they will be glad that they knew me, and were touched by whatever small magic I brought into their lives. And in the wake of this divine sampling, the bite of sweet tomato and lettuce grown on our own farm, touched by cheeses bestowed from Heaven's Delight, I am forced to confront the third part of the truth—that I have no family, and I am as a stray dog found on the street, brought to the house and tolerated for company, and for whatever diversion I can provide.

The reality of my life weighs heavy on me, as I prepare this Mexican American feast in Japan, burdened by revelations of the spirit, bestowed to me from screams I have heard in the night, and voices from somewhere forward in time. From an unknown future, to the pain and sorrow of the present, Fate hath intervened on my behalf, perhaps, speaking through Mika Yung earlier this very day, telling me *"You may take water to the girls in the field. Breathe some fresh air."* And I had taken the bucket and old silver ladle in a spirit of hope and renewal, feeling the cool wind flow in from the east, brushing across my face, blowing my long, black hair up behind me. And I had carried the bucket of water to them one by one, past Mary Anna and the two remaining Japanese girls, all happy and surprised to see that I was allowed out of the house by Ni Li and Mika. But when I approached the girl with the fiery red hair, I was pricked by a spark of fear when she turned around and looked at me, a pool of blood in one of the whites of her eyes, and a scar on her forehead unhealed.

"What *happened*," I had said in horror, too afraid to touch her, or touch my own chest in apocalyptic shock.

"Mika," she says defeatedly, bending down to pull the stubborn weed, that simply would not be chopped and pulled away by her garden hoe. I walk away from her in something close to fear, looking back at Emma Rose till the soil, undone by the knowledge of the first part of the truth.

I approach the beautiful blonde in a spirit of total apprehension, staring at her face when she looks up at me, unable to keep my hand from my own mouth this time, as I see her eye bruised dark, and her top lip cut and swollen.

"I can't take it anymore," she says. A tear dripping from one of her eyes, taken and swallowed up in the dry earth. "You don't know how bad she hurt me, Sarah. She's crazy. I'm so scared."

I listen briefly, fearfully, to the cause of metal pliers at a girl's nipples, and of what inglorious pain they might cause. Briefly, I hear tell of a fiery red head's foolish attack, whacked away by a punishment stick across the head and face, then the power of a leather belt wrapped around this selfsame throat and twisted until the redhead coughed like a choking cow. Briefly, I listen to the pain of a blonde escorted away in private, bound with her arms out and topless in the barn, while a pair of metal pliers were pinched hard onto both her nipples, twisted and pulled ad nauseam as she screamed. I listen briefly, at how she was held tight by Ni Yung, and punched by Mika in the stomach until she nearly vomited, then punched in the face many times besides. All of this, while the brunette and redhead were locked in the workhouse, marveling the nature of violence and fear. I listen to her descend the third part of the truth down upon me, heavy as I turn away in defeat, stumbling back toward the house in the same dreadful fear I have come to know.

Jade

As I serve my Japanese hosts in the bounty of their Mexican cooking feast, I glimpse the happy, satiated smiles on the lot of them, ruling court over their little farming kingdom, being served by the obedient house slave with the long black hair. I give them their meal in the humility of servitude, excusing myself from them, taking my own dinner up to my lonely room, to contemplate the third part of the truth, echoed in my memory by the voice of Annabelle Blue *"if we stay here, we are going to die."*

I place my plate on the bed, taking a moment to look out the window into the night. To consider the third part of the truth.

Which is cataclysm.

he middle of the night descends upon my resolve. Rising me up from my bed of uneasy rest in the dark. I raise the second floor window softly, unable to breathe while I inch the window up as wide as it will go. With my beautiful Jade robe slipped on over my old, faded blue dress, I slip one leg quietly over the windowsill, positioning myself for this tragic leap into the dark, summer night.

The half moon casts little hope at me, as I fly through the darkness down to the grass, knowing somehow when to bend my legs and roll onto the ground. I had expected to feel maybe a broken ankle or knee, even though I felt as if I were carried on the wind. With the key in my hand, stolen from the key chain while doing the dishes after dinner, I hurry through the dark, country night toward the workhouse in the nearby distance, loomed over by the black, ghostly silhouette of forest trees just behind it. Whether or not the girls are awake, I do not know, as I fumble clumsily, noisily in the dark in pure terror at the lock, finally sliding the key in its place, making the fateful, clicking turn to freedom. I pull the lock free, tossing it into the grass, opening the door to the workhouse and hurrying inside. I touch Annabelle gently on the shoulder, then shaking her until she rises awake suddenly, looking at me frightened in the dark, as if I were her nightmare transcended into reality.

"What are you doing," she says.

"We have to go. We have to go now."

"Go where? Our lives are over, Sarah. We might as well stay here."

"I know that. But that's why we have to leave. You said yourself if we stay here we're dead."

Emma suddenly appears beside us, having already changed into her plain, faded burgundy dress.

"Why are you still in bed Annabelle," she says, handing her the blue denim dress she is cursed to wear. "We have to get out of here now."

As if guided by a force beyond her control, the blonde girl slips her dress on over her sky blue night shirt, slipping into the faded, gray athletic shoes. Emma hurries over to the beautiful, brunette Mary Ann's sleeping form, waking her up startled in the dark. Mary Ann hurries into her ivory colored cloth and her shoes, knowing only that it is the middle of the night, and the door to freedom has been opened.

"Where are we going," she says.

"I don't know. But we have to go."

"Why?"

"You *know* why," Emma says. "Because if we don't we're dead."

The four of us gather ourselves as best we can, even trying to convince Tina and Kyoko to grab this last rope cast down into the abyss. But the two Asian girls refuse, warning us that we are in the middle of nowhere, with nowhere else in the world left to go.

On this current of exhilaration and fear, the four of us hurry out of the work shed into the waiting country night. Running helplessly across the nighttime field towards the safety of the distant woods, away from the house of Pain. Fear.

And Death.

In the Forest

East of Eden

*I*n the forest east of Eden. Somewhere, in the woods of the Japanese countryside, four are lost in a flight for freedom. In desperation to live and breathe again. Four American girls in Japan, one in hair of spun gold. Another in strands as red as fire. One with hair as black as pitch, above porcelain skin as white as snow. The other tressed in hair the color of midnight silk. Deep inside the late night forest, we find a place in a small clearing in the moonlight, the four of us settling together in the darkness and fear. Four western girls lost in a dream, lost somewhere in the far east, with no way of knowing whether or not the sun would rise again, or wherever it is in creation we are going to.

In this grassy clearing, under the faint moonlight, the four of us huddle nearby one another, unafraid to sleep like two pairs of spoons for comfort on the grassy floor, where the red head protects the brunette from terror, and the blonde sleeps in uneasy comfort, under the arm of her Asian eyed liberator. The four of us are a victim of the night spirit's whim, whom some have called the Sandman, who sprinkles the dust of exhaustion over our minds and bodies, that we may rest for whatever traumas must still remain. The four of us are bound under the stars, bound inside a deep and inescapable sleep, where we are tormented more by the voices of our captors than by the ghosts and spirits that haunt the night woods around us.

In the glow of the jade cloth in the moonlight, somewhere between life and death, I know that two spirits of the forest walk among us, sniffing at us in the guise of two deer, a mother and her fawn, out for their own version of a stroll through the moonlit forest, emerging from the underbrush that will glow so bright and green in the daylight. Emerging from the nighttime sea of fern, to see what manner of human tragedies lay asleep in the soft grasses in the clearing at their feet. In my mind's eye, I see these two deer nearby the house of my tormentors, observing the house at sunrise amidst the chaos of sound, when a mother and her three daughters comb the property in confusion, with the oldest daughter grabbing one of the Asian girls hard by both sides of the head, screaming at her to tell the truth of what has happened. I am tormented by this in my nightdream, by the fearful rage in the hearts of the farmer's wife and her three daughters, riding up and down the lonely, isolated roads in the light of the rising sun, desperate to find where the four condemned American girls have dared to hide themselves along the road, imagining what brutal punishments there must be. Imagining the crucifixion of each of them, where they will be bound to support beams in the barn, where they will be whipped to bleeding, and then have their legs broken to ruin. Legs fixed and allowed to heal, so that they can stay alive long enough to work themselves into exhaustion, until such time that they are hit over the head with a stick, or held down and smothered, and then buried alive in a wooden box in the back woods nearby their farm.

The sound of hammering and the smell of pine torment me into a pitiful night scream, a wailing that hurries the two night spirits away like lightning, waking me up in the clearing inside the night woods, where I can see the three girls nearby, still in the cause of the Sandman's whim, in this nighttime forest east of Eden.

From the throes of our troubled sleep, we wake up in the dawn over this new world, in grieving to learn where to go, and what to do to keep from dying. But somehow, we know that perhaps this is only another path leading to our same dark destiny. We know that we can never go back. Back through the woods toward the sunset, which might lead us back to the farm, and the shackles of torture and certain death. The only thing for us to do is to keep traveling east through the plush, green jungle forest, through the hidden growth of tall, fernlike plants that wave in the swirling breezes as we travel. We can do nothing more than travel onward, thankful for when the growth thins out enough for us to see further ahead, so that the trunks of the tall trees are visible all the way to the bottom, and we can see where we are going. These daytime woods are pristine, pleasing to the senses, to bathe us with false security, to trick us into believing we are not condemned, and lurking our last miles of forest green to our deaths.

Sometimes, I wonder where the mother and her fawn from my dream have gone, and why they will not appear to us in the light of day, and guide us to some oasis of life nearby. We are all in the midst of a powerful thirst as we keep walking, even mocked by the pebbles of a dry creek bed we passed, but knowing better than to dwell upon it on our journey. The sun climbs high over the thick forest leaf canopy, in suffering to burn us alive with hopelessness, and bleach our bones in the aftermath of despair. The thirst we feel burns us from within, causing us to move deeper into the forest, and further away from the cold touch of humanity.

Surely, there will be some seasoned woodsman out and about. Someone who is no stranger to these woods, someone who will come along and help us find our way back from the land of the dead. But we press on in this false hope, watching the forest shadows shift through the passing of another day, until we see them vanish in their nightly calling, in the dark of the early evening twilight, where the evening day beckons the echo of the coming night.

We find another place in these thick woods to settle down for the night, this time among the sturdy trunks in the community of trees, where the green ferns grow shorter, allowing us to see further into the hidden landscape of our bleak future. There is no comfort for us in this life beyond one another, as we take another uneasy rest in deep thirst and hunger, barely able to discern the stars that mock us from high above the blackened forest leaf canopy.

In the haze of this brutal slow motion dream, nearby the rising light of the eastern Summer Moon, I am again tormented by the Sadist's Call, standing behind me in my dreams, gripped around my neck until I am awake into reality again, holding my hands at my throat in clutching, barely able to draw a raspy breath in the dark. Only the company of my traveling companions assures me that I have not died, and awakened somewhere in the pits of Hell, where I would begin Eternity's wait for someone to dip their finger in the river that flows nearby, and touch it to my parched tongue.

In and out of sleep we drift through this next night, lost somewhere between Yesterday's hope and Tomorrow's despair, beginning to wonder what tragedy is this that hath befallen, and whether or not we will live to taste another drop of water. But the fading of the night into another dawn strengthens what relief we have left, telling us to go farther than we ever thought possible, to trod our misery into the forest earth, to walk and pray silently to ourselves, that soon we will come to a river or trickling stream, or even a road that we can follow out of these thick, dark woods back to civilization, back to the blinking lights of earthly progression, where at least there is hope for some kind of reprieve from death.

But for all of this third day in the forest we walk, until the porcelain skinned brunette falls with the setting sun, and the four of us realize that we can go no further, and we all settle into our requisite places for the night, understanding that there will be no walk when we wake up tomorrow, and this is the place where Fate has chosen for us to die. We languish at the edge of breathing through the night. Adrift in the world between sleep and awake, where time has no meaning, and a thousand years is as the turning of a day.

The break of dawn touches upon the tragedies draped in cloths of ivory white, crimson burgundy, tropical blue and emerald jade on the forest floor, all having taken our places nearby a chosen tree for our final rest, to wait for God to grant us mercy, and allow us to soon drift into the mist of a final sleep. The rising of this sun brings with it a sense of resignation from the four of us, that we have suffered enough for one lifetime, and now it is time to wait for a final reprieve.

I am about to drift away, into the comfort of this early morning sleep, when I am shocked awake by screams loud enough to wake the forest dead. I stand up immediately, clutching the tree with my golden haired maiden, while the fire haired girl clutches a nearby tree with the screaming brunette, all of us frozen by the *white tiger,* emerging calmly from the plush, green undergrowth nearby, gazing at us with eyes the color of winter, nearby stripes as black as midnight, across a coat of fur as pure and white as arctic snow under the Mountain Moon.

45

Father Blake…sing thy song to me
In the heart of this fearful memory:

Tiger, Tiger, burning bright
In the forests of the night
What immortal hand or eye
Could frame thy fearful symmetry?

In the heart of this fearful memory
Father Blake…sing thy song to me!

Jonathan Lovejoy

When the stars throw down their spears
And water'd heaven with their tears
Did he smile his work to see
Did he who made the lamb make thee

Tiger Tiger, burning bright
In the forests of the night
What immortal hand or eye—
Dare frame thy fearful symmetry?

The cold hand of death touches the four of us in fear and grieving. Walking toward us in black and white striped form, a look of angry curiosity in its eyes, threatening to morph into a scowl, foreshadowed by a deep, rumbling growl, and a soft padded stepping towards us in stalking. Who among us is truly brave enough, or stupid enough to run?

Fate decides to have mercy on all our stupidity, holding it in check, so that it is impossible for us to move, as this enormous, beautiful thing is at the edge of crouching, as the scowl we have feared begins to appear on its face. And at the edge of reason, at the edge of our sanity, there appears the rumbling from within this animal's instinctive soul, followed by the turning of his angry curiosity into a scowl of controlled hatred.

"Kai!"

It is a cold, sharp voice from just out of our sight, that seems to startle this beast into immediate calm, causing it to relax and stand up straight, as the voice steps out of the tall brush just behind it, in the form of an Asian woman of mature, breathtaking beauty.

"Hira *Kai*," she says sharply, tapping her leg with the same authority she speaks, causing the animal to glance at us once again before it turns obediently, calmly walking around behind this beautiful woman, then resting itself on the ground with its head up. Gazing at us in Olympian beauty and power. As the beautiful woman walks toward us, the look on her face is a masterpiece of non verbal communication.

Her mouth opens, but she cannot speak.

"W... we came here from a farm," Annabelle says. "They were holding us captive and we escaped."

"How long...how..."

"We don't know. We're so thirsty. Please help us."

Her lovely face is suddenly awash with compassion, motioning us away from our trees of safety, telling us to follow her. Every step we take is on a cloud of fear, neither of us being able to take our eyes off this monster of a snowy white creature, lined with such a glorious black striped pattern. Do tigers roam the golden streets, and the rolling green fields of heaven? Of this sort, maybe.

This heavenly killer follows behind and beside her, while we keep our safe distance *far* behind, causing her to stop once and assure us that she is a good cat, and that we can come closer. We walk cautiously behind this beauty and her beast, both out for their morning stroll, who found four lost somethings deep inside the forest.

She leads us confidently through the beauty of this dense greenleaf forest, whose treachery is disguised in the loveliness of jade. Before long, there is a greater light at the end of this daytime dark, at the end of this tunnel of woodsy green.

We step out of the forest into another world. A place where tranquility touches the green lawn and perfectly landscaped bushes and nearby trees. We follow her and her furry white companion across the green lawn to the massive, enclosed area, the fenced in space where this snow beast can roam, and play with the spirits of its calling. I see a large, jade ball in the middle of the enclosure nearby its wooden house, and a white ball a good distance away, near the other side of its wire fence enclosure.

"She would never hurt you."

"She?"

"Her name is Shi Hira Kai," she says. She is a Siberian tiger. That's why she's so big. She may be the last white Siberian tiger in the world."

"She was going to eat us," Emma says.

"That is how she plays. She was going to get up on her hind legs and knock one of you to the ground. I'll show you one day, so you'll be able to trust her. If an animal like that decides not to kill, she means it."

"Has she ever killed anything?"

The lady smiles. Lowering her eyes.

"Not yet," she says.

Emma Rose Rides the Wind

*E*mma Rose rides the wind. On the eve of eschatology. In the wake of a doorbell chime.

Fiery red headed beauty. Mother of one; a strawberry blonde whip with a fencing sword. Scholarship to Yale. Promises of a future too bright to behold.

Emma Rose rides the wind. Suburban capris pants as red as blood. Matching T shirt the same color of death. Skipping down the stairs of her suburban palace, to answer the doorbell. The chimes in her Connecticut home. The home of a blonde physician. Yellow haired, red headed loving beach bum turned doctor. A graduate of the Bowman Gray School of Medicine. A glorified nothing of a white toothed, boy toy ears, nose and throat man. Grabbed and thrown up the ladder to success everywhere he goes. His beautiful blonde haired fencing daughter. His red headed housewife. Poison Ivy, lifted from the pages of fantasy and reality. The Desperate Housewife dream in the real world.

Emma opens the door of her suburban palace. In disbelief at what she sees. The somber, beautiful face of a blonde from her past. A blonde aged 20 years into the future. Eyes as blue as the ocean. Skin the color of ivory cream. In company of two daughters of like prowess in suburban beauty. Emma hugs the two beautiful girls, inviting them into her home. Tossing them quickly from her presence in fungalooga smiles and chiming promises of fruit punch in the kitchen. So she can be alone with their mother.

Emma Rose rides the wind. On the Red Wing of a memory. Stepping across this tiny space, this chasm of a separation. As if blown from somewhere back along the timeline, forward to the present. Grabbing her blonde visitor around her waist. Clawing her hands in hugging into her back. Shoving back the flow of tears to their appropriate place deep inside.

The blonde asks to be taken to the nearest computer in the house. A private computer. Yelling after the girls to bide their time. Going upstairs to the computer in Emma's master bedroom. The queen's palace in burgundy cushion cloth.

The blonde woman goes to the computer. To search the archives of tragedy. The affluent Washington Township, in Roanoke County Virginia. The fearful story dead and buried. An end of the world tragedy come and gone. A grand, bloody darkness. Forgotten.

Emma reads the story flashed on the computer screen. The story of a small time, small town female mayor and her grown daughter. Found murdered in their wealthy suburban home. A murder unique to the modern day. Evil passed down from the mind of Eve. Tragedy bestowed from east of Eden. A wealthy female mayor and her daughter. Nailed naked in death to the walls of their grand suburban home. Their gullets carved with a large X in bowels and blood.

The flood of fear from head to toe. A wave of terror in ice and cold. Lady X, as they recall. Lady Wolverine, in the heart of their tragic memory.

Emma Rose rides the wind. On the eve of eschatology.

Jade Silk Assassin

The four of us follow our hostess and savior from the tiger sanctuary, across the grand and picturesque lawn, that runs behind us far off into the distance, running beside a great woods on one side, and a great meadow of green grass on the other, with tall shade trees growing in isolation here and there. Fifty to a hundred yards to the left of the house is a large pond where two of the biggest, whitest swans on earth swim, walk and flap their wings, nearby a few white ducks and some brown ones, with the one requisite mallard with the special green head, swimming in easy confidence of its own unique beauty in nature. Nearby the pond is another building like a small guest house, painted as brown as the earth, in sharp contrast to the bright green grasses that surround it in every direction. Whether or not this is another dwelling or storage house I do not know, but believing that surely, no storage house could bear such an alluring, domestic tranquility.

The four of us file in nervously, exhaustedly past our kind and beautiful host, standing helplessly in the middle of the big, spacious area that must be the livingroom. Above us is the smooth, beige ceiling that seems to extend forever to the far wall, where two doorways are covered by elegant sliding panels the color of pearl, with Japanese symbols for *love* on one, and *judgment* on the other. The wall on the right is softly lit in the morning dark, to display the huge, beige canvas hanging down from a black rod, on which an elegant bonsai silhouette is painted entirely in sepia tone.

The tiles beneath us are laid out in elegant gray marble, to contrast the cushion seats of tan shades, married to the soft, like color of the ceiling and the walls, and even the coverings of the lampshades in the corners near the bonsai painting. The wall to the left of us is partly a large, patio door window, where the view of the swan lake and the forest is pristine. We walk under the bell crystal light fixture hanging down from the ceiling, the upside down bell shaped crystal, past the brownwood staircase banister to one of the sliding pearl doors, with the black symbols painted over the white pearl, watching our hostess slide the door of love open, where we see another extension of the heavenly beige décor trimmed in brown wood, accented by a Brownwood dining table with four matching cushioned chairs.

We strain our sore legs and backs to sit on the low things, basically chairs with no legs, having to cross our legs under the low, narrow table so we can have room. The framed symbol on the wall across from me, behind Annabelle's beautiful blonde hair, says *"the spirit of Christ is the spirit of love."*

"My home is your home," she says, bowing elegantly, traditionally, closing her eyes. I notice the brunette among us gazing at her in wide eyed fear, bowing her head as if she had been screamed at to do so. Our hostess turns to leave us alone for a moment, to give us time to breathe and recover from the shock, and to realize that we are not inside of a dream.

Our hostess returns with a silver tray with four clear glasses, and a glass pitcher with what looks like something that truly cannot possibly taste as good as it looks. She pours this magical looking drink in our glasses one by one, the lemon slices held in the pitcher by the spout at the top as she pours carefully, handing us all a glass of this natural metaphor, which we all stare at in mouth watering uncertainty.

"Please drink," she says. "I hope you like it."

How can a soul in Hell not wish to drink? As long as it is liquid and safe to swallow, I suppose. But when I turn this glass up to my mouth, amidst the smell of lemon in my nostrils, when my lips taste this sweet, tart elixir, both of my hands go to the glass, and I am resurrected again in citrus life, this time in lemon sweetness, of a kind that may truly be among the best ever made, perhaps uniquely at this moment, to welcome me assuredly back to life, as I bid farewell to my dignity, and pledge to drink the entire glass without stopping to take a breath. And this, I do, opening my eyes to see the other three variations on this theme, who are rescuing themselves from the fires of certain death.

*T*his morning has mercy on our fragile, feeble psychology, moving us along with angry insistence that the last year of our lives has come and gone. The four of us were bathed and fed, and filled up to our eyes with the best lemonade this side of Heaven. Hers is the most delicate hand in the kitchen, Asian food so light and tasty, vegetables stir fried and served over rice, all seasoned to a place of indescribable beauty. Even so, my craving for a thin crust pizza still haunts me, but only as a small price to pay for a journey into paradise. I wander through her lovely house alone at the moment, having already looked disappointedly in the freezer, seeing no Freschetta or DiGiorno delight inside. *Does she eat ice cream,* I wonder, as I drift from the kitchen through the spacious and elegant living room, drawn toward the sliding pearl door of judgment.

I slide the panel smoothly open, stepping into what looks so strangely like a warrior's room, with every wall decorated by daggers and swords of all types, and framed captions that say *vengeance is mine saith the Lord, I will repay,* and *a warrior's heart is forged in the fire's of suffering.* Of what purpose could it serve, I wonder, such a brave and bloody display room, in the home of one so elegant and beautiful? I cannot help but touch the Samurai sword, understanding that pictures and films cannot do it justice, as it is true with any manmade or natural wonder. How can something so deadly be so beautiful?

"That's not the Jade Dragon," a beautiful voice speaks, startling me to the core. I turn fearfully, gazing at my lovely host, so exquisitely displayed in her long blouse of plain, black silk from top to bottom, draped over her pants of the same shiny, midnight cloth.

"The Samurai sword is beautiful," she says, her English heavy with her native tongue. "But it is heavy and clumsy. Not the sword of a true assassin."

Nayomi Hahn steps slowly into the room, walking towards the opposite wall, where many traditional swords rest both bare and sheathed. Among these is a sheath of the brightest, purest green, colored exactly as the emerald green handle.

"It is said to be hundreds of years old. Thought to be the only one of its kind ever made."

She lifts the curved, polished sheath from its place on the wall, sliding the curved, shiny blade into view.

"Can I hold it?"

With only a brief, enigmatic look, she hands me the Jade Dragon sword without a word, with the emerald green handle pointed in my direction.

"Its so pretty," I say. Taking it by the handle. "It looks brand new."

"As it did when it was given to me. Over 20 years ago."

"Did it belong to your father?"

"My teacher. He was a master swordsman. He told me that the sword was mine before we ever met. He told me to care for it, until I met the one who would wield it at the end of the world. A Jade Silk assassin."

I look up at her beautiful face, in time to see a tear roll down her cheek. As to what pain it betrays from her, this, I do not know.

"Are you okay?"

She lowers her head, turning away towards another wall, where the caption reads of divine retribution.

"Last night, I had a dream. In the dream, the edge of the forest was burning, an explosion of green and black fire at sunset. And there emerged from this fire, a jade dragon as tall as the trees. I saw the fire coming from its mouth. It was the most beautiful dream I ever had."

A pause...

"And then, just this morning, Shi Hira Kai walked deeper into the forest than we have ever gone. I was worried because she would not come when I called her. She would only stop and look back at me, and would keep walking when I got closer. Then, she disappeared into the tall brush. I followed her in, angry with her, ready to grab her by the fur of the back of her neck, even though she is a tiger and can kill me. I heard her growling, and I thought that finally, I would see her give away our innocence, in exchange for the blood of some poor animal she saw...

"Then, I came into the small clearing where she went. Then I could not speak. But not just because the four of you were there. It was because my dream flashed so bright in my mind, when I saw you in your beautiful, jade silk robe."

I can only stare at her in utter confusion, from halfway across the room. Holding the sword, waiting for her to return to reality.

Waiting.

Jonathan Lovejoy

Mary Ann

White

Rides the Wind

51

Mary Ann White rides the wind. On the eve of eschatology.

Divorce. Mother of two. A son who has abandoned her forever. Abandoning her for his wealthy father. Calling her "too pathetic." Leaving her that day in tears. In pity.

Mary Ann White. Mother of one. Living alone with her fifteen year old daughter. All the money from an old life dead and gone. Living modestly on her divorce settlement. Alone with her daughter. A small, two story house in a working class neighborhood. Nestled comfortably nearby a wooden fence and a cropfield. A cropfield at the dead end street. Country on one side. City on the other.

In her undersized, overpriced livingroom, Mary Ann and her daughter hear a knock at the door. There is always so much to fear, from a fateful knocking at the door. On the wings of smiles less bright than normal, the White Raven, a.k.a. Snow, opens the screen door to her modest, Cherokee County home.

In flies the Red Hawk, a.k.a. Redwing, on a current of hidden fear and grieving. Hugging Mary Ann and her daughter. Ignoring the suburban secrets that burn in blue and black fire.

In the wake of this hidden sorrow flows the Blue Dove, a.k.a. Seabreeze, flown on the same current of grieving. Hugging Mary Ann and her daughter with nary a smile past a tiny grin. The fifteen year old can barely breathe through the nervous tension. Unable to take her eyes from the two beautiful women and her mother. Having never before seen the like in real life. Petticoat Junction, revisited. Hair as yellow as gold, as red as fire, as black as midnight silk. Beauty unrivaled, these three. Except for one they know. One whom they remember.

The brunette mother releases her daughter from the tension. Allowing her to go upstairs to her room. Escorting the two wayward visitors from afar to their cushioned repose. To the plush, ivory seats of suburban delusion. Of lower middle class how de do. The three women sit close together. The redhead on the right. Taking the hand of the brunette in the middle. Both of them staring at the blonde, blue eyed beauty. Whose eyes are as the sky. Deep as the ocean blue.

She's coming for us, the blonde says.

How do you know?

Because of what happened in Virginia. To a female mayor and her daughter. I know it was her, she says.

But why would she come after us? That was so long ago.

I can feel it in my bones, the blonde says. *In my blood. We have to be ready.*

The types of fear are many, and uniquely distinguished. Among these is the fear of Death.

Mary Ann White stands up in stunned silence. Walking from the livingroom into the kitchen. She stares out the kitchen door, arms crossed over a healthy bosom. Hips spread wide in her black jeans. Unable to see the fearful looks on her visitors' faces in the livingroom behind her. Staring at the green of trees. The burning of green and black fire in her memory. Braving the memory of the Jade Dragon, a.k.a. Jade Silk.

Mary Ann White rides the wind. In the wake of tragic recollection. Of what comeuppances are overdue.

At the kitchen window door, the first droplets of rain begin to fall. In the pain of recollection. In the armament of jade.

Mary Ann White rides the wind. On the eve of eschatology.

The League of Shadow Assassins

*T*he League of Shadow Assassins. The spirit of Ninja. What tragedy of human existence hath this been, these four years of our paradise in the woods?

"It's your ballet training," Nayomi says. *"Your body responds uniquely, much better than the others. You move faster, jump higher, kick harder than anyone I have ever seen. Wing Chung and Choy Li Fut have made your body the most lethal weapon imaginable, your finger jabs and punches strike like lightning, your kicks explode like thunder."*

In the four years that we have been immersed in her training, I have cracked a dozen set of ribs with my kicks; men and boys brought in to test us, to block us from, or take us to the next level.

"Until you can beat these men," she says. *"You are not ready."* And she has pulled the hair of each one of us many times, furious over our tears, disgusted at our weakness, caning our backs and shoulders ad nauseam, until we understand how to kick, how to punch, how to block and counter punch, until the moves are so natural that we can perform them in our sleep. *"Lazy American doll babies,"* she'll say, which always brings a smile or a laugh to her lips, once knocking Emma down and taking her place in front of Mary Ann, managing to land slap after slap to her face, punch after punch to her chest before eventually kicking her in the stomach hard enough to bring her to her knees, coughing and crying.

"Awww," she says. *"Baby Barbie want hospital? You bleed inside? Then, you die. And I bury you in the woods. Stand up."*

Mary Ann had stood up slowly, reluctantly, her face wet with tears and crimson with humiliation and pain.

"Baby Girl stand in one spot until I tell you to move. If you move, you will practice nunchaku until your arms cannot work again. Do you understand?"

Mary Ann had simply nodded, squeaking out one single sob to go with the tears, standing in the same spot without moving for two hours in the hot sun, Nayomi putting a large, traditional Japanese sun hat over her face after the first hour, daring her to move. Truly, nunchaku practice is brutal on the arms, after just a few minutes, sending a burn through the muscles all the way down into the chest and abdomen. The three of us could not contain ourselves from laughing as quietly as we could at her that day, standing in her black gi with her white belt and white grand grandma hat in the sun.

"Watch Sarah Green," she would call me, as I would endeavor to destroy whatever boy or man she would bring. Our fights with Nayomi

were worst than the fights with the men she brought in, until I begin to wonder if they were not set up to be easy wins for us. *"You are better trained,"* she said. *"Therefore, you fight better. You train the way I was trained. And I was trained by a Chinese master of Choy Li Fut and Wing Chun, and a Japanese sword and Ninjutsu master. It was he who gave me the Jade Dragon."*

But before I was ever allowed to touch this beautiful sword, we were all immersed in pure hand to hand combat for two years, until we were able to match her when she was at her most lethal, without getting knocked to the ground and choked by her legs around our neck for being *"slow and stupid"* she would say. I watched her hold back on the other three so much more than she did with me, until it was something of an unspoken conclusion that when we fought, the spirits were going to gather and watch it happen. Mary Ann and Emma always told me, *"I don't know how you can block all her punches without getting hit, she is so fast. When you two fight, its scary."* And though I try not to notice, Annabelle sometimes will force a smile over an obvious irritation, the source of which, I truly do not know. I have not been boastful or proud, knowing that I am a child of the dirt, having been lower than a dog, rescued from the jaws of suffering and death by the mercy of God.

"Power without humility is corruption to the soul," Nayomi says. *"If you are not humble, you are not an instrument of God. Christ was the most powerful being who ever walked the face of the Earth. Yet, he humbled himself, and died so that we can go to Heaven when we die, even though we are all evil to the core of our rotten souls. When Christ first came, it was in humility. And love. When he returns, it will be in glory and judgment. Those among this evil generation, those who are*

meant to be judged for their wickedness, must die at the blade of the chosen, those who have humbled themselves before God and Christ, so that the anointed sword of battle may be guided by his mighty hand. Those who will someday die by your divine blade are chosen to do so, and you will be chosen to execute the life from their bodies. You will be humble, or you will die."

As to what varying degrees of acceptance this is, as to how deeply this seed of humility is planted in each of our hearts, this, I do not know. We push forward the best we can, training so deeply into Wing Chun and Choy Li Fut Kung Fu in the first two years that we were all shocked when we fought so called "advanced masters" of Karate, Taekwondo and Judo and Jujitsu, and found that the sluggish, stiff, *"fancy dancing"* she calls it, was no match for either of us. *"And these are so-called tournament champions,"* she says. *"They make me sick. They know how to fight for points and belts and trophies. But in real combat they are stiff and awkward. Relying on training and technique rather than the spirit of survival. When this spirit takes over your training, you become invincible."*

We were witness to this on one occasion, when one of the karate masters, a Japanese tournament champion, challenged Nayomi Hahn to a full contact, no holds barred fight, which frightened the four of us from the outset. We could tell that this traditional looking man was no slouch, simply by the way he carried himself—with quiet confidence, hands always behind his back, always looking at Nayomi with a disgusted expression. Angry because all four of his best karate students were handed their asses by the four of us, though they were four of the hardest fights we ever had, Mary Ann only winning hers because she resorted to biting, and Emma from the most effective eye gouge.

"Chinese bullshit!" he finally bursts out and says. *"They fight like scared rabbits! I could beat all four of them at once!"* The four of us look at Nayomi, and I can see her struggle to cover the wave of satisfaction that flushes through her body.

She unfastens the loops on her top, one by one, slipping her black top off, revealing her tight, black sports bra pulled tightly over the D cup breasts, then bending over, sliding her lose pants down, folding her body in half all the way down without effort, sliding the pants away, loosely folding both pieces and laying them off to the side. She walks confidently in her full length, black stretch pants and matching bra over to the center of the practice floor, her extraordinary figure on full display, one of the finest examples of feminine athleticism possible, both tightly muscled and deeply curved at once, with full, shapely hips and a waist tiny in the middle of a cinched, inward curve that is remarkable to behold. It is the silhouette of God's inspiration, when Eve was formed from the rib of Adam. Her loose, modest clothing has hidden this full truth from us these two years of close quarters living and fighting with her, and I think the four of us are as unnerved by this woman's body as much as her balls to fight this man.

To counter her audacity, he removes his top and tosses it gracefully away, walking his well muscled, middle aged thickness to the center of the floor with her. He bows deeply, respectfully at the waist, while she only nods her head in like respect, staring at him the whole time, affixing her stance with her legs slightly apart, standing up straight, her hands behind her back. He goes into his deep, ready stance, turned to the side, knees bent, fingers stiff and extended, with one arm stretched out in front towards his lady opponent.

In thin mustached determination, he lunges an impressive punch directly at her face, which seems to activate a program in her body, causing her to flip backwards; several full bodied flips all the way to the other end of the floor, then not stopping to rest at all, employing the most elegant hops, leaps and kicking turns on the way back toward the man, with long leg extensions easily over 10 feet high. She whirls back to where he is, but not throwing a punch or a kick, waiting for him to gather his senses again—standing toe to toe with him, blocking every strong, precise punch of his at close quarters, needing only to move her head slightly, frustrating the poor man by blocking every punch and close quarters kick, suddenly striking his face with blinding speed with the palm of her hand, then once again with her fingers extended—both moves which cause him to back up and bend over, covering his face with both hands. When he stands up, the poor man is blinking wildly, with the requisite blood having already appeared at his broken nose.

In a rage, the man yells his best karate yell, lunging at her again with a flurry of punches more hopeless than the last, while Nayomi stands with her side to him, one hand behind her back, the other blocking every angry punch thrown. She blocks a forward kick to her stomach with both hands, holding his leg, hitting his face again with the back of her hand, then engages him full on again, slapping both of his hands away, slamming a barrage of quick, loud punches in full, spanking sound against his bare chest, then shoving him back very hard, in the spirit of masculine power channeled through the feminine, then hopping a side kick directly in his face, shrieking one loud, sharp yell, stumbling him backwards.

He stands there out of breath, looking her up and down, refusing to be beaten by a "cheating bitch," as he calls her, running at her as if to grab her, shocked by the extreme height of her body lifted off the ground in front of him, as she spins a back kick into his head at the temple, snapping his head violently, knocking him down on his back to the floor. She stands in full, classic form, with her legs deeply bent, with one arm extended far out towards him, with the other arm up slightly behind her head, staring at him as if he could pull out of this stupor and stand to his feet. He does not surrender, but his body does, refusing to allow him to stand up, forcing his head back to the mat, rolling his eyes unfocused in his head. Along with his shocked, so-called master students, the four of us watch our lady master stand up straight and bow her head to him, barely able to breathe from the pressure of fear and awe in our chests, as we watch this beautiful, shapely Asian woman walk calmly over to where her silken black cloth was laid, and calmly dress herself in casual modesty once again.

"It takes seven years to defeat the devil," she says. Walking slowly around us, the four of us standing in a line, wearing the requisite colors of our calling; which are snow white, crimson red, royal blue and emerald green. With stretch pants, sports bras and ponytails all in place, we stand in 4th year confidence, listening to this beautiful, mature Asian lady, this woman in black, relate to us the eighteen disciplines of the Art of Shadows, she calls it, telling us that fighting a warrior trained in Ninjitsu is like trying to fight an angel in the dark, which is as a shadow come to life.

"A Ninjitsu assassin with a sword is certain death. It is the wrath of God."

We stand still in the breeze, listening to the chorus of the leaves, the messages blowing wildly through the forest trees nearby, to foreshadow the coming storm.

"Already, your prowess with a sword is deadly," she says. "But you are not as good as you think you are. A real Samurai or any other trained warrior would cut you to *pieces*," she says, snapping at Emma, as if the poor girl had actually said something aloud. She didn't.

"You will not fight any more gifted amateurs. No more pathetic, Samurai and Ninja wannabes. Today, you will turn your Katana swords... on each other."

At that moment, the approaching storm gives an account of itself, rumbling loudly enough to shake our insides with warning.

"If we get wet, we get wet," she says. "If we die in lightning, we die in lightning. It is God's will."

She tells us to take the gold coins we hold, and flip them, catching them and turning them over on the back of our other hand. "The first two who are alike will fight."

From the left, Mary Ann is the first to reveal her coin. Tails. Then Emma shows Nayomi her coin. Tails.

"You two, *fight,*" she says.

The two of them stand in the rising wind, the brunette and the red head, both holding the long, curved swords with two hands, the blades crossed and touching. Characteristic and typical of her fiery demeanor, Emma attacks first, bringing the sword down toward her brunette lovely's face, angry at this futile attempt, as the sword clangs against Mary Ann's blade raised in blocking stance, who counters with a quick swipe that Emma blocks as well. They go on like this in the rolling gray, clanging and banging ad nauseam, until Emma at last swipes a cut across Mary Ann's arm, making her lower her sword and look at the bleeding wound.

A few seconds later, she is stumbled backwards from a massive slap from Nayomi, who glares at her with the fires of Hell. "You *never* lower your sword in a fight."

"I couldn't help it, she *cut* me!"

Another slap elicits a scream, and she pulls Mary Ann's hair violently, holding her head back and staring at her face in disgust. She takes Mary Ann's sword hand, biting the back of it hard enough to make her scream, snatching the sword from her hand and throwing it to the ground where it sticks blade first. And then, remarkably, she *spanks* Mary Ann on her bottom like a soccer mom in a South Carolina Walmart, lurching the crying 21 year old young woman forward like an unwanted foster child.

"You act like stupid baby I *beat* you like one!"

After at least twelve of the hardest spanks one can imagine, she shoves the crying brunette back towards us, kicking her *very* hard in her backside, causing her to stumble forward and loose her balance, falling flat onto the ground. The girl gets to her knees and crawls back to her spot in line, where Annabelle and Emma help her to her feet.

The four of us stand still in the rising wind. Seeing a streak of lightning arc in the distance. Feeling the first drops of ice cold rain on our faces.

"Annabelle! Sarah Green! *Fight!*"

Crossed swords mark the beginning of our journey through this brief tragedy. We stand ready, glaring at one another in the pouring rain. The spirit of what must be descends on me with the falling mist of rain, drenching me with sudden instinct, and inherent knowledge of what it is that I must do. She raises her sword, striking it at me in the rain, but to no avail. *Do not waste a single motion,* are the words I hear, *she is nothing to you.* I step back slowly, watching her as if she were a spitting cobra. I lunge at her, dropping my body in the rain, sliding underneath her sword, grabbing her legs with mine, making her fall like a clumsy sack forward to the ground. Standing up, placing my foot hard into the middle of her back.

"Submit," I say, over the chorus of rain and thunder. But she flips over quickly, clanging her sword hard into mine, climbing stubbornly to her feet, the front of her blue sports bra and pants stained dark with wet grass. She leaps up, coming down on me from above, which seems to bring my sword up in a twirling flash on its own, blocking it so hard it pulls her body with it to the side, allowing me to slice a deadly gash across the front of her thigh, touching the blade to her neck in the rain.

"Submit!" I say, this time in Japanese, to appease the growing spirits of the storm, and their quest to see me obey their beckoning call. But in the wake of Annabelle's fervent scream, she forces herself upright again, more afraid to lower her sword than not, being foolish enough to lunge at me again, this time with designs on stabbing me in the gut, to which my body responds not with a block, but with a flying, floating leap backwards in the storm, as if caught up in a gust of wind, much to the shock of all present and accounted for.

Now do it, I hear the spirit say, and I find myself in another strange leap, but this time after a running step forward, disorienting her as I turn upside down over her head, blocking her sword, my legs high in the air, my head just above her own. Landing on my feet behind her, twirling the sword once in my right hand as I bring it down sharply across her back diagonally, taking hold of it with both hands instantly, then crossing her back again diagonally from the other direction. Emerging from this slow motion dream to the sound of another fervent scream from the blonde girl, as she falls to her knees, trying desperately to touch the pain she feels burning her back like fire in the rain.

"Submit!" I say, touching my sword to her neck in warning. But she only screams "Nayomi, *help me!"* Trembling, drowning as she stands up again. Stubbornly holding the sword with both hands, as I walk around to the front of her. When she lunges at me again, I block the blade to the side, then kick her hands hard enough to send the blade flying, then spin kicking her in the chest with all my might, with a full leg extension, lifting her off her feet, flying her backwards through the air, landing her in a sickening thud on her back in the pouring rain.

The next scream I hear is from the fearful Mary Ann White, music set to the image of Emma Rose with both her hands over her mouth, Annabelle Blue on the ground unconscious, with me in dragon stance over her body, while Nayomi Hahn stands frozen, drenched in melancholy and awe, as the rain pours down in waves, and the lightning sparks streaks of light across the entire sky amidst the rolling thunder, and the rising gusts of wind and rain.

The Mountains

of Tragedy

*T*he earth turns upon the River of Fate, born from the mountains of tragedy east of Eden, flowing us in bondage toward the Sea of Destiny. A mere seven painful turns of the earth have happened since Annabelle was cut for life and knocked cold by what spirit had taken over me, more completely than at any time I remember. The jumps and moves I did seemed to come up on their own, pressing upon me severely, until I had felt as if I had no choice in the matter.

"You flow," Nayomi had said. *"I saw it with my own eyes. When you retreated back from her third strike, you spread your arms like an eagle and the wind took you like a kite. I swear to the Holy One of God, it happened."*

"We thought you had killed her," Emma had told me that same night a week ago, while Annabelle rested for three days, saying it hurt her to take a deep breath. Nayomi had reluctantly taken her through the violent storm in her sleek, black luxury ride with its tinted windows to the hospital north of Nara in Kyoto, fearful that I had broken one of her ribs.

Its just a bruise, the doctor had said. *She may be fine in a few days or it may take a little longer—sometimes it may linger for a month. What she needs is rest, and no more soccer practice for a while. My daughter tried out for the professional team,* the doctor had said. *She twisted her ankle during the tryout, so now she is where she belongs. In medical school. Going to be a surgeon,* he had said proudly, while he gave them a prescription for pain pills and sent them back toward their hidden country paradise. Annabelle had not been able to speak of what she saw me do, and had simply cried in the car on the way here, while Nayomi had tried to comfort her.

"*Do we know enough to kill,*" Annabelle had said.

"*That depends,*" said Nayomi, "*on whether you want to be good. Or the best.*"

"*What kind of people did you kill? Who where they?*"

"*Condemned souls,*" she said. Not speaking again until they arrived back here many hours later.

In a quiet daze, she has been since that day. Assuring us that she is okay, and that she holds nothing against me.

"I was so scared at what Nayomi might do if I held back," I say. "Please forgive me Annabelle."

"Of course I forgive you," she says, hugging me tight as I cry quietly in her arms, patting me gently on the back. "Fighting you, I should have known what was coming. You've cut every swordsman you ever fought. You're wicked with that thing."

"I was only obeying Nayomi." I would *never...*"

"I know," she says. "I know. I'm scared of her too. If she wanted to, she could probably kill us all without a thought. I asked her about who the people were that she killed. What kind of people they were. She wouldn't tell me."

In the wee hours of the morning, I languish in and out of the world of dreams, missing my roommate in the dark, whose bed lies empty in the night, as the storm returns with purpose of intent. It seems to have arisen as quickly as it had before, but with a greater fury. The loud, rumbling thunder serves to drift me back into the land of dreams, until I am suddenly shocked awake by a heavy weight slammed down on top of me, pinning me under the sheet, seeming to knock the wind out of me. Images of shadows come to life threaten my sanity, enticing me to shriek Nayomi's name. But the breath that I draw is taken by a cloth pressed firmly over my mouth, making it impossible for me to draw another life giving breath in the dark. I can only manage a quick, muffled scream into the cloth, unable to follow the voice in my head that tells me to *lie still and let sleep have its way*. It only induces a greater panic and struggle, as the weight of two shadows press down on me the length of my body, while the third shadow lays heavy across my chest, pushing the cloth hard into my nostrils and my mouth.

I squirm again the best I can, hearing my inner voice *say there's no need to scream,* at last giving in to the heavy swoon, that swirls the three shadows into a haze in the nighttime storm. And even in the throes of this burden of sleep, I feel myself being carried away, transported by demon spirits slowly above the floor, seeing the sliding glass door approach in the otherworldly dark, but being unable to stop myself from being taken. And in this paralysis of motion, I can feel the cold, open air of night, and the punishing attacks of the cold drops of rain on my face. High above my head, as I drift low to the ground, I see the streaks of lightning illuminating the clouds in the dark, followed by the cascading, screaming mountains of thunder crashing down upon the world, in bitter knowledge of what takes place beyond the feeble sight of women and men, and what tragic truths do emerge from the shadows. These inhabit 3-D space around me in the rain, drifting me though the elements as though by magic, away from the safety of my country home, past the mysterious roar of some lonely, desperate animal in the night.

These shadow demons drift me to the unfamiliar edge of the nighttime woods, turning me left from the safety of the clearing, transporting me through the gates of Hell. I am suddenly aware of the nighttime tree canopy, which seems to be lit up by streaks of lightning in the storm. In the haze of this slow motion dream, I can feel myself being lifted upright, feeling as if pressed against a tree by a cushion of air, which takes hold of my throat so that I can neither breathe nor swallow. I feel the shadow demons thump hard against my face and my stomach, hard blows that carry no pain, stopping as suddenly as they began, as the shadow demons move menacingly around me, then drift stealthily away in the nighttime rain and cold.

The rain continues to tap me on my face, gently, incessantly in the whistling forest wind, until I am again aware that I have eyelids, and that they are closed. With a mighty push and struggle, from a strength found from deep within, I strain my eyes open, gazing into the reality of the nighttime forest wood around me, feeling the bark of a wet tree pressing into my back, as I slowly come to realize that yes, I am wide awake, and I am somewhere deep inside the forest in the raging storm, roped and bound tightly to a tree.

The roar of a Siberian tiger haunts Nayomi in the rainy morning dawn, on the third day after she discerned that my bed was empty.

"She was feeling guilty about what she did to Annabelle," Emma had said, with Mary Ann nodding in fervent, fearful agreement. She never told us she was leaving."

Nayomi stands at the glass door this Sunday morning, glad for the impending day of rest and recuperation, listening to the culmination of the tiger's agitation, which began three days ago. But I am not privy to the sounds she hears, understanding that there will be no orange juice or lemonade resurrection for me this time, and that this is the hidden sunrise of my final day. Every new awakening brings me closer to my last ounce of strength, my body on fire in the cold, to at last tell me that I would rather be dead than feel this pain. I understand that my next sleep will be the sleep of death. To at last carry me away from the pain and suffering of this life, to receive the promise from my spirit that this is my last and greatest trauma.

At her isolated country home, Nayomi Hahn can endure the pain of my absence no longer, though she has no idea where in God's creation she can possibly begin. *Maybe I abused her too much,* she thinks. *Maybe she finally left me.* But even while she is haunted by this thought, the tiger will not cease its loud, disturbing call in the morning rain; a deep cavernous roar of strength and power, so uncharacteristic of her, having never done this in all the years since she was grown. For the better part of an hour, this tiger Shi Hira Kai, roars several times a minute, until Nayomi must drape her long, black rain cloak and hood over her body, to go the front of the tiger's lair. The huge, white Siberian tiger walks briskly back and forth, growling now instead of roaring, seeming undeterred by the heavy rainfall, and slightly appeased by her presence at the gate.

There are those who refuse to look beyond what they can see. Those who stubbornly cling to the five senses, and the logic and common sense of the ridiculous world around them. Those have no understanding and belief beyond the logical, beyond the natural world, having no belief in the force of destiny, and the power of fate, and the workings of forces beyond their control. These have no fear in a dark room at night, no understanding of a child's terror at the darkness that peers out at them from the closet door ajar, or the shuffling and scratching they hear in the walls at night. They have no understanding of predestiny, and the parchment of their life that is unfurled among the stars, a thousand years before they are born. These are they which could stand in front of this tiger from here to forever, and never hear the voice that tells them *"open the gate and obey,"* not understanding their own inadequacy, and their unbridled ignorance of the rule of the supernatural world.

But Nayomi Hahn is not one of them. Raised by a practitioner of the dark arts, a woman who gloried in the shadow of necromancy, and so-called communication with the dead. Looking upon those spirits with disdain, knowing that some of them are demons, whose only purpose is to steal, kill and destroy. Looking on the other side of their darkness, to honor those spirits born from the light, who are sent by the spirit of the Almighty God, to bring messages to the hearts and minds of hopeless women and men unawares.

Nayomi Hahn stares into the white eyes of a tiger. Who sits calmly now. Staring at her with eyes of knowledge. Nayomi Hahn stares at the eyes of a tiger. The eyes of an angel.

She opens the gate to the tiger's realm. Not surprised by her calm stroll out of her fenced in paradise, and her turn toward the house. Nayomi Hahn is not shocked by the tiger's walk past the house to the edge of the forest wood. Nor by its long walk down the edge of it, towards a place where they have never walked together inside. She is not shocked by the tiger's inevitable turn, following it deep into the unfamiliar daytime dark, the thick and foreboding forest wood, following her glide into the unfamiliar spread of trees, wondering briefly what dark magic has reached up from her past, and finally taken her sanity forever.

But at the momemt of truth, Nayomi Hahn glimpses a flash of unnatural green, the darkened forest green of a nightshirt she finds deadly familiar, touching a tree trunk where there are ropes tied, and a pair of white arms bound immobile. Nayomi Hahn runs past the white tiger who sits, moving no further in the rain, staring in horror at the face of death, upon a young Asian woman bound to this tree by her neck and the rest of her body, her arms pulled behind her around the sides of the trunk, her head hung at the near edge of her final sleep. The near edge of the sleep of death.

Catch a tiger by the tail

In the beauty of the forest green
Ride him to where the truth prevails
In the hour of their darkest dream

The scent of wet tiger fur is strong in my nostrils, in keeping with this otherworldly impossibility. I can hardly open my eyes to this bizarre entry, which is the sudden end of the rain on my head, and the sound of my own wet body flopping to the floor. And I was not privy to the look in three pairs of eyes when the glass door slid open, and the largest white tiger in the world walks into the house with a soaking wet Japanese girl on its back, who sits there leaning forward as long as she can, before slipping off and falling to the floor. The tiger screams a full roar into the house which is deafening, causing the brunette among them to go running into another room, while the other two stand frozen in something beyond terror.

Nayomi leaves me lying wet on the floor beside Shi Hira Kai, who licks her chops and glares at the two girls in a look as cold as ice.

"Kai," Naomi says, tapping her legs, walking toward the glass door again. In her black hooded rain cloak, she drifts out into the pouring rain, a lonely figure dressed in black, leading the snow white, black striped beast calmly through the rain to her fenced in home place, where she roams free in captivity. I can barely see, let alone move while she (Nayomi) is gone, unable to tell how completely their awe swings in one direction or the other.

This odd and tragic awareness is soon met by Nayomi's silhouette returning from the rain. Drifting through the glass door slid open and shut. Moving slowly towards the wet, broken down nothing in the middle of the floor. Lifting her up, escorting her trembling, resurrected body to her own bedroom. Changing her into a dry, white cotton nightgown. Lying her on her back on the comfort cushioned, queen sized bed. Floating with malice, down the stairs again, ghostly and disillusioned, calling the girls from their hiding and their stupor. Sitting them on the hard cushioned, beige sofa. Sitting on the wooden coffee table in front of them. Not yet looking them in the eye. Blinking once to clear her vision.

Weeping.

"For what you have done, the three of you deserve to die. Even among killers, never have I seen such profound dishonor. It is a ruthlessness. A cold, vicious savagery that I am not capable of. And neither would I have believed it of you, if I had not seen it with my own eyes. One of Christ's sayings is: *Those who take up the sword, shall perish by the sword.* Among these is the sword of betrayal."

From the mists of sorrow, Nayomi looks up slowly, locking eyes with Annabelle. Braving the itching on her face, flowed down from both her eyes in the quiet of slow, steady streams. Beyond the flash of lightning, the thunder rolls across the forests and fields of the Japanese farming country.

"You are as ready as you need to be," she says. Finally sniffing. Wiping her eyes. Joined by both Mary Ann and Emma. Annabelle's single tear is silent.

"I cannot allow you to see her again. Of this, what apology could there be?"

Mary Ann finally plays her melancholy tune. With one, loud sob, as if a wave of agony has suddenly passed through. Guilt? Sorrow?

Fear?

"I will take you to the airport in one hour. Your clothes are all that you may take with you. You will have plenty of money for many months of comfortable living. At the airport, you will meet a man named Chow. He will introduce himself to you. He will say *"I hear that you three girls are ready."*

In the aftermath of grieving. In the pain of trauma come and gone. Three deadly flowers in partial bloom, riding the wind and the rain. Ready to join the Shadow League, where they will bloom in the shade. Where the art of shadows will accompany their deadly skills, to sharpen the blades of their calling. To hone their natural ruthlessness to a deadly poison. To make them killers of women and men.

The three blossoms disembark their windy chariot in the rain. Among the busy lights of earthly progression. In the sorrow of regret, three young American women roll the bright lights of civilization. In full and easy command. Imagining already, how many they could do away with if they should so desire. What pathetic fool carelessly adrift in a bathroom.

Stuck in a stall with them. The place where piss and blood do meet. A place that could mean certain death to them. A choking. A broken neck. A pocket blade to the jugular. To a child, a smothering by mere hands alone. To a stolen baby, a drowning in the toilet, while the mother is held by another. When sometimes two are better than one. When sometimes, two flowers bloom together.

On the eve of the Second Coming. Three flowers ready to bloom sit in the bright lights. Approached by a man named Chow. Chow plucks three flowers in partial bloom. A white rose. A rare blue rose.

Ready to blossom.

Jonathan Lovejoy

Sarah Green Rides the Wind

*S*arah Green rides the wind. On the eve of eschatology.

A black rose in full bloom. Leaf petals in the armament of Jade. A rose the color of death. Seven years removed from the lemonade resurrection. The girl she was being long gone. A reputation already, as the deadliest swordsman ever known. A swordswoman. Flying and flipping, cutting long and deep. Wounds that gush blood. Lives on the edge of oblivion. Trained masters at the edge of death. Having finished Ninjitsu training with the Lady Hahn. Moving like a shadow. Appearing from the woodland brush like a spirit. To place the dagger blade at her lady master's throat. Then to throw the dagger into a nearby tree. To make her mistress afraid. Afraid of what could be. Afraid of what might have been. Watching her perform balletic moves in every form. Leaping, kicking, striking the air in graceful beauty. Throwing the daggers with the accuracy of the bowman's arrow. Throwing the stars like bullets shot from a gun. Done with speed difficult to resister with the eye. A power and accuracy too fearful to behold. A sword touched by lightning. Hands and feet of thunder. Burning fists of fury. Ready for the game of death.

Sarah Green rides the wind. Satari Sakara. The seventh Jade Silk Warrior in history. The last of her kind.

On the eve of the Second Coming. On the eve of eschatology. Nayomi Hahn pulls her sword in fear. In the deadly shadows of the night. Ready to jab her blade at the living shadow in front of her. The shadow that holds the Jade Dragon. The weapon of an assassin. The greatest assassin of all time.

In the darkened raining room. In the meager light of the storm. In the flash of lightning from the windows high above. In the glow of natural lamplight from below. The two women circle one another in scant cloth attire. Pieces of black cloth for modesty. Breasts exposed for this deadly game. A single, bleeding cut to the victor. A cut where the blood must run. Anywhere on the body, save the neck to preserve life. Or the breasts, to preserve a woman's dignity. In this game, cuts to these places have no honor. No victory.

In a flurry of steel. In the sparking of blades in the firelight. In the clashing of metal in the storm. Nayomi Hahn senses the death of Sarah Green. The death of the white blossom. The autumn of the white woods. The birth of bloodlust. The eyes of Satari. An avenging angel. The deadly hand of God. With all her power summoned, Naomi blocks the flurry of blows with a gift. Unleashing her truest inner voice with the blade. To give Jade Silk her final test with the blade. To see if she can truly do the impossible.

Jade jumps her fearful overhead flip. Feeling the confused wind of her mistresses sword. Stopping to look at her waist, just beside the naval. There is a cut. A cut red with unfulfilled promises. A painful cut, with not a trickle of blood.

In Satari's piercing eyes, her mistress slows down to a crawl. She leaps at her mistress, blade extended in the dark. Aimed at the shoulder for piercing. Letting Nayomi's instincts play. Feeling Nayomi's blade knock hers to the side. Stopping her momentum just enough. Dropping in full leg split beneath Nayomi's raised sword. One leg far out front. One far out back. Topless Asian Barbie on the floor. Seeing a canvas of flesh in front of her. From the bottom of Nayomi's wobbling D cups, to the curved waist and naval. To the widened front of the hips in the patch of black cloth and string.

In one motion, blocking the blade above her head, bringing her own down in a deadly, stabbing strike. Piercing inches into the thigh. Like a dragon's tooth clamped down. A move only possible with the *Wakizachi* sword. The shorter blade of the Jade Dragon. Over immediately in a yelping, stroking regret. Her lady master. Breaking her own tragic rule. Stumbling backwards in defeat, her blade lowered pathetically. Long breasts dangling heavily in the dark. Lifting her hand away from the dragon's bite in her white thigh. Watching the warm blood run. Watching it run down her leg in the firelight.

Satari Sakara rides the wind. On the eve of eschatology.

In the Advent of the Storm

$\mathcal{N}$ayomi's deep, womanly scream continues to haunt my mind, down to the core of my spirit every day since that stormy night, when I achieved my victory in blood. I held her hand as the lovely female doctor stitched her up, watching the middle aged woman enjoy the pain as Nayomi tensed up with every stitch, only half numbed by the local anesthetic. I could feel the doctor's own sadistic pleasure flowing, as Naomi had refused to take the stitches with me out of the room. The lady doctor did not seem to mind, however, seeming to enjoy causing Nayomi this mildly intense suffering in front of me. I can remember the doctor's smooth, lovely hands on Naomi's white thigh, in contrast to the red nail polish worn by the physician, in tandem with the red lipstick she wore. She was a pretty woman, made up to be beautiful, stroking Nayomi's leg in soft reassurance in their native tongue, then gleefully pushing the big, hooked needle through her skin, poking through the other side and pulling the thread through, while Nayomi's lovely face bore the anguish of it. Watching these two beautiful, older women in this act made me have to take a deep breath, which I struggled to keep hidden from plain view, as if either of them were really watching me anymore anyway. The cut had been so deep that she could barely walk. I had enjoyed her limping repose, her pitiful resignation that yes, at least in part, the teacher must bow down and call the student master.

I serve her my American version of vegetarianism, thin crust cheese pizza and French fries, which she always eats with a look of hungry fascination, having gone nearly her entire life without even so much as a taste of this before I arrived. "Such food you eat," she says. "No wonder your breasts are so heavy."

Mock me, Mother dear. Chime that sweet lady voice to me. I will hear you scream again, this very night, my queen. Of this scream betrothed to me. Of this, I truly swear.

Fruit cocktail and strawberry Jello are the cure for what ails her vegetarian craving. As if in answer to a prayer I did not know I prayed, the skies have devoured the moon and the stars again, to begin to rumble another warning to the complacent inhabitants down below.

"This is the worst storm season I remember," she says. "The skies are angry almost every day."

At the glass door, she is startled at the reflection that appears so suddenly behind her, holding her chest and blowing a deep breath.

"You move like a ghost," she says. "Not necessary to walk like Ninja all the time."

"You taught me too well," I say. Stepping close behind her. "I just wanted to thank you for everything."

"Why? You leaving?"

"Oh, no. Definitely not."

"Why you act so strange then? So mysterious?"

The next moment of her life is filled with the terrifying sensation of cupped hands at her hips. Sliding their unmistakable message across her black silk dress.

The types of fear are many. And uniquely distinguished.

"Satari. What are you doing?"

"I'm thanking you."

"That's not necessary. You don't—"

Her breath is cut off, by a sharp pressing of my thumb to her ribs. My other hand finds its way to the smooth, pearly white skin of her throat.

"This is beneath you, Satari. Stop it."

"Nothing about you," I say, shaking my head no, "can be beneath me. That is not possible. My master."

These words are breathed into her ear, as I sense her close her eyes in a last ditch effort—a last, pitiful attempt to avoid surrender.

"Shadow warriors do not do this," she says. "It is beneath us."

"Tonight," I say, in the accompaniment of rolling thunder in our midst, "tonight, we are *women.* "

And upon this sentiment grows the fearful, fervent pinch at her nipple, to spark a response in flashing from the clouds, and a loud, mother's shock of drawn breath from her. As if I were her daughter after a Sunday church service when the father is out of town.

"Satari san—you cannot do this," she says, in her native tongue, shaking her head no. Oh, but Nayomi, my dear. I most certainly can. I am a motheress, my darling. A mother lover of the highest order, I am.

"I know how to make you scream."

"I will not scream for you," she says. Trying to push my arms away. Trying to run. But the pinch at her throat, and the twist at her nipple say otherwise.

"You will stand *still*. You will obey."

"I will *not*," she says. In another bold attempt at rising above the drowning wave. To draw one last breath of pretense. With both hands, I cup her breasts through her dress, squeezing them hard, causing her to grunt a trembling breath involuntarily. I move from her breasts after another squeeze, sliding my hands slowly, firmly down her silken black dress, down past her hips to her thighs, past the place of the healed scar hidden, sliding her dress slowly, carefully up her legs, past her thighs in the advent of the storm, where the rain falls unseen on the darkened countryside door window.

"Please," she says breathlessly. "Have mercy."

"No. I cannot."

And in the next moment, in the chiming of apocalyptic thunder outside. I slide my hand inside her black underwear cloth to her chastity.

Feeling her push hard back against me with strength and power, her head thrown back beside mine. The warmth, the wetness, the swollen cushion of her surrender is extraordinary. Her face, her body, her spirit is as one who has been deprived of life giving water to drink, and then has it suddenly thrust upon them. The poor woman is helpless in my grip, which arouses my pity for her, and the desire to cause and ease her suffering.

I oblige her weak and begging spirit, with a fervent and steady rubbing of her down below, watching her ride the waves of this inevitability, not knowing whether or not she will have the power to keep her promise, to not allow me to hear her scream. But I am privy to the loss of what dignity she has left in the strong, desperate grip of her hand to mine, and her other hand to my hips, as if being pushed over the edge of a great fall, where she must hold on in futility for her life.

And suddenly, in the midst of nighttime thunder, I feel the strike of lightning in her poor body, and she jerks and spasms back against me, her face twisted in the mighty effort to hold her voice, as she seizures an Armageddon quake from head to toe against me.

Oh, but Nayomi, my dear. I am a motheress slut from east of Eden. Oh yes, Nayomi, my dearest love. Oh yes, Nayomi. You will scream for me.

And in the wake of these end of the world spasms, I rub the cushion of defeat without ceasing, rubbing the erect proper place, her improper place, to begin her grunting anew, which she strains to prevent from pouring out of herself from deep within, but to no avail. And then, at the threshold of her endurance, what pleasure there is crosses over to a pain unfamiliar, and I am blessed with the power of a deep and tragic woman's scream, a scream twice born, as she pushes her lips to mine in a quest for relief, bellowing her agony onto the conduit of my tongue, trembling the remainder of her body's energy into me from top to bottom.

From our apocalyptic tragedy at the downstairs window view. Up the stairs to her plush and cozy bedroom. Allowing her epic vulnerability to show in full surrender, as she feels me ice cream lick her neck as we stand by the bed. Licking her shoulders, her arms, sucking her fingers, taking hold of a single breast, nursing it, pulling it far out from her body in my mouth, until she cannot resist her body's tell tale shudder, and the sign that she has been thrust high again, where there is another threat to be cast down to ruin.

I lift this healthy hipped, full breasted woman up in my arms, throwing myself onto the bed on top of her, hearing her breath escape in the impact, a loud, fearful grunt that takes hold of my body like I have never felt, and tells it what to do on its own. I raise up, sliding her around roughly to her proper position on the bed, ice cream licking her at the naval, to feel her entire body quiver in the agony of waiting, raising up just enough to glimpse the massive little girl cock, and it's beautiful thrusting up at rapt attention. I touch my own, opening the place where it hides, touching the tip of mine to hers, shocked by the spark that hits us both, which appears as anguish on both our faces as we look down, amazed by the feel of this miracle we see. *Fuck your mistress*, is the whispered voice in my spirit, which caresses me in places unseen, guiding me to lie down on top of this beautiful woman, pressing both my breasts to hers, nipple to nipple, feeling our girl cocks intertwine, twitching my buttocks in pre-lightning strike. *Fuck her*, are the words whispered again, causing me to have to pin her arms tightly to her sides, slightly underneath her so that she cannot break free, instantly finding a long, grinding thrust, a motion that creates another upon itself, to guide my hips into a rocking, sliding cadence of four/four time, to establish the dominance of my spirit over hers, and the surrender of her spirit to mine.

And I must take all of her essence into myself, refusing her the breath of life, clamping my lips over hers as I grind, feeling the complete merging of one soul into another. And of this, I am aware of my body's certain need, and I must abandon thoughts of her pleasure, and I begin the slamming, humping rhythm down onto her, feeling her breath already begin to lose control again, colored by sobs of quiet pleading, as though she understands that the trumpet of her voice will soon blow again. But of this, I am unaware, only concerned with what must happen to my own body, of what fires in my tragic soul must be reawakened, as I hear her sobs give way to a full weeping, as though the well of misery in her spirit hath spilled over, and devastated her mind and body to ruin. I hold this steady, pounding rhythm, my hips slamming up and down as she weeps, perceiving somewhere in the haze of feeling her voice gather upon itself, until the weeping becomes a pitiful howling, a wailing cry for a mercy that can never be given. And this cry of agony from deep inside her reaches into my tragic spirit, to activate the fire the color of blue and pitch, causing my breath to escape my control, pulling the words *help me, oh God please help me* in her native tongue, words born of their own volition, until the logic and sanity of them is morphed into the blaring trump of God, and the power he hath seen fit to flow through the human female body. In the burning of this tragedy, in the fires of this judgment, seven years of pent up energy explodes into my body, flowing out of my voice in a severe, high pitched soprano shriek, taking over my body's motion until I am no longer aware of how to move, or even begin to know how to stop this devastation of my spirit, soul, mind, and body.

Jade

On the second day of this bizarre, divine honeymoon, the two of us find ourselves of, at all places, a ridiculous sex shop. Browsing the grand, impossibly well lit and put together megastore of every perversion known to man. Walking past the handcuffs, whips and chains attached to nipple clamps, ball gags and lengths of new rope and bondage instruction books with bound Asian women on the cover in pretend peril, so reminiscent of where I have been in reality. Seven floors of kink, cute and corkscrew carnality, schoolgirl this and school teacher that; from books on how to kiss to erotic wrestling mats, paddling board bliss and a nurse's white hat, women who like to piss and pull their own breasts when they have shat, all of this we walk past, in quiet awe of every this and that. Until we come to the section of boxes and sealed packs of what speaks to our perverted souls, which calls to us in perpetual and phallic girl erection. Of this eight inch thing attached to its leather hip harness, we cannot easily dismiss, stopping to stare at it, and then each other, like two mischievous Siamese cats.

Before too many turns of the clock, we make our journey through the rain, sneaking a kiss here and there, a hand holding or two at the traffic lights on our way out of town, a caressing of one another's legs and thighs ad nauseam, hands gripped and kissed ad infinitum, until at last we are in the world of the swans and ducks, woodland trees and a white tiger in the rain. We make our way hurriedly into the house and directly up the stairs to her bedroom, where our clothing is removed without ceremony or pretense, even before our packages and presents are opened and admired.

I am in motheress heaven when I slide the realistic, skin colored member up to my hips, nearly twitching when she tightens the straps for me with such clinical care, then getting to her knees in front of it, stroking it amused, saying in her worst English, so heavy with her eastern accent, *"big girl cock,"* stroking it lovingly, watching me hold my head back and take a deep breath with my eyes closed, savoring the pull of her hand upon it, feeling it take a deep breath with my eyes closed, savoring the pull of her head upon it, feeling it take hold of the nerve endings in my body as if they had become attached to it. I watch my beautiful, older mistress slide her mouth upon it, tasting it, stroking it by natural instinct, saying, "in my entire life, I have never done this to a man. Only to my sister and my mother."

As to the feeling this revelation flows into my body—of this, I do not know. I gaze down on her in the spirit of shock, watching her push every inch times eight down her throat, holding it there until she gags, sliding it out unashamedly, letting the spit fall from her lips to her breasts down below. She does this a second time, letting the spit fall again, stroking it harder, looking up at me as a guilty whore, proud to be judged over her sin and depravity. She slides it back into her mouth, in and out, bathing it in her spit, which runs down from the member to her lovely hands, which grip the slippery when wet, sliding it back down her throat in one last show of what churns beneath cultured civility.

She pulls it out, and stands up. Turning her back to me mysteriously, stepping slightly forward and away.

"I'm going to do a backward handstand," she says. "Grab me tight, then lift me up till my clit is at your face, so I can suck your cock like a mother whore."

She stands still, her legs together, her widened hips on full display. Leaning all the way back to the floor, delivering her promise, her breasts flopping toward her upside down face. Her smooth, white chastity and legs high in the air. I grab her tight, and she tells me to lift her high up, anchoring her legs over my shoulders, so that we are an upright yin and yang, where the view of her immodesty is unique and pristine. I cannot see what I feel down below, which is her upside down, with the member pulled into her mouth, sucking it for whatever nourishment it may provide. And I must wait a moment, observing what I see with rapt attention, watching it seem to dampen before my eyes, as the energy of it grows in profound length for a woman. I have to put my lips around it, feeling her leg twitch strongly, then taking it all the way into my mouth again in a harder sucking, hearing her groan loudly and deeply with desire. I can feel her upside down sucking grow more intense, as does mine, pushing the member against my body just so, which threatens to shake me prematurely. And though I try not to let it happen, my breath betrays me loudly through my nose, as I anchor myself, feeling my whole lower body quake as I stand still and strong, grunting loudly through my nose so I can hold my place, having to release my sucking so I can breathe, and hold her up without losing my balance. I hold her steady, with her hanging upside down, feeling her continue her hard sucking rhythm, amazed by what I see, when I see the middle of her tense up violently, squeezing out the tiniest bit of clear fluid, as I feel her grab on to my hips as hard as she can, releasing her sucking so that the loud, quick scream can be free to pass from her mouth, and noisily into the room around us.

Our third night of perversion bears witness to the rise of pain, and a phallus strapped to a long, jade green pillow in waiting. Having already been made to choke upon it in punishment, she stands upright now, facing the bed, her hands cuffed in front of her, with the matching silver nipple clamps attached painfully to her breasts, with a tiny silver chain dangling between them. Even the mildest pull on these is enough to make her shake her head no, in a genuine plea for mercy, not wanting her precious nipples to be scratched to blood upon a reckless pulling.

"Stand up straight," I say sharply, my own jet black phallus hanging down in power and glory. The folding of the leather belt, the tinkling of the buckle inspires her to a deeper breathing, knowing already that she is going to understand the nature of fire lashed upon her skin. With the speed and power of my calling, I bring the first of one hundred blows down upon her fleshy backside, watching her body flinch once in a shock of terror. And before I continue, I notice already the changing of her skin, the bright redding of it in a full stripe across her hips, soon to be raised into a welt of sorrow. I continue upon this theme, not holding back her discipline, listening to her breathe to endure each passing blow, until she is easily bruised and marked from top to bottom. And when the seventeenth blow whacks her across her backside, I hear her breathing give way to what I had thought was pain, until her buttocks betray her with a violent quiver, which she tries to swallow and hide in her voice, breathing out a deep, breathy grunt in shame. The eighteenth blows is a hard, angry response to her already, while 19, 20 and 21 accompany the words "filthy…nasty… *bitch!*" and then "dirty… nasty… *whore!*"

I continue the blows, some in silence, others accompanied by the music of my inner frustration, stopping once to twist the belt around her neck, to bark insults at her in her native tongue, until I know she is genuinely defeated in her spirit, continuing the hard, uncompromising blows, until her skin bears the marks of deep discipline, in bruises and welted places, and the cutting of her white skin to blood. The one hundredth lash is built upon the chorus of her quiet weeping, but done genuinely and without pretense, as a grown woman broken down from the humiliation of a deadly belt whipping.

"Why you cwy," I say, mimicking her thick Japanenglish accent. "Mama san no like belt? Too much hurt on bwuised bottom?" But her quiet sniffing tears can inspire no pity, as I shake her head by the neck and order her to shut up. Pulling on the nipple clamps still in place, which is painful enough to elicit shaking of her head, and another pleading for mercy. Carefully, I release her nipples from the painful metal clamps, unlatching them one at a time, each unlatching causing her to groan loudly in relief. Leaving her hands cuffed, I gently lick both her sore nipples, gently pulling them deeply into my mouth. "Touch yourself," I say. "You cum." And this, she does. Rubbing herself in obedience while I gently, deeply nurse her nipples. Holding one in my mouth without releasing it, holding it there still, while she rubs herself in obedient, lightning rhythm, her face anguishing over, until suddenly, tension breaks in her body, causing her to double over in deep, breathy grunting from the trauma. In this, I nurse her breasts without ceasing, until I feel her body completely recover from the trauma.

"Such a good mother whore," I say. Studying the severe exhaustion her face without pity. "Get on the bed," I say. Watching her crawl helplessly and handcuffed onto the bed. I follow her immediately, guiding her to the phallus attached to the pillow. "Get on it," I say. "Slide it deep inside." This, she does. Straddling the long, round cushion pillow, guiding the member inside herself. Grimacing its now unwelcomed desire. "Sit still," I say. Getting behind her on the pillow. Letting the spit fall to her rectum. Touching the tip of it to her improper place, pushing it impossibly inside her bottom, listening to her cry out as she lowers her head, to endure the arrival of the Queen of Sheba, and the burning of blue and black fire. Every dark inch slides deep up into her backside, to elicit squirms and loud cries for a reprieve, and for salvation where none can be given. I push my whole body tightly up against hers, holding her around the waist, so I can feel the depth of this last and greatest trauma, and to feel the fires of new sadism that burn.

I take hold of her hips, and do a slow, in an out motion, sliding the black serpentine in and out, in and out, in and out inside her rectum, watching her get used to the rhythm and the feel of two cocks pushed inside her body, beginning to move herself as though the pain of what she feels is now her darkest dread of pleasure. I roll my own eyes back just once, the feel of this being enough to satisfy me, craving only to see her body once again shaken to devastation and ruin. I take the key from its hidden place in my leather strap, undoing the shackles of her past, tossing them unceremoniously to some other lost place nearby.

I take hold of her breasts, squeezing them softly as she settles in to her humping rhythm double penetrated, pulling her back up against me, breathing hotly into her ear as she rides herself to a plateau of near madness and frustration, placing my hand to the front of her, to find the stiff and swollen little girl cock down below. Causing her to hold her head further back, grabbing me by the hair and at my hips, as the remaining energy buildup in her body strikes an unknown chord inside her, sending her entire body into shaking, quaking spasms, while she babbles helplessly, gruffly in her native tongue, as the spasms shoot in waves through her body, trembling her senseless from the crown of her head to the soles of her feet.

For seven days, we ride the heights and depths of perversion. Variations on themes of pain and pleasure, harmonies of pain and suffering. We trade orgasms ad nauseam, under this storm of powerful and protracted duration, until we find ourselves listless and spent, laid together in the nighttime voice of this endtime rainfall, and the warnings heard in the rumblings of distant, rolling thunder. I lay draped nude across my mistress laid upon her back, with my arm and leg laid heavily over her, resting my head on her shoulder, in the shadow of her lovely bosom in my vision.

"What kind of people were they? The ones that you killed?"

"I call them condemned souls. Either in this life, or the life beyond the grave. Adulterous wives and their lovers. Evil corporate giants. Whole families sometimes, of those who betray their own crime bosses. They call us through certain people who know where to contact us. The pay is enough to last a lifetime."

"One of us could kill anyone in the world then. I mean, in my country, even the President wouldn't be safe."

"There are forces. Unseen powers that control what we do. Who it is that we have to kill. We are merely instruments of the Hand of God. And he will judge us in due time."

"You killed women and children?"

"I never liked having to kill children. But I drew satisfaction in ridding the world of their evil fathers. But I'll have to admit, that killing women gave me the greatest pleasure. I killed many wives in bed with their lovers. I would drive my sword through the woman's bodies into the mattress. If the sheets were white, the blood would spread outward like wings from underneath them. Some of the men, I would cut off their heads. Whatever I felt led and guided to do, I did."

"How many did you kill in all?"

A corporate mother and her daughter were number 26 and 27 for me. They were the last. Spread out over eleven years. The killing of this wicked woman and her daughter quenched the fire in me. I knew it was time to stop. There are more requests for killings in the world than there are killers to do the job. There are not enough assassins in the world to satisfy the bloodlust of wicked men."

"What makes us any better than they are?"

"We are no different from them. Except that we were chosen by God to kill, and their enemies were chosen to die."

"But what made you want to start doing this in the first place. What made you become an assassin.?"

"Like you, I was abused by my mother, and also my older sister. I was beaten and enslaved by the both of them. I did not know that I was filled with so much rage inside. When I was seventeen, I stabbed my sister in the stomach."

"Did she die?"

"No. But I was sent to jail for a year. After, I was approached by a man who said he could make me rich, by training me to be *"a secret agent,"* he said. Since I had no job and nowhere to go, I went with him, thinking that I was probably going to be turned into a whore, and maybe even be raped and killed. But I did not care. I was lost, I had no one, and I wished that I was dead."

"What happened?"

"He took me to a beautiful mansion. Inside, a handsome older man said, *do you want to be rich?* Then he said, *follow me.* He took me to his fine office, and there was a man who was not in a suit, but in a Chinese style dark blue shirt, pants and soft shoes. He said, *an assassin is chosen by God, young woman. You have been chosen."*

Outside, the voice of divinity rumbles a message of eschatology from the clouds.

"Satari Sakara," she says.

A low, whispery sound.

Jonathan Lovejoy

The Motheress Call

he rains of our fervent discontent do rise and fall, from our journey along these tracks on our cross country train ride, over the forests and fields of the countryside where we roam. In the tragic 24 years I have lived and died on this doomed planet, I cannot remember a time of such peace and tranquility in my soul, through it is touched and colored by a mild, continuous depression; a melancholy that encompasses us both, and drags us inextricably together as one. Though I wonder when the wind of my impending departure will take hold and carry me aloft, there is a part of me that will not allow this idea to take hold, making me cling to false hope for dear life, that Nayomi and I are somehow married, and will be together forever.

On the plush seats of our luxury train ride, I sit as close to her as I can, so grateful for the privilege of our private car, where we are the only ones around, languishing together on the plush sofa, freed from the prison of the lower class cars, where we would have to endure the stares of everyone, gazing nosily at the older woman and the younger, wondering why they seem more like sisters or lovers, and less like mother and daughter.

Twice, Nayomi was approached at train stations on our way from Nara, by way of Kyoto east to the far city, by other curious women her age, women of what empty status that can be acquired by money, and of what shallow beauty it can buy in fancy clothes, fancy hair and fancy makeup. Wives and daughters of wealthy men, they were. Set to brave their luxury train ride to nowhere, such as we, having spent a lifetime buying off unhappiness, bribing it to leave them alone through the pain of their earthly season.

"Your daughter is so beautiful," one of them says with a desperate boldness, her own skinny, Asian Olive Oyl looking daughter smiling and agreeing so enthusiastically, even though her mother was clearly saying it as a direct insult to her. I reached out to this painfully thin young woman with my eyes, with a stare of tragic understanding, but seeing that she herself had none. Whether or not this was intentional, I do not know. I only know that this young woman in her early thirties was already under lock and key, a prisoner of the phony life and smile bought and paid for, where money is the medication for the disease of Truth, a panacea drug for the cancers of pain and sorrow. The glassed over, happy go lucky deadness in her eyes caused me to have to tilt my head just once, as

though looking at a curiosity I couldn't quite process or understand, while she and her mother smiled and stared at the two of us like they had seen us together on the movie theater screen. But before long, we are rescued by their flitting, restless spirits distracted, lured into some happy, empty conversation with some other rich men's wives and daughters nearby.

On this melancholy train ride, here at the end of the age, I take the hand of my new mother, my mother wife, pressing the back of her hand to my lips, my eyes closed, expression anguished, unable to even look her in the eye, lest my delusion of future happiness vanish in my sight. In the wake of this dying, rainy world speeding by outside our window, I lay my head in my mistress's lap, feeling her caress my hair and the side of my face, both of us surely drowned in uncertainty, which rises up above our head like the waters of Fear, that surely we can never be lucky enough, be blessed enough to have found happiness, a refuge from the coming storm of eschatology.

As she gently rubs her hand across my hair and the side of my face, I am haunted by the mother daughter image of a road less traveled, where *fungalooga* has not been bought and paid for, to medicate the pain and sorrow away. It is the image of a younger mother in the train station from over an hour ago, an Asian mother in the company of her twelve year old daughter, both of them lost in the throes of this same rainy melancholy I feel. These two are heavy burdened on my soul and spirit, the lovely mother and her quiet little daughter, hiding in public, in plain view, carrying their secret with them as an invisible curse ghost, sitting with them in the form of gray death in long, black hair and angry sorrow about her deathly features in beauty from beyond the grave. It is the motherline curse, the mother daughter curse, the motheress, the ghost of mother daughter perversion, shown to but a few souls unlucky enough to see her in the company of them she has cursed—sometimes standing behind the mother, with both her arms wrapped around the mother in invisible tragedy, or sometimes behind the daughter in like manner, or at times merely standing in their presence, to keep them infused with the pain of a tragic need to exercise themselves in the depth of behind closed doors secrets upon each other, leaving them spent and guilty, and primed to do it again when the mood arises.

This lovely mother, I remember, who had a bosom much heavier than my own in her white collar shirt, somewhere between my own heavy F's and my mother and grandmother's light J's. This heavy breasted mother in the train station, I remember, in the presence of The Motheress, the ghost of Mother Daughter Perversion. And as I allow sleep to take over, here in Nayomi's lap on the train, my heart and mind are so clearly burdened with the truth they have hidden from the uninformed. Those that cannot see, that cannot feel the truth of what goes on behind closed doors, and of what churns beneath cultured civility.

They are not privy to the truth of the train station mother and daughter as I am, that can see clearly, *feel* clearly the hidden trip up the stairs in the endtime rain, while the Japanese father is away on business. They do not see as I do, the lonely trip into the mother's bedroom, where the twelve year old girl is obliged to remove her mother's blouse and bra, to expose the gigantic, low hanging bulbous breasts, then to take them both in her young hands for a mighty squeezing, clapping and slapping them together, then taking one of the mother's huge breasts into her mouth to give suck until the milk is made to run, the milk of their secret perversion so recently born, pulling the milk so fully into her pretty little mouth,

The spirit of mother daughter perversion looms over our journey to the far city, hanging low in oppressive melancholy and gray. The rains of this endtime warning continue to fall, haunting us every step of the way, along our journey toward tranquility.

Our time in the restaurant had been spent focused on each other, both of us daring even to embrace the silliness of wine glasses, though the juice of the grape we drink was as unfermented as what was created from the water at the wedding by Christ the Lord. In the restaurant in Tokyo, we had enjoyed taking our place as the strange, close mother and daughter couple, whom no one could quite figure out, wondering why if we were mother and daughter, why were we holding hands so much across our table, and looking into each other's eyes with such quiet longing and such deep, melancholy understanding. I notice that my mistress' hands are both sturdy and elegant, strong yet unmistakably feminine. Across the restaurant table, I stare enamored at eyes of great beauty and wisdom, eyes that burn as wise as those of a serpent, but as innocent and harmless as a dove. She suddenly seems like an elegant stranger to me, like some exotic and world weary traveler, who has stopped along the way to indulge my pathetic self because of a heart filled with pity and compassion. No world leader could possibly be diminished by her presence at their side; an Asian woman of such elegant maturity and extreme, radiant beauty.

Part of me is still afraid to embrace her fully. To accept her beyond her role as caregiver and martial arts master, knowing that my luck has never allowed another human being in my entire life the space to have ever given a damn about me.

Back at the high rise luxury hotel, the two of us are prisoners of the strange love we feel for one another. Standing together at the still rainy balcony door, watching the lights shine through the mist of the rainy Tokyo night. With the balcony door slid open, where we feel the breath of warning flow in from Tokyo Bay in the gray dark, she stands behind me as closely as possible, her arms wrapped tightly around my waist, her lips at my ear as I look out over the lights of the rainsoaked nighttime city.

And I am amazed how the thunder seems to acknowledge the feeling inside, the inevitable move of our faces toward one another, where we are gathered upon a current of fear, moving to this fearful destination, which is flashed in warning in the storm—as our moving cages open, to disembark the two of us into the bright land, the promised land, the land of milk and honey, where the taste of her kisses are sweet to the palate, and the nourishment of them is milk for the soul.

In the wake of mother daughter energy screamed at us from the clouds of warning, under the burden and torment of the motheress ghost in our midst, our lips come together in epic declaration, in exaltation, in quivering resignation of what fate has bestowed to us, that we are two that have been joined as one before God, announced by the brightest energy from the clouds, and the roaring of thunder from one side of creation to the other.

*Y*ou are my mother, Dear Nayomi. I am your daughter.

I see the epic confusion you try to hide. When you wipe the tear away from my cheek while we stand at the balcony door. Looking at me from my hair to my chin, at my shoulders and my neck confusedly, in anguished confusion at what desires must torment your soul. At what desires you must now torment mine with all the same. You have to make me understand, I know, that what must happen tonight is not mutual. What pleasures you must give, what pleasures you must receive are born from selfish instinct, from the core of burning desire.

I am your daughter, Nayomi. You are my mother.

With your eyes open, you kiss me on the forehead. And then the cheek. Touching both my lips with yours, one at a time, to quiver my spirit and soul unseen. Staring at me until I understand, Mother Nayomi, that no, I am not your equal. My pleasure must not be your concern.

She takes hold of both my wrists. Placing them behind my back. Pinning my arms tightly in this hug, her face in grieving to hide her pain. Pressing her lips to me again, this time in the full on kiss, pushing her tongue in deeply, squeezing me, enough to take my breath away, causing me to have to whimper so quietly, in such quiet desperation for mercy. But in the rising of her strength, is the falling of her compassion, the death of her tolerance for my audacity, for my foolish belief that I am little more than her possession. Her delicate plaything. A mere slave to what cravings she must command.

Have mercy on your daughter, Dear Nayomi. My dearest Nayomi, remember to have mercy for me.

Upon the release of this kiss, I am escorted from the balcony window door, over to the plush, king sized luxury bed, where this beautiful older woman sits me down in such naïveté of who she is, in such fearfulness of who she has always been. She leans to my mouth in what gentleness she requires, to touch my lips just enough with her own, to make me wish that I could be blessed with a kiss. But no. She instead takes the top button to my Jade silk dress (the single button over the cleavage circle in front), then reaching around behind me to zip it down, sliding the top of the dress all the way to my waist. Stopping there. Looking at my breasts in their black bra without shame. Looking at them as one possessed by possession, by her obsession to claim them as her own. She lowers the straps on my black bra, reaching around to unlatch the bra from my bosom. Exposing them. Watching both the great areolas shrink by attrition—watching the nipples grow in cold and fear.

Still fully clothed in her black evening cloth, she begins to slide my dress down and away, past my black underwear and black silk stockings, past the six inch heel black pumps, then making slow and easy work of the shoes, placing such a firm bite to my toes, just enough to warn me of what dreadful place I have been reduced to, of what place of subjugation I am in. She slides both stockings down and off my feet, placing my toe in her mouth in deep sucking, with her face anguished over in profound suffering, her cheeks drawn in from the heavy sucking motion. From this borderline crossed over, she raises up tall and strong, still fully clothed, looking at me exposed, topless in my black underwear cloth, looking up at her in nervous awe, not knowing whether I am going to be slapped or stroked softly when she moves her hand. But she takes me by the shoulders, ushering me onto my back on the bed, unable to take her eyes from my flouncing, flopping breasts laid to the side. I have never felt quite so exposed to her as I do at this moment, watching her stare at both my breasts as if they carried a message that could be read.

She climbs onto the bed, still wearing her black dress, stockings and shoes, climbing upon me in full, pressing her kiss fully to mine, where I am unable to stop myself from whimpering, nor the whorish raising of my leg in hopes that she will accommodate my desire. But she releases this kiss, pushing my leg down, her expression at the edge of a determined frown, her features burdened by melancholy, and the pain of a lifetime of unknown, unrequited desire. She sits astraddle me, reaching back to unzip her dress, sliding it off over her head, showing the mature, voluptuous shape framed in the glory of the black bra and underwear cloth, a waist that bears the power of the Nova Curve, both fit and fleshy besides, to deliver the silhouette of extraordinary femininity, enhanced by hips spread out to their glorious, straddling infinity. She takes her shoes off, tossing them away, sliding both stockings down and off, wearing nothing but the scant black underwear cloth and black lace bra.

As if unable to resist, she locks her gaze at my F cupped bosoms flopped to the side, and begins to grind herself in such smooth, serpentine motion as to be remarkable. Lowering her head to one of them, pulling the nipple deep into her mouth, stretching the breast high up, her brow wrinkled in great stress. I can feel the swollen warmth of her, pressing, grinding against me through both her cloth and mine. Releasing the breast in a long, kissing pull. Letting it fall wobbling back into place. Making me want to move, but knowing that I must lie still, lest I break whatever spell she is under. She lowers herself again to my breasts, but not to give suck, but to press her bra fully against them, moving my hand into her underwear, telling me to *hold it there, hold it right there,* as she grinds helplessly, awkwardly against my hand in her underwear, as if desperate to find her most perfect rhythm.

As if hearing an inner command, she raises up to straddling again, reaching back to remove her bra, her entire body tense in this plateau from somewhere along the timeline, born from the roots of her family tree. She tosses her bra away, lowering her breast back to mine, her body laid slightly diagonal across me, resting upon it nipple to nipple, inspiring a new anguish in her face, and a new and powerful motion in her hips down below. I hold my hand steady, watching her do this thing as though a prisoner of it, feeling the impossible wet upon my hand, closing my eyes to preserve the dignity she has abandoned, as she begins to whimper upon the advent of pain, grinding and humping herself to my hand in a frenzy of motion, until her voice at last betrays the depth of her desire, pouring out of her in animal grunts deeper than what I have ever heard from her before, as her entire body begins to shake violently, and the remainder of her pain gushes powerfully onto my hand from underneath her swollen desire.

The Green Destiny

The break of dawn rests among these clouds

In amber waves of earthen beauty

To caress the world in hope for another day's passing

Where Redemption through Christ is a solemn duty

The highest mountain in Japan rises the height of our love for one another, on our stroll through the rolling green tea fields of Shizuoka. When the melancholy rains from Tokyo Bay took their brief hiatus, from whatever endtime prophecies they were in grieving to make, Nayomi was inspired to rent what she called *an assassin's car*, which saw us cruising down the highway from Tokyo in a black Mercedes convertible, complete with our requisite selves in sunglasses and hair flying, feeling the power of who and what we are, and the dark strength of what churns beneath cultured civility. Knowing full well that briefly, we can get away with it, and obey the cliché, and bring grief and the sorrow of envy to those lucky enough to pass us by. On this brief stretch of highway, on this part of our journey through the timeline, we are the beauty of the Gaboon Viper, strange and deadly to behold.

Somewhere at the foot of the mountain, we stroll in the leisure of this rare day free of the haze of summer mist, where I can still remember our journey west from Tokyo down the big highway, with all its strange looking signs and trucks of such otherworldly design, seeming so surreal to my pampered American vision. And I can remember the sight of the mountain in the far distance, approaching as though something out of a far away dream, like a promise with no intention of delivering itself into reality, until I noticed that this mountain high began to loom taller over our horizon, until the pictures were put to shame by this rare early summer snow capped view, where the drowning rains had fallen at the top of the mountain in one last desperate attempt at winter white, rising majestically above our windy flight along the highway. Nayomi had left her sunglasses on as she drove, while I took mine off in shock and disbelief, as this mountain gave an end of the world account of itself in full, snow capped glory, rising high over every jaded, tragic soul passing by. I cannot speak upon such towering and unearthly beauty, which is truly a glimpse at the glory of God in creation, and one last look at the power of his grace and mercy come and gone. I can remember putting my sunglasses back on, sniffing, and crossing my arms to try and pretend it wasn't happening, until Nayomi took my hand in good natured pity for me, that I must be the only person in Japan who cried when she passed by the Holy Mountain.

The beauty of this green tea plantation gathers me up and carries me aloft, into a place of brief hope and tranquility. The glory of God can be seen in brief glimpses throughout nature itself, which might be disturbing to some, when confronted by the truth told by the many rows of jade green bushes that stretch far into the distance, untouched by the hand of manmade effort and skill. Of what message in this truth is beauty? What is the truth of this rolling beauty I see? That underneath the heavens that declare the glory of God, beneath the firmament that sheweth his handiwork, contained within the first heaven is the microcosm of who he is, which is the beauty of nature in Creation.

With nary a word that need be spoken, we stroll arm in arm, my wife mistress and me, both of us enraptured by the light of morning, by our hope that maybe, we have been granted a reprieve in this life, that a lifetime of unearned suffering is truly redemptive after all. I suddenly feel as though I cannot breathe, when I think of the possibility of leaving her side, causing me to grip her arm that much tighter, as she points to the far left of where we stroll, to see the first light of the sun caress the sky in amber, while the Holy Mountain looms in glory behind us, over the rolling green fields of our desperation, and the sunrise of our tragic love for one another.

This is the Green Destiny of our perversion. The double dong of legend, shined so brightly in crystal green, as we sit facing each other on our bed of hidden depravities, away from the Holy Mountain, and the rains of the far city. Tucked away again so deeply in farming country.

Both our lips are wrapped around this jade form, each of us deeply concerned with the feel and shape of it in our mouths, the shape of that which pertaineth to a man. We both push it as deep into our mouths as we can, pushing it well past this gagging reflex, with Nayomi being able to swallow all of a full eight inches down her throat in hungry repose, so that all of the 12 inches of jade double dong are made to disappear in our mouths. We sit with our legs apart, the center of ourselves pushed together in classic scissor style, not moving at all, so that the heat flows from one to the other on its own, as we slide our mouths upon the Green Destiny of our perversion.

I believe it is true for her as well, that if either of us were to move a muscle down below, that it would be all she wrote, and one of us would be doing the Armageddon Quake prematurely. So we sit in the heat of desire, in the depth of torment from a craving to move unrequited, pouring our lust upon this jade dragon of our want and need, sliding it in and out of our mouths at the same time, mouths open so wide and so deep, to receive every flexible inch of the foot long double dong into ourselves. I can hardly go past the fifth inch without a need to gag, while she devours the rest of what remains, making every emerald green inch disappear in a wide mouthed kiss, where a foot long double dong phallus is completely hidden down our throats. I hold it still in my mouth while she slides all seven inches out from her throat in full abandon, allowing every drop of spit gathered to fall.

And upon this note, we seem ready to build this part of our perverted symphony, with me holding a scant four or five inches of the foot long thing in my mouth, as the beautiful older woman makes smooth and steady work of it over and over, sliding her mouth down the length of it successfully every time, until I know her throat craves even another perverted inch or two. She slides her beautiful mouth over every inch times eight, letting the spit fall again as I hold the other end still. Taking the big double dong, our Jade Dragon fire into her hand, placing it between my breasts, telling me to push my breasts together, so that she may take her part of the Virgin's Intercourse, which is to watch the emerald sword cut its way through the white breast flesh, working herself into a controlled frenzy of motion with her hand, sliding the emerald thing rapidly between my breasts, telling me, *"spit on your tits... let the spit fall on your wicked breasts."* And this, I do, hearing in her the rise of a spirit bestowed to her from days long gone, and sprits passed from one generation to the other. I watch the pretense fade completely as her expression grows frustrated, even intolerant, spitting violently upon my breasts in full, spitting angrily a second time, as though frustrated that the Green Destiny is not attached to her body down below.

She moves the jade phallus to the side for a moment, pressing her lips to mine for the slurping kiss, a kiss replete with tongues and wetness, where she cannot stop herself from grabbing my head with both her hands, and dog licking my face from top to bottom. *"Open your mouth,"* she says sharply, splitting angrily into it, then grabbing my tongue, sucking it as through it nourishes her body for Christ's sake, then spitting with quiet rage into my mouth once again. She returns to her dog licking of my face again, enjoying the sweet and salty taste, treating my nose as if it is the flavor of a banana pop, licking my cheeks, even both my eyes, until I am blinded by the rage of her desire.

"What happens to bad girls," she says. Taking firm hold of my throat. And I know not to try and disrespect her with an answer—looking into her eyes with fear and pleading, watching her lose herself in the spirit with which I am so familiar, which causes every mistress I have ever had to eventually want to choke the life out of me. "Inside of you, is a disobedient little *cunt,"* she says. Shaking my head on the last syllable. Filling me with fear. She grinds herself once into me down below, which anguishes her expression over with awe, grinding once again, causing her to roll her eyes upward, then shake her head in refusal. As if to say *no, bitch. You will not make me cum.*

"On your hands and knees," she says. Sliding her groin away, taking up the Green Destiny in her hand. I move obediently onto all fours, my big, long breasts hanging down toward the bed. Feeling a single, hard *whack* to my backside, done with such force and purpose as to be shocking, designed to cause real pain. It is the note of a perfect spank struck in the flow of time and history, so that we both understand that to deliver another would diminish its force and power; and I must lower my head in impending shame, as the truth of my sluttish soul comes forth in a single, mighty twitch that I pray to God that she will have mercy on me and pretend she didn't see. But as it is with most prayers, this one too, goes unanswered.

"You see," she says. Grabbing my hair, raising my head up to hers. "Disobedient *slut.*" And all I can do is look at her in humiliation, finding no mercy in her bitter expression. Intolerance and disgust power the strength in her warrior's hand, pushing my head back down. In the next instant, I feel her fingers at my rectum, spreading it open wide, spitting her anger upon it without mercy. Then, I feel the onset of the impossible, as when a little green snake slides its tiny head nearby an egg in hunger, to make the onlooker have to declare in their soul, *'no way.'* But yes. I feel the head of this thick, Jade Dragon Dong pushing into my rectum as I languish on all fours, making me understand that surely, even the Lord must have cried out in agony at the Cross.

And this is my noisy cross to bear, as I let out an angry warrior's cry, screaming in rage as the green serpent slides itself into my rectum without mercy, to remind me that yes, to be born is to be cursed, and to live is to suffer.

I fully expect to hear her tell me to shut up, but this, she cannot do, as the sound of my screams is as meat and bread for a perverted soul. This is the Green Destiny of our perversion. The Jade Dragon Double Dong of our desire. This is the emerald fire burning inside me, that calls to the sadist's heart, and the soul of the masochist, causing her to move herself into position on all fours, where our backsides are facing each other. And before very long, I can feel the Jade Destiny pushing deeper inside me, as she slides it into her own rectum, unable to resist the same warrior's cry that she had heard from me, pushing back against it until our backsides are pushed tightly together, with the Jade serpentine deep inside both our rectums at once, holding us both captive to a unique pleasure born from pain, a unique pain born from pleasure. And she is unable to resist an immediate and powerful slamming back against me, sacrificing her dignity to the cutting room of this part of her life, bellowing like a wild animal in the effort, bouncing herself against me hard enough to rattle me in a place beyond my physical body, using me as an outlet for an inner rage stored, to deliver us this angry comeuppance overdue. I know to keep myself still, to rest firmly as an anchor for her in this storm, as whatever demon this may be is exorcised from her soul, and passed from her motherline tree into mine. She does not touch herself down below even once, having no need to take such an easy road out of this wilderness, knowing already that what treasures there are here to be found must be gathered at the end of this path chosen.

With a fevered intensity bordering on rage, she slams this hidden message home, this unhidden message from the end of the age, of what depravities are born from the heart of woman, and bestowed through the generations of Eve. And it is not long before the spirit of this punishment

312

seeks me out to completion, and the feel of her buttocks slamming against mine have their desired effect, and I am unable to gather control of my breathing, until I hear the sound of a human female siren wailing in the air around me, so loudly that the noise shocks me, as though I were suddenly a projection of myself in spirit, watching it happen from outside my body.

And from my spirit repose, I am privy to the warrior woman's despair, as the spirit of her own impending destruction takes hold, to settle her into a final, butt bumping rhythm in 4/4 time, to warn her of the dangers of fires gathered anally, and of what devastation they may be to the soul. The tragedy of an *anal orgasm* rises from the siren of mine, into every inch of her flesh, until she can only lower her head in the throes of a lady warrior's cry, an angry yell screamed into the end of the age, passing through every bouncing, trembling inch of her, through the walls of our hidden depravity, and over the forests and fields of Japanese farming country.

Dance of the

Sugarplum Fairy

71

$\mathcal{I}$ did a dance of the sugarplum fairy, in the prairie green beyond treetop tall. Much to her shock and disbelief, I think, she has watched me hop and prance my way through this divine ballet suite, in the fine echo of our former training room, where I have allowed myself full ballet regalia and attire, so that it is as a full and formal dress rehearsal displayed for one. Through every characteristic dance, I skip and I prance about, immersed in the private training of my youth, where the pain of what I know was channeled and displayed. As to whether any human being besides myself could every appreciate me as a ballerina, I do not know. I only know that as the music builds up to the epic finale, the end of the final waltz of *The Nutcracker* that I have not heard in many a year, I feel the descent of a power come over me once again, allowing me to jump and soar in my glittery fairy costume as though inspired, finishing on a spin as of yesteryear, where the world around me vanishes as in a blur of speed, until I slow down and stop as the music fades, with my arms and back leg raised in classic arabesque, held stiff in place by the hand of God's mercy on my poor soul. I can expect no applause, to be sure, being that there is only one other being present besides me that is not a spirit. And so I allow my inspiration to fade and gradually return me to renewal in near total silence, my only applause being the noisy rain on the world outside, and my only bravo's being the noisy cascading thunder. But when I open my eyes, I see my only audience put her head down into her hands, hearing the requisite and loud sniffing that comes with epic weeping. In full pink tights and tutu, I run over to where the woman in Asian black silk sits with her head down, touching her on the shoulder. She raises her head enough for me to see her lovely face twisted into the classic ugly cry, shaking her head and resisting me slightly with a wave of the hand.

"Was I *that* bad?" I say, genuinely worried that I may actually given the worst solo in dance recital history.

"I was just hit hard with the tragedy of who you are. The pain. The suffering. The beauty of what you could have become. I have never seen…"

Then the poor woman puts both her hands over her face, and allows herself one great and powerful display of sorrow, that escapes her voice in full blown sobs of misery. I take hold of her arm, coaxing her to her feet, hugging her tightly and comforting her the best that I can.

"It was the most beautiful thing I have ever seen," she says. I thought I was going to see maybe a talented amateur. But you are the same as a professional. But with long, Barbie Doll legs and a beautiful China Doll face."

"So, you liked it?"

"I... I don't know what to say."

She hugs me again, returning to her sobs of misery. I do not discourage her, holding her in my arms, being that shoulder to cry on everybody's heard so much talk about, but have rarely ever seen. Before long, she is able to return to her senses, apologizing to me for her "foolish crying," as she puts it. But I assure her that no matter what she says or does in my presence, the word 'foolish' can positively never come to mind.

"I once read somewhere," she says, "that *the tragedy of human existence is Fate*. I don't know if I truly understood what that meant until this moment. I thought *my* life was a tragedy. But I was not potentially a world famous ballerina dancer that was stolen from her home by fear and pain, and plunged into a nightmare of hellish suffering. I was just a gook girl who stabbed her stupid older sister because she was going to beat me up, because I was taking too long to cook dinner. I probably would have just been a girl cook in a restaurant if my life had not led me here. I was nothing. But you, Satari, you are a prima ballerina, cursed by God to be forged in the fires of suffering. You were chosen to a dark destiny. What have I done to you?"

"You rescued me. Without you I would have died. I probably would have never made it as a dancer. Nobody really does. I probably would have just been a cook, too, like my great Auntie Lin. That's about all I can really do anyway."

"No. You have a special gift. Your ability with a sword is unreal. You are unmatched in the world. Your speed and precision are unique. I have watched you train these last seven years. And even the greatest masters I know have said that you are the best they have ever seen. And I know that even though I do not want you to leave, I know that soon, you must find, and fulfill your destiny."

"I've already made up my mind, Nayomi. I'm never leaving you. I can't."

Nayomi looks at me with desperate gratitude, a look where hopeless longing dies, and the joy of an inner promise fulfilled takes over. The two of us hug tightly in the voice of this twilight storm, barely able to contain the flow of blissful satisfaction born from one to the other.

Deep inside the forest

There's a door into another land

Here is our life and home

We are staying here forever

In the beauty of this place all alone

We keep on hoping

Jade

Maybe
There's a world where we won't have to run
And Maybe
There's a time to call our own
Living free in harmony and majesty

Take me home...
Take me home

Thom Pace

73

*D*ays of Heaven tempt us with hope for the future, even as the wind and rains of eschatology continue to blow. We have enjoyed every fun and foolish diversion we can think to do that we can stand, learning that ice cream licks are best reserved for the real thing. Movies and malls and museums and mountains all over Japan, in and out of the rain seemingly everywhere we go, until it seems that the earth is under the curse of a divine warning of things to come, and a tragic reminder of what things once were, at the end of the first age of mankind, when man was eating, drinking, marrying and giving in marriage, until the Great Flood came, and took them all away.

Back in our country paradise, the two of us languish together on a rare, moonlit night, where the parting clouds are aglow in the silvery light of the Prairie Moon. A good distance from the house, the white silhouette of the Siberian tiger strolls mysteriously in the confines of its fenced in paradise, moving ghostly in the pale moonlight.

"Please tell me that you'll never ask me to leave."

"I won't."

"Promise me, Nayomi."

"With all my heart, I hope you'll stay."

But even while I hug her in this strange, moonlit night, I can sense her hesitation at the thought.

"You think I'm going to leave, don't you?"

"I didn't say that."

"You don't have to. You don't trust me."

"Satari, I do trust you. It's very possible that we were meant to meet, just so that we can be together. To rescue each other from a lifetime of pain."

"That has to be it. I *know* it is. Why else would we have met? Just because you were an assassin doesn't mean I have to do it."

"We have to do what the spirits have called us to do Satari. There is nothing we can do to stop it."

"Oh yeah? You just watch me. For the first time in my life I feel like I have a home. Somebody who loves me. This assassin thing might mean something to you Nayomi but to me it's nothing. You were the one who was called to be a killer, remember? I'm just a girl you found in the forest and taught how to fight. Maybe I can enter some tournaments. I might get lucky and win some. If I win enough tournaments, then I can open a school or something. I'll called it, *Shi Hira Kai Kung Fu.*"

323

"And spend the rest of your life taking Middle Class Momma's money, to train her fat daughter to stomp around like little Sumo wrestler. Her eyes half closed all the time 'cause she so fat."

Truthfully, the image brings up a mild chuckle from somewhere deep within.

"Well, I wouldn't have to do anything like that. I could audition for a dance academy or something. I'm too tall to be a real ballerina but I could go to school and study dance. You said I could dance, remember?"

"Already, you are probably one of the best solo ballerinas in all of Japan. You should never give that away to a community of jealous failures who will try to dominate and beat it out of you until you lose all of your confidence. It would kill me to see that happen. And it's your height that makes you so unique and special in the first place. You can just stay here forever with me if you want. You can cook American hamburger with American cheese. We get big and fat together."

I smile while I hug her in Mare Luna's cold, indifferent stare. A look with every emotion hidden, all intertwined with a grieving to warn every soul of what is coming upon the face of the earth.

"Tell me this is my home, Nayomi. Tell me this is my home forever."

"This is your home forever," she says, hugging me tight, gazing at the face of the Moon, struggling to resist its mournful gaze, and what it knows of truth itself, and the perpetual sufferings of women and men.

  *T*he rains return in grieving over the forests and fields of southern Japan, to color our days of Heaven with somber reality. I wake up from last night's revelation of truth in my dreams, only slightly comforted by the unfamiliar smell of bacon in our vegetarian house, which draws me out of bed immediately and into my Jade silk robe. Everytime I slip into this fateful cloth, I am reminded of just how beautiful it is, and just how powerful its tragic symbolism is concerning my reality.

  In black night shorts and matching tank top, I stroll, or rather *drift* down the halls, with my Jade Dragon robe open as I walk, which seems determined to ride the current of air moving around me, flowing the green fabric in tiny waves of motion against my skin. I leave these long, silky smooth, white legs of mine exposed to immodesty as I make my way down the stairs and into the kitchen, where my loving mistress is hard at work preparing our special "American style" feast.

I drift slowly up behind her at the stove, wrapping my arms around her waist and kissing her firmly on the mouth, distracting her the slightest bit from the non vegetarian duties. The Oscar Mayer bacon I love so much sizzles quietly in the pan.

"I hope I get this right," she says. "I've not cooked bacon in many years."

"It looks perfect. You can probably cook it better than I can." I kiss her on the cheek, turning toward my Simply Orange redemption waiting for me in the refrigerator. After a detour to the cupboard, I go to the refrigerator, crystal glass in hand, pouring myself a sweet orange elixir, intrigued by the merging of East and West on the label. A sip of this magic nearly rings my ears with its perfection, to leave the orange groves of Tropicana in the dust of a distant memory.

I breathe in another long sip of sweet, Amber West, allowing it to grow into a gulp as I move quietly to the small, round kitchen table of shiny dark wood.

"You so quiet this morning," she says. "No talk of where we go today."

Poor thing. Doesn't she know that the impending ice cream cone is inevitable? I smile quietly at Nayomi-san at the cooking stove, enamored by the simple, elegant beauty of the white silk robe with its black sleeve tips and front seams, highlighting the black dragon pattern.

A white dragon flew the land of dreams. From my homeland to infinity.

"You a million miles away. You feel okay?"

"Sure. I'm fine."

"Then, why you look so sad? What bother the Jade Silk Warrior today?"

She has never called me that before in jest. Never in casual conversation. Matter of fact, she has never mentioned it to me since the miracle of the throwing stars, which happened just a few long weeks ago. When my training was complete. All I can do is lower my head. Smiling in agreement with the spirits that I know.

"You haven't called me that since that day."

"What? Jade Silk?"

I take another sip of my sweet orange elixir. Marveling at what is possible in God's creation.

"If the name fits," she says. "That beautiful robe you wear is no accident. Are scrambled eggs okay?"

"They're my favorite. I'm bothered by this dream I had last night. Boy, if only I could draw, or paint pictures."

"What did you see?"

"I've seen it before. But never quite this vivid. It was the Jade Dragon again. Not the sword, but a real dragon."

Nayomi stops the noisy *plop, plop, plop* of the fork in the egg bowl. Staring off in the distance, like a mother whose daughter just revealed a dream about a man the mother is terrified she is going to marry.

She returns the plop, plop, plopping to the egg bowl again. With angry enthusiasm.

"I was in the field at the farm we ran away from seven years ago. And this big, green dragon taller than the trees came out of the forest. I was scared at first, but I didn't run. I just stood there and watched him come out of the forest into the middle of the field. He drew his head back. All the way back, then blew this explosion of green fire out of his mouth like a rocket. It was the prettiest green fire. It set all the crops on fire. Then he stepped forward through the flames. He reared his head back again, then blew out a stream of this fire again like a flamethrower into the farmhouse. And then I woke up."

Nayomi stands there. Her fork motionless in the mixing bowl again. Without another word, she pours the eggs into the hot pan, and begins to stir them almost immediately with the black spatula, salt and pepper notwithstanding.

"I know what you're thinking, Nayomi. And I'm not gonna let some dragon nightmare tear us apart."

"What if this 'dragon nightmare' comes again? What will you do?"

"Ignore it again. Ignore it until it goes away."

Nayomi looks defeatedly at her little domestic breakfast. At our sad little attempt at tranquility. Heavy burdened by the past and the future. Of doves, hawks and ravens, the inevitability of dragons, and of what comeuppances are overdue.

redestiny falls as the gentle rain, on our walk along the covered trail through the Great Botannical Garden, where every color and kind of flower seems to grow with grace and intrepidity. The two of us take this lovely, leisurely stroll on this ice cream high, Nayomi already having made quick work of the chocolate coating, devouring the soft serve vanilla ambrosia underneath. In the periphery, I secretly watch this beautiful older woman give her ice cream such a good tongue lashing, punishing it for being as irresistible as any food on God's earth, opening her mouth wide when the ice cream tower is small enough, sliding it as deep into her pretty mouth as she can, unaware of what vulgar beauty it entails. Not since before I was born, she says, has she tasted anything so divine as this, having only indulged in the rare bowl of orange or lime sherbet after a meal.

"I can feel my hips spreading out," she says, crunching the chocolate coated top of the cone itself, delivering the start of its impending death at her hungry hands. There are so many examples of the touch of God's hand in the human struggle, where the dark clouds of mediocrity are pierced through with the light of inspiration, where such small tokens as an ice cream cone rival the flavor of any wild fruit in nature. But ice cream is not harvested in a natural state; it is manufactured through the corrupt hands of man and womankind, so that the taste of it puts an echo of the divine spark in the heart and mind.

But what manmade vision may capture the human eyes such as these? This, the field of tulips and roses, even the blue and purple flowers that have no name I need to know, what ridiculous attempt at beauty can man produce to rival any one of these? *Consider the lilies of the field*, Christ said. *They do not sow, they do not spin, yet my Heavenly Father feeds them. And yet King Solomon in all his glory was not arrayed as one of these.* Even before the second heaven catches the eye, even before the sun, the moon, and the stars go flying by, every part of earthbound nature shows us the hand of the Almighty, and the power of his might in Creation.

The beauty of these flowers lifts my mind briefly in the rain, to where I can see the white beast pacing the limits of her kingdom in the country. Oh, Shi Hira Kai, Queen of the Jungle, what immortal hand or eye, indeed, dare frame thy fearful symmetry! Everywhere in earthbound nature: in the trees, in the flowers, in the beasts of the field, even in the taste of fruit from the garden grove, the light of God's power in Creation is evident, and obvious to every human heart and soul.

As we continue our walk in this grand and gentle rain, sheltered under this walkway through the Great Botannical Garden, my heart thinks upon the joy of my loving mistress with pity, as I come to terms with the call of Predestiny, and the pain of what tragic course must be. I wait until every bite of her cone is eaten and stored in her memory, before I must raise the sword of inevitability, and bring it down on her joy and tranquility born. I hug her tight even before I say a word, unable to keep the tears of my inner heart from betraying this secret, that yes, the dream has returned again, to let me know that this was our last meal together, and that I must be caught up in the winds of time, and be carried to where it is that the Lord himself has ordained me to be. And the wave of disappointment and fear I see in her eyes, brings a pain to my heart in stabbing fear, and I can only hug her again, unable to speak, only able to cry and sob, knowing in my heart that even this very night, as the rains fall in weeping over the countryside, I will have to gather my sword and sorcery, and stars of agony—I will have to gather my instruments of death, and go to the edge of the forest wood. For I know that there is a journey that I must take, as there are corrupt and tragic lives that I must take in his name.

The two of us leave our heavenly stroll in the mists of our joyful and painful memory, to go back to the house of paradise, which is now a house of deadly sorrow in waiting. In our home by the sea of country green, in our cabin by the sea, the rest of the day is spent in a drowning mist of sorrow, as I prepare myself for this journey that must be, waiting until the last of the evening day has come and gone. I gaze one last look upon the eyes of winter white, the eyes of an angel in divine and fearful symmetry, bowing my head quietly to her majesty, then strolling through the last remaining light of day, head to toe cloaked in black, in what may keep the silvery moonlight from my skin.

At the edge of the forest, I stop and look down the treeline toward the house, seeing such a powerful, lonely figure dressed in white, in mourning for the passing of joy into her past, and in grieving for the loss of a loved one in the twilight. At this edge of oblivion, where the evening day is deep twilight, nearby the edge of night, I wait until the last second of light fades away, and I leave her ghostly silhouette behind, stepping into the woods of this tragic future, unable to perceive the swooning of a soul lost in grief, and her collapse on the wet ground, as the Jade Silk Warrior descends into the shadows, in the forest of the evening day.

Nayomi Hahn Rides the Wind

ayomi Hahn rides the wind. On the eve of eschatology.

At the edge of the forest of dreams. In the wake of her lover's departure. Her newest reason for living. The daughter she never had.

Languished in the throes of a rainy sleep, at the edge of the nighttime forest wood. Having been knocked into a brief coma by the demon of a heart bruised and broken. By a spirit tattered and torn. Her mind betraying her yet again, in the new and darkn'ed twilight rain. Lifting from the rains of her present, to the rains of a forgotten youth. Raised in Nara farming country, nearby the forests and fields of southern Japan. Raised by a bitter mother and older sister, scratching out a living from the farmer's dirt. Having no tolerance for the weird and quiet Nayomi, whom they tolerate because of her cooking. Whom they have no kind words for, nor passing warmth of compassion. A mother who claims to have over heard her daughter say *"such a bitch,"* Though it was only a teenager's quiet, passing complaint,*"it sucks cleaning that kitchen."* A complaint that opened the tragic, mother daughter door. The portal to a dark future.

Nayomi Hahn rides the wind. In the heart of this dark and rainy memory. Dreams of a mother's fervent slap in her bedroom. Then drawing her hand back again, hitting her with such a powerful turn of the hand as to be genius, spinning Nayomi into the air off of her feet. Picking her up off the floor by the throat. Grabbing Nayomi by the throat with both hands. Pulling her up to her feet. Screaming for her oldest daughter. Slapping her daughter again, this, with the back of her hand. Leaning down low, bringing the back of her hand up again. Stumbling Nayomi into the bedroom wall, at the moment her older sister comes into the room. Staring at the scene in bitter satisfaction.

The mother tells Nikki Hahn to hold her youngest daughter. Nikki holds her from behind. Her arms up under Naomi's shoulders, clasping her hands behind her neck. Holding Nayomi still and tight. The mother proceeds to slap her daughter repeatedly. The front and the back of her hand ad infinitum. Slapping streaks of lightning into her vision. Punching her in the stomach many times. Punching her to coughs and nausea. Taking her fist, and punching Nayomi in her face. Slapping her many times again.

Let the bitch go, she says. Watching Nayomi fall to the floor. Kicking her in her stomach, bringing a sickening yelp from the sixteen year old. *Help me pick her up,* May Hahn says. Taking her by the arm, her daughter Nikki on the other. Dragging Nayomi, the two of them. Dragging her down the hall, through the uncleaned kitchen in question. Out the back door. Dragging her through the pouring rain. Taking her to where the dog is tied to the tree. Yanking the dog out of his house.

Taking the leash from his collar. Tying the leash around Nayomi's neck in the twilight rain.

Go bring me my belt, the mother says. Waiting patiently for her oldest daughter's return. Kicking her daughter in the stomach again, pushing her head down. Taking the belt from her oldest, who hurries back in sheer, bitter delight. Watching her mother beat the little bitch with the buckle of the leather belt. To place a bleeding reminder in every place. In every place upon her daughter's skin.

In the haze of this slow motion dream, Nayomi Hahn opens her eyes. In grieving in the twilight rain. Unable to move. Unable to stand. Unable to care.

Nayomi Hahn rides the wind. On the eve of eschatology.

Shadow Warrior

*T*hrough the forest, and into the future I travel. Braving these end of the world rains returned, through the dark of the forest leaf canopy. Glad for the frequent flashes of lightning to show me a glimpse or two of the treacherous path unfamiliar, moving more on instinct than anything else. Not even sure if I am going the right way, but knowing as I knew seven years ago, that I must keep walking. But something tells me, even in the midst of my uncertainty, not to go too far to the left or right of where I travel, as if the location of where I am going is implanted in my mind, as it is when one drives the streets of their mundane suburban errand, having it implanted in their mind where it is they need to go. All through the night, I move steadily, unable to slow completely down, feeling a sense of divine urgency, though not for the preservation of my own life, which is insignificant to me. I am an instrument of Fate. To be used to deliver dark destiny to a chosen few.

I move forward through the nighttime forest, undeterred by the unfamiliar surroundings, the cold, uninviting dark of the forest wood in the storm, where it seems that I am mocked and pushed along by spirits that will not allow me to grow confused or complacent, or content to languish without moving forward. I can feel my seven year paradise fading into the past, crossing a mysterious, unseen barrier into another part of the timeline, which is the beginning of the end of what I have known. The spirit of bloodlust hath descended already, moving me through the forest at such a mighty clip among the trees, which will not allow me to even stop and rest, moving with more certainty than was ever shown seven years ago, when we wandered lost in these woods for three days, until we could go no further. This time, there is a touch of ice cold water to drink, and the speed and assurance given to me by this calling, so that any ordinary soul moving with me would have been lost and left behind many hours ago.

Throughout the rest of this rainy night and into the day, I continue to walk and run, eventually coming to the biggest, brightest sign on this hapless journey, which was the empty creek bed of some tiny, trickling brook that I remember from before, but this time, swollen into the course of a small woodland stream. Somehow, I know that my calling lies in the direction I am traveling, and that I should be there by the fall of night. Around me, the brush and trees do the Armageddon sway in the daylight, swirling and swishing in the eschatological storm, which blasts through the air on a brackish stroke of lightning, crashing in the sound of the sky split in two. This storm has a determined life of its own, refusing to die, as though it understands that what must be done lies underneath a weeping sky, and the wailing of mournful winds and midnight thunder.

On the other side of the stream, in partial shelter among the trees, I take the only cold sip of water I have had, and the only one I will have, until my destination glows the light of another nighttime storm. Oh, what tragedies have befallen these poor souls, as they wait for annihilation from the four winds! I move forward from my brief, rainy hiding place, my body still protected by the thin, black rain gear pulled from the tiny travel bag I carry, moving now with equal determination as before, resting from my running with merely a walk, finally beginning to give in to my body's need for rest and sleep.

But at the moment the decision is made, the loudest blast of thunder I have ever heard screams over the forest, admonishing me that the last mile is often the most difficult. And so, in the agony of what must surely be, I begin my hopeless walk forward, craving a place to lay my head, that I might renew my body with lifegiving rest and sleep. But as the new daytime rain begins to fade into the twilight, the forest around me is less menacing and hopeless to be sure. Until I am at what is clearly the edge of this endless forest, nearby an open cropfield in this early evening rain. In gratitude to the spirits of this righteous calling, I am in awe of this latter day miracle, at a workhouse I have known from my past, and a small farmhouse disturbingly familiar, at the end of this last mile's journey through the wilderness of suffering.

The rage of my arrival has cursed my body's need for sleep, pushing me beyond the barrier of sanity. Our slow, pitiful walk of three days through these woods from seven years ago I covered in less than a third of the time, driven forward by some angel or demon I could not resist, but certainly *did* understand, making me realize without fail that there is blood that must be taken. In the fall of night, covered by this unrepentant storm, I peer through the window of the locked workhouse, seeing that there are 10 girls crammed inside, with no hope of escape past these grill barred windows, nor the heavily bolted door up front. From the spirits that lift and carry me forward in this tragic life, I already know that this is a prison of depravity, lorded over by the curse of Mika Yung and her mother. As to what manner of beatings these girls have received in the name of discipline, of this, I cannot tell. As to what manner of rapings these girls have received, as to what bloody tortures they have endured, of this, I cannot tell. As to how many of their bodies populate these southern woods, of this, I cannot tell. All I can tell is what manner of pain and death they must suffer, of this, I *can* tell.

Having already seen them settling down to the gluttony of their dinner hour, after the slave girls have been meagerly fed and forgotten, of the condemned souls, I see the father, Sao Yung, and his wife and two of his three daughters, Mika having blossomed into her mid thirties, with the younger aged into her twenties, there to assist in the family calling. To record these young girls being raped and beaten, and to see these recordings into the hands of a certain police chief's wife.

By the spirits of indignation, whether righteous or unrighteous, I perceive the cauldron of fear stirred among them, when the window nearby their kitchen dining table shatters into a million pieces, and they see a woman dressed in skintight black, her ponytail flying behind her as she flies over their supper table, landing hard into the man's chest with her feet. I am bathed by the screams of terror as they scramble helplessly, the youngest daughter not escaping my dagger flown directly into her throat, as I run quickly to the familiar living room and swing my sword across the back of the older woman's thigh, slicing it so that she collapses in screaming agony. When I return to the kitchen, I walk slowly in the cacophony of a woman's screams, and a daughter's stunned silence, as Mika Yung stands still with her mouth open, watching a face so familiar walk slowly over to her father, who writhes on the floor in a futile attempt to endure a cracked ribcage.

"Sit," she hears, doing so without hesitation. Watching the thing in the ponytail and tight black pants and black bra top point her sword unsheathed, with a razor sharp blade slightly curved, and a handle the color of emerald green. Quickly, in eyesight of the Mika Woman, in earshot of the mother's screams, I pull two short lengths of rope, tying the man's feet together, and his hands behind his back.

"You live…because the blood of a man, is not worthy of my sword."

I stand up straight and tall. Glaring a gaze across the kitchen. Burning green and black fire.

My sword in hand, I step, I glide to the living room view, to see the crying woman on the floor. Then I step, I *glide,* over to the beautiful, sensual woman who sits in awe and fear, her face anguishing over suddenly with something beyond fear.

"Sata- san?"

I step around the table, as I once did as a slave, pulling the knife from her dead sister's throat. Wiping the blade on her dead sister's white blouse.

"Stand up. Go to your mother."

This, she does. Her entire body immersed in the spirits of hopelessness and dread.

"Take her by the hair. Drag her to the barn."

This, spoken in her native tongue, watching her reluctantly grab hold of her bleeding mother's hair, dragging the screaming, scrunch-faced woman in shock and disbelief through the house, and out into the nighttime storm.

In the barn of this shameful memory. Among the old wood, and rusty old tools and equipment stored. The women I knew are stripped naked of their clothing, and tied with their feet together and their arms spread apart, side by side roped to the wooden fence, each on a sturdy wooden beam. The two women stand nude, mother and daughter, babbling incessantly about how sorry they are, and about how much money I can make if I will just have mercy, and join them. In response, I go over to the mature, healthy hipped woman tied to the cross beam, lifting her breast, and nursing it with as much gentle skill as I can muster, which is the call of every motheress, to know how to put the divine spark of pleasure into the breast of another woman. Tied with her arms spread out, the woman cringes, as if she has been rubbed with the cold of a handful of snow.

"For the pain you bring into the world. For the curse you have passed down to your daughter."

Upon this last word, my arms are powered as if on their own, removing my black sports bra made top, slipping it off with comfort and ease, placing it carefully on the beam, nearby the two of them. With my breasts hung natural and free, above this deep, sensual curve they see, I take up the Jade Dragon from its sheath of emerald green. Holding it still in front of me with both hands.

"Sata-san! Sata-san!" She screams my name with deep fury, the kind caused by fear. To the music of this woman's death screams, I welcome the spirit of the sword in my body, twirling the blade rapidly in my right hand in lightning display, with the prowess of a heated up majorette with a fire baton, swinging the blade up diagonal from her gullet to the bottom of her breast, seeing the blood pour in the periphery, bringing the blade down for another twirling and whirling of steel in the air, taking it into both hands in raised position, whishing it down diagonally in the other direction, a deeper cut which elicits a loud, yelping grunt from the woman. In her eyes is the stare of madness, the trembling helplessness of one who is lost in the cold and dark, looking at last at me in defeated surrender, lowering her head, to allow her spirit to go to its eternal

reward, to be judged for the life she lived, and whether or not her name will be found in the Book of Life.

"Sata-*san.* Sata-*san,*" Mika says. A quiet, pleading tone. "Let me worship you Sata-san. Let me be your life long slave."

"Do you want to live?"

"Yes, Sata-san."

"Then, put your tongue in my mouth. Let me feel your repentance."

I stand with my nipples at the barest touching of this condemned woman. Allowing for no further intimacy beyond this breast touch. Feeling the trembling of her lips and tongue. Her tongue pushed and probed so deeply in her death kiss, to allow me the taste of fear so sweet, and the feel of it caressing my naked breasts with power.

"My queen. My queen Satari-san."

I lay my sword on the heavy beam nearby. Retrieving the sledge hammer that was hidden from her sight.

"Satari-san…"

"Do you remember when you told me, what a sledge hammer could do to a piece of wood board?"

"Have mercy Sata-san! Have mercy!"

In the midst of these Hellish pleas, this final begging for mercy, I take the metal hammer firmly into both hands, bringing it down with all my might upon her shin, hearing the bone snap like a piece of wood, seeing her shin fold backwards, as if the bone were as flexible as a bent plastic straw, or a green bamboo reed. Seeing her body seem to drop lower, as her eyes light up in the self same madness as her mother. Her death scream powers my hands to their course of action, lifting the hammer again, hearing the bone of her other leg snap, renewing the power of her fervent shrieking and screaming in the storm.

I retrieve my blade before her insane eyes, and with both hands on the handle, I come down with the diagonal blow, whirling the blade up with my right hand alone, with the other diagonal cut in X across her bleeding abdomen, whirling, twirling my dragon's blade in the show of strength, and the power of cold hearted steel in flight. Then I stand in unique warrior's stance from within, a winged stance with my sword aloft in back of me, born from somewhere back along the timeline of the centuries, when the other six Jade Silk assassins were called into tragedy, and cursed by Fate to ride the winds of time.

$\mathcal{I}$ am the Jade Silk Warrior. My sword is born from the shadows of the night. My blade is touched by the light of the Moon.

The stench of the city is poison to my nostrils. The souls of the condemned are scorched with fire and brimstone.

What meteor rock hath crashed through this corporate glass at night! Into the fancy, high tech nonsense in the haze of corporate sleep? What is this figure in black, whose face is masked as the Ninja warrior, that leaps through the window like a great rock thrown, coming down in the rain of glass upon the nighttime floor? What is this demon, who moves like lightning flashes unleashed, amidst the screaming police hiding their faces, when the silver stars are thrown?

One hundred, one thousand of you would not matter to me. But there are only ten. Four of you on the floor with stars in your eyes, unable to pull your guns of stupidity. And then the fifth and sixth of you approach the shadow in foolishness, to receive the recompense for your unbelief, with swift kicks to your middles that break your ribs without thought. Engage the Shadow Warrior, thou seventh fool of the corporate cop conundrum! Pretend to know how to kick as the warrior! Provide thine arm of weak skill to me, to raise my knee to thine elbow, to make your arm as the letter L in the backwards way! Endure the flattening of thine nose, and the crushing of it to bloody ruin!

My destination is in sight, as I move down the hall of offices. Why do you approach the shadow warrior, thou eight fool, to endure this whirling kick, that lifts you off of your feet with my leg extended high, slamming you through the glass of a night office in the dark? Take out your gun, thou ninth fool—brandish this fiery weapon into history, that the cameras may record for all time, the greatest warrior ever born, who moves like a ghost in the wind. These *sparks* that you see, my dear lady fool, my dear corporate city she-cop? Is it the flashes of your *bullets* from my blade brandished in the haze of my calling, where your movements are as molasses to me, and the bullets of your gun are as rocks thrown from a child's hand? Brave this impossibility, my dear lady cop, for it is the last thing you will ever see, thou ninth fool. My blade slides from its Jade sheath at thee, my dearest lady cop, to lift thine head from thy body in a flash of motion.

I am the Jade Silk Warrior. I am a living shadow in the night. You cannot hide from me, thou tenth fool. You, the chief of police. The husband of the witch who took me into the gates of Hell. Do not bother to run into your office. You will not make it inside. Feeling the door kicked open as you try to close it. Knocking you hard into the wall of the cramped space. Pull thine foolish fire weapon, condemned soul of latter day corruption. Turn thine hand to me. Now, feel the wind whistle by your stupid face. Feel it slice through your arm. Scream a hopeless scream, thou tenth fool of city cop corruption, as you grieve to hold your firing tool, to spit the bits of fire at this shadow, this dark angel from the moonlit night. Scream the music of the squirting blood, thou tenth fool of the corporate corruption. Pray that you do not die tonight.

I am the Jade Silk Warrior. Returning to the shadows of a moonlit night.

$\mathcal{S}$even years after the fact. Seven years after the gates of Hell were opened. After I was pulled from my ballet fantasy in a Japanese airport, and thrust into dark reality. Seven years after my journey into the forest, after the lemonade resurrection in paradise. I am in the darken'd home of the police chief's wife and daughter, hearing the sounds of deep depravity, even in the wake of the father's painful absence, in the hospital intensive care. Having very nearly bled to death in his office, before the medical people came to save his life. He who will study the security cameras ad nauseam, to try and convince himself that it was not real, that the sparks flashing when the gun was fired was not the unspeakable. That there are no shadow assassins in reality. That the eyes that bore down on him, were surely not the eyes of a woman.

These eyes are in the home of his condemned wife and daughter grown, in the throes of a noisy diversion. In the throes of a perversion too wide and deep to know. I can feel the spirit of the modern mother daughter dynamic unrestrained, in the womanly yells of ecstasy coming out over and over again, from the woman who hath cursed her daughter with this sin.

Down the hall I creep. In Death Girl face and ponytail braid. Sword unsheathed for what price that must be paid. Black pants stretched as tight as my skin, bra top holding the F- bombs tight in their place. I step to the mercifully unlocked bedroom door, easing the door cracked and open, undeterred by this apocalyptic shock, of the daughter in her thirties on top of her mother, the police chief's fancy wife, slamming this end of the world message home into her. Their depravity is so intense, the throes of their passion so violent, they do not see the angel of death in the dimly lit space of the bedroom. And I am privy to the power they possess, as the daughter who has learned to time her orgasm, to coincide with the explosion that occurs inside her mother's body.

And I can hear this inside the two of them, on the edge of being expressed into their little world, to where in their native tongue, I hear the daughter saying to her mother *"I can't hold it Mother, Mother I can't hold it…"* And this time, at the end of their life's journey, I hear the blaring trumpet pour in soprano shriek from the daughter first, a scant few seconds in front of her mother's dreadful scream, and then, another scream from the two of them in tandem, from the cold, sharp agony they feel pierced through their spine! The sword of their perversion hath pierced them through, through the daughter's naked back, through the mother's stomach underneath, as I hold it tight in place, gazing into their death stare, a gaze too lively with the fear and desperation of hope, a survival instinct too strong. Of this, the remedy is quick and easy for me, pulling the blade up and jabbing it through once more, to get the sickening yelp I crave to hear from the both of them, watching the life leave the daughter's eyes first, and the beauty of blood from her lungs creeping from her open mouth. She lays her head down onto her mother, who still struggles to breathe, to escape the pull of whatever devil that has come to take her to the place where the river runs parallel to their thirst, where they are tormented in this flame. The mother lays there. Her mouth and eyes wide open, gazing at the ceiling, an expression frozen in terror, as the last of her life's breath gurgles from her body.

I slide my sword from their corrupted flesh, to sheathe it bathed in their blood, watching the blood obey a prophecy, as it spreads out from under the mother's body like bloody wings, to echo their tragic flight to eternity.

81

"*olice in Tokyo are baffled by an attack on their main headquarters last night, in which a single assassin armed with a sword killed one police officer and injured nine others. The bizarre event was captured on security cameras, showing the assailant fighting ten police officers, including the chief of police, eventually killing the only female officer on duty. The video appears to show the assassin somehow deflecting the shots being fired from the female officer's gun before the officer was decapitated, prompting some to anoint the attacker as 'the greatest assassin in human history.' The nine surviving officers are all recovering from their injuries at Tokyo Medical Center, with the police chief in intensive care, having suffering a severed hand in the attack. The surviving officers report that the masked assailant appeared to be a woman, and was armed only with a sword. One Japanese reporter has called this real life Ninja style attacker 'Lady Wolverine.' Cora Leeds, the Associated Press.*"

Jonathan Lovejoy

In the Shadows of a Moonlit Night

Twenty years, and twenty five miles down east. A score of years and two, from the beginning of my journey at seventeen. When I learned that the tragedy of human existence is Fate, and that where the will of man ends, God's will begins, and one cannot change what is meant to be. On the current of this River of Fate, I ride, with the blood of fifty nine women and their daughters upon my sword. Corporate witches and adulterous bitches. Hypocrites of the end of the world mother daughter secret, and the curse they are spreading to a condemned generation.

Those who walk the world in smiles and white, but whose heart is a bitter frown, as black as coal from beneath the earth.

My sword burns with a jade flame in the shadows of this night, at the Connecticut mini mansion of Emma Rose, and her blonde fencing champion Amanda. Emma McDuffee by marriage, a.k.a Emma Rose waits in repose of fear, having kept her fencing champion daughter close by, afraid to let her out of her sight, in the shadow of the Lady Wolverine.

In the fading light of the evening day, the red headed beauty answers the complacent call of the door bell, going to the front door of her suburban palace, opening it to the echo of a warning breeze, and a cold chill up her spine.

"Amanda, she's here," are the words that find themselves flowing freely from a fearful soul, and a heart struggling to pump blood iced cold with regret. Regret for twenty years ago. Regret that she did not hear Annabelle's warning, and gather the three of them together in one place, to prepare for the coming storm of eschatology.

Amanda convinces her mother to allow to her to brandish her own cutting blade, to maybe distract the shadow that approacheth, so that it can be dealt with by the Red Hawk's fiery blade. From my easy entry through their fine, sliding patio door, from the circle of glass cut and removed, I drift this suburban paradise as an avenging spirit, an echo of fear and fantasy come to life, to see the mother and the daughter's souls leave this earthly plane.

From my place in this palatial kitchen, I can see the beautiful mother and daughter sitting fearfully in the dimly lit livingroom, trying not to appear terrified from their posts on the sofa, waiting for what they know is coming, neither of them stupid enough to be anywhere near a gun, nor even a phone for a futile call for mercy in the twilight.

"There she is!" Amanda screams. "Look!" Gazing in strawberry blonded terror at the woman in skin tight leather battle gear, pants designed to show much skin on the sides all the way up the thigh and buttocks, waist fully curved and exposed, with black ponytail braid long and ready for the tragedy of their impending demise.

"If you come near my mother," Amanda says, "I swear I will kill you."

I approach this living corpse in the rage of judgment, held in check by my sword left in its sheath on my back, walking from the kitchen to the livingroom without a word. Stopping in the middle of the carpeted floor in waiting.

"I *know* I can beat you," she says. "I'm the best goddamned swordsman you ever saw, bitch."

Upon this, she delivers an impressive flurry of Westernized nonsense, flash and dazzle designed to please the eye, but as fragile and brittle as a crystal skeleton warrior's blade.

"Jade," Emma says. "In the name of God."

And upon this hopeless pleading, her fencing champion daughter lunges at me with her sword raised in both hands, unprepared for the speed of my feet meeting it in the air, knocking it to the side, then a flash of motion, in which my sword is unsheathed and twirled once in my right hand, and brought down across her beautiful neck, to lift her beautiful head in shock from her body, causing what is left of her to fall bloody and helpless to the floor in bizarre inevitability, to the music of the death scream from her red head mother in despair.

"You murdering—we should have *killed* you when we had the *chance!*

I walk slowly to where this woman stands too stunned to move, eyes as red as her locks of crimson hair. I take my dagger, and proceed to cut every strand of her suburban MILF fabric from her body, from the tight, burgundy button down blouse and black bra, to the black capris pants and tight black underwear, until her white skin is as bare as it was the day she was born. I gather a twirling of her fiery red hair in my hand, escorting the naked woman roughly through the livingroom and out the back door, into what remains of the evening day, into the world nearby the edge of night. Across the grand and beautiful lawn we take this death march, neither of us able to speak again, both of us bound by the course written in the stars, that described this night a thousand years ago, written upon the ethereal parchment of the Almighty God.

At the edge of this backyard forest grove, the tree chosen for us stands conspicuous in the coming night. In the fleeting hope that her life may be spared, the healthy hipped, tiny rose bosomed woman strands obediently against the tree, feeling her neck be constricted by the length of white rope pulled tight. Feeling her feet bound, and then her hands pulled tight around to the back of the small trunk, barely bigger than her own body glowing in the twilight. In the growing dark, I can hear her struggle to breathe in desperation, her neck pulled tightly against the tree. And then, in the light of the star that rules the evening, I unsheathe my blade, whirling it up diagonal in one hand, to hear the shriek escape her voice, whirling the sword down the other way, to hear a shriek less vivid, colored with a groan as one punched in the gut. This death groan delivers a message in the starlight, in the rising light of the Prairie Moon; that the sword of betrayal cuts both ways, from the past, into the present, and far into the future of an accursed body and soul.

I am the Jade Silk Warrior. I am Death, in the shadows of a moonlit night.

83

*R*evelation descends upon the White Raven, in the light of the Prairie Moon. Hardly able to eat or sleep, in the wake of news from the world wire, of the killing of a Connecticut millionaire's wife and daughter. The daughter's head was cut clean off her body, they say. And the mother was tied to a tree. An X marked the spot from her waist to the bottom of her breasts, where she bled to death in the light of the Moon.

An entire night has passed from this, until the Moon has made another journey, and the face of the Desert Moon looks down upon her. Nearby the stroke of midnight, a *scream* from upstairs strikes her soul with a lightning bolt, turning her from the kitchen door window, running upstairs quickly to her daughter's room, carrying her sword with her as though prepared for battle. She bursts in the darken'd room in all readiness, running over to the bed where her daughter sits in the dark hysterical.

"I saw a shadow come in the window," she says hysterically. "It was a shadow with green eyes Momma, I swear."

Mary Ann White hugs her daughter. Sword laid to the side. Understanding the power of dreams, and their potent touch upon the chords of sanity. *This talk of a Jade Assassin is driving my poor daughter crazy*, she thinks. Hugging the girl. Kissing her full on the forehead, shushing her in the suburban nighttime dark. "It was just a bad dream, honey. You can go back to sleep. We're safe."

"But you don't really believe that, Mom. You brought your *sword* with you."

"I was just looking at it when you started screaming, that's all. I told you, nothing's going to happen."

"But you said you know who it is that killed Emma. I heard you talking to Annabelle on the phone. You said her name was Sarah and that you knew she was the one who killed that mayor in Virginia too. You can't deny it Mom because I heard you. Where do you know her from? Why is she coming to get you?"

"Honey, you're just being silly, now. Go back to sleep. Nobody's coming to get us."

"How can I go back to sleep after the dream I just had?"

"I'll leave your bedroom door open and the hall light on. Don't you have a big day planned with your friends tomorrow?"

"Brittany's getting a car for her birthday. We're all going with her."

"See there? That's all you need to be worried about. Just lie down. Close your eyes."

Mary Ann White leans down to her daughter. Expressing her comfort in the kiss that lingers. In the kiss ripe with years of secrets untold. She picks up her sword, and walks back down the stairs to her place in the nighttime.

In the grieving light of the Desert Moon. In the wake of false hope come and gone. In the shadows of complacency, I move from my hiding place, from somewhere in the ghostly realm of the night. From the nighttime space of another room upstairs, I emerge again into the hall, moving as on a cushion of air into Emily White's bedroom. Gliding across the floor unseen, unfelt in her new nightttime attempt at slumber. Getting on the bed quickly. Pressing my hands over her nose and mouth. Laying full on top of her. Laying there, feeling the fear course through her body. Watching her eyes go mad with terror. Then feeling her young body stiffen, as it reacts to the loss of life giving air. Holding her still underneath me. Watching the life now fade from her eyes. Feeling her spirit lift from her body. Holding her there. Until I know her soul has left the earthly plane.

The next moment in time sees the fervent touching of my blade to the dear girl's bedroom mirror, and the realization to the woman downstairs, that the types of fear are indeed many, and uniquely distinguished.

From her place nearby slumber on the nighttime sofa, she picks up her sword again, rushing upstairs in knowledge of the Green Eyed Shadow, and what possibilities that it was not the product of her daughter's nighttime dream. Oh, what ghosts and spirits from a score of years do fly, what shadows burn the fires of emerald vengeance in their eye?

Mary Ann White walks the nighttime steps of revelation. Holding her sword in the form of one who is no stranger to the feel of it, nor the motion of it through the barrier of a victim's skin. Mary Ann steps slowly down the hall in stealth inspired by terror, her sword raised and ready as she approaches her daughter's room.

Now, step violently into the room, White Raven. Brandish thy blade to the shadows. Look in terror at the shattered pieces of your daughter's mirror on the dresser and the carpeted floor. Look to the figure under the sheet in your daughter's bed. Walk cautiously, reluctantly over. Peer down, Mistress Snow, at your 15 year old daughter's eyes. Look down at the eyes of Emily, that gaze lifelessly at the darkened ceiling. Call her name. Reach down, dear Mary Ann. Shake the life back into her. Shake the life into your daughter's body.

The White Raven stands up in the dark. Aware of the presence of evil. The presence of a shadow in 3D Space. The shadow touches a blade to her throat. She screams to both God and Christ in the confines of the upper room. Jumping as though sparked from head to toe. Having to stand still from pure terror. Dropping her sword to the bed in surrender.

"Annabelle made me do it," she says. "She was jealous of you and Nayomi. She was just trying to teach you a lesson, I *swear.*"

With the sharpened dagger blade, the fabric of this suburban pretense is quickly cut away. Witnessed by lifeless eyes. The lifeless eyes of her daughter. Eyes that see her mother's clothes cut and pulled away, tossed into the netherworld of the darkened room.

The two of us walk together. Shapely, naked white flesh through the nighttime abode. Moving through the livingroom and the kitchen, out into the backyard of her suburban paradise. To the tall tree, that beckons to provide a place. A place for her to die. Facing the cropfield on this dead end street.

The shapely, naked brunette is bound by her neck, arms and legs to the tree. Her face tormented by terror that will not subside. By pleading that will not manifest itself. By a begging for her life that will not come. An assassin whose stock and trade was little girls. Smothering them with a pinch to the nose. With her lips clamped over their mouths. Feeling them jerk and kick underneath her. Feeding. Feeling their life slip away in the night.

From the bosoms hung heavy in the key of D Major. To the top of thighs heavy with womanhood. The Jade Dragon blade finds it way diagonal from top to bottom. Then diagonal again, from the bottom to the top. Done to the music of two sickening yelps in the night. The sounds of one kicked in the gut by life. Kicked in the gut by death. By the light of the Autumn Moon, X marks the spot of death in blood. Running in heavy streams down her white legs to the ground below.

I am the Jade Silk Warrior. From the shadows of a moonlit night.

84

Rising above the trees of life
Despairs life Autumn's fervent night
Burdens of pain in weary strife
Drift beneath the Harvest Moon

Spirits of a tortured few
Elite in chosen misery
Beyond suffering unfruitful labour
Rest beneath the Harvest Moon

Jade

Reprieve falls under cloak of night
Promises from the healing land
Mercy relieves grieving years
Underneath the Harvest Moon

Spend your last days in fear, Annabelle Blue. Listen to the world talk of the killer they are calling Lady X, because of what manner it marks the spot of death brought into the world. A suburban mother and her daughter found dead in Cherokee County, North Carolina. The mother was tied naked to a tree, was she not? The X was carved deeply into her naked gullet, was it not? Gaze in fear at the rising of the Harvest Moon. Push away the cold premonition that torments thee. Walk the ground of your southern brick mansion in stubbornness. Tell yourself that you and the lovely Danielle and Nicole are not going to die.

High school girls were your specialty. You loved to infiltrate their world as one of them, when you first began. The blonde headed beauty from nowhere. Smiling at you, inviting you carelessly into their lives. Even going on vacations with them and their families. Getting the girls off to themselves. Taking walks with them at the edge of a lake alone. Getting their confidence. Drowning them in the waters of secret. Mourning with the families at the burial. Then mysteriously disappearing from their lives forever.

Oh, what tragic necessity is sleep, Annabelle Blue! These are the eyes of Jade you see, when you open your eyes in terror! Laid heavily on top of you in your sleep, to pull you up from slumber in the night! Arise, Annabelle. Walk with me to your daughter's rooms, at the behest of my Dragon Blade!

"Oh, my God, where is she—Nicole! *Nicole!*"

Now, let us go to the sixteen year old's room, my dear. Let us look upon the empty bed. But why do you not scream her name? Why do speak it in such quiet and sobbing defeat? The dragon blade is sheathed, Blue Dove. The dagger now craves the taste of your white skin. The dagger makes easy work of your sky blue nightshirt and matching underwear. Walk with me naked and thin, suburban queen. Let the night spirits see your rib bones and laugh at thee. Let them see your shrunken breasts and narrowed hips, your bony face starved into suburban conformity. Walk with me in the dark, skinny suburban queen, through this nighttime Virginia brick mansion. Thy millionaire husband has abandoned thee forever.

Walk with me, skinny suburban witch. Walk thy sickening stick figure down the stairs, and out the patio door. Lie on the brick tile beneath your feet. Do not even wish to fight the living shadow that binds your hands and your feet. Now, watch the Jade Shadow drag your crying sixteen year old from her place in the locked pool shed, her hands bound behind her back. Watch it happen, naked Mom. Watch me fall backwards into the pool with her.

Thirty seconds. One minute....

Watch me emerge for a quick and powerful breath. But where is the daughter?

I disappear again. One and a half minutes. Two. Two and a half minutes. Three.

Watch me climb out of the pool in skin tight black. Asian eyes burning.

Fourteen year old Nicole pleads in begging. Your muffled screams vibrate every cell in my body, Annabelle. Scream into the cloth gagged in your mouth. Scream your gagged, guttural scream, as I pull the bound Nicole lamb into the pool with me, whose mother was once called Annabelle Blue. Count the seconds, dear Annabelle, until you see my face again. I am the Jade Assassin, Annabelle Blue. I am death from the shadows of Indian Summer, underneath the Harvest Moon.

The shadow emerges from the water again. Grabbing the blonde Assassin turned suburban queen by the hair. Dragging her across the tiles, the grass. Dragging her across the great lawn, inch by inch, foot by foot, yard by yard, to the nearest tree of our calling. Pulling her up, slamming her hard against the tree. Leaving her mouth gagged and sore. Pulling the wet rope around her neck, to secure her to the accursed tree. Unbinding, then rebinding her arms around the sides of the big trunk wider than her body. Securing her bound feet to the tree.

Your sensuality hath been corrupted, suburban starvation witch. Your womanhood cannot live on blowpops and water. Unsheathed, the Jade Dragon glistens in the light of the Moon. *Send her in a flurry of steel*, the voice says to me, prompting a mighty flourish of whirling, dazzling display in the air nearby her condemned flesh, that she may feel the wind from my blade, that she may see the Jade fire that burns the wrath of the Almighty God in the night.

From this one handed whirling and twirling from the netherworld, of a swordsman's display of demonic ingenuity. I leap up upon the winds of this calling, slicing her diagonal from the B minor bosom to her hip bone, hearing the muffled scream of being kicked in the gut by Death; then a quick and mighty slash diagonal in the other direction, to hear again the sickening yelp muffled by the cloth in her mouth, backing away in the demonic, finishing flurry of steel in the southern, suburban light of the Harvest Moon.

I am the Jade Dragon. I am Death. Burning the Jade fires of vengeance. Underneath the Harvest Moon.

Sumi Sakara Rides the Wind

86

$\mathcal{S}$umi Sakara rides the wind. On the eve of eschatology. A.k.a. Sue Green. Mother of Sarah Green. Mother of the Jade Dragon Warrior, unbeknownst. Languishing alone after the death of her own mother, and other husbands come and gone. Wondering every so often where in the world it is that her beloved daughter could have gone.

In the Virginia land after sunset. At the approach of the evening light. Sumi leaves the tasty kitchen treat being prepared, the simple yellow cake with banana crème icing, leaving her dessert mixing to go and answer the front door.

On the other side, standing in the Asian dress cloth. Black dragons woven into a Jade silk fabric, standing in the fading light of day, is the embodiment of a dream long gone. A memory transcended into 3D space. Sumi's beautiful, careworn face morphs into the requisite awe and shock. Stepping out into the fading light. Hugging her daughter tight. Telling her, "you grew so tall and beautiful. I always dreamed you had left me to become a dancer. It is the biggest regret of my life."

Sumi invites the Jade Princess into her home. Telling her, "come to the kitchen, Sarah. Tell me about your life while I make my daughter a banana cake."

The Jade Silk Warrior follows her mother into the kitchen. Watching her closely. Smiling, listening to her chatter. Knowing where and when it must happen. Hiding the golden dagger behind her back.

"Don't look so sad," her mother says. "The past is the past. We will start all over again, you and me."

"Yes," the daughter says. "We will."

The mother is suddenly burdened with pity. With regret for the sorrow she caused to young Sarah, a score of years ago. She leaves her banana cake surprise to itself, moving away from the counter, walking to the beautiful woman in Jade silk cloth. What a privilege it is to have such a beautiful daughter return! What a privilege to have such a daughter that loves her! She takes a final step in her ivory dress, to the lovely daughter in Jade. Reaching out to hug her again. Feeling a cold, piercing shot into her abdomen. Trying to pull away. Being held tight, as the woman in Jade pulls the dagger up diagonal, across her abdomen, up to her breasts. Holding her mother there. Staring her in the eyes. Feeling the well of tears form on their own. The Jade Woman quickly moves the knife, jabbing into the ivory mother again. Hearing a brief, howling shriek.

Pulling the blade up and across. To mark the spot of their reunion. To complete this circle of time. To join together the centuries. To complete the flow of their family's history.

The Jade Woman pulls Sumi close. Shushing her on the lips. Braving the flow of water from her own eyes. And the flow of blood from her mother's dress to her own.

The two women lower clumsily to the floor. Both in shock and disbelief. The daughter lays full on top of her mother. Comforting her. Kissing her gently. Loving her.

Sumi Sakara rides the wind. On the eve of eschatology.

In Gold Silk Cloth

In the land of the far east. In the land of the rising sun. I find again the woman who loved me, by the forests and fields I once knew. Having found a respite from the four winds. Having found a place to rest my grieving sword.

All day, I have wondered where she is. Desperate for my new wife, my new Mother to return.

The lovely Nayomi finally arrives, after such a long time away. Telling me mysteriously, "Satari, there is someone here I would like for you to meet."

From just outside my view, she pulls a lovely young woman into the living room. A face so familiar, as though I have a sister I did not know. A younger version of myself, I see.

"Hitori," Nayomi says. "I would like you to meet your mother. Satari, this is your daughter."

I stand still, unable to move. Afraid that she might disappear, and I will wake up from a dream. The dream walks to me in gold silk cloth. Hugging me tight. Calling me her mother in weeping.

I am the Jade Silk Warrior. In the shadows of a moonlit night.

ABOUT THE AUTHOR

Jonathan Lovejoy is a graduate of the University of North Carolina at Greensboro, with a B.A. in Religious Studies, and a graduate of Liberty University with an M.A. in Theological Studies. He currently lives in Winston Salem, North Carolina.

For more info on the author's life and career, visit jonathanlovejoy.com